The Mirror in the Ice Cream Parlour

Nick Hooper

Wordandnote Publishing 2019

Copyright Nick Hooper 2019

ISBN 978-1-9997848-4-3

A CIP catalogue reference for this book
is available from the British Library

Printed and bound in Great Britain by
4edge Limited

Cover design by Sonja Burniston

For further copies of this book, and other books
and CDs for sale, go to:
www.wordandnote.com

*To all my friends and relations who read
The Occasional Gardener and encouraged me
to write a sequel.*

*And in memory of
Richard Cocks,
writer of memorable songs and a gentle musical
companion.*

3.15pm 15th November

The sea – the sea is like my breath.

The sea pulls back, gathering its forces – I breathe in, filling my lungs with air. The sea rushes up the beach, slowing to a light film of water as it reaches as far as it can go – I breathe out, my breath slowing to a whisper as it leaves my body. The sea pulls back again – I breathe in again; it rushes up the beach again – I breathe out again. This rhythm lulls me, and makes me realise why I always long for the sea: it is the rhythm of life.

Sitting on the beach in November, sketching the grey clouds coming in above the cold Welsh sea, I'm getting chilly, and the dog's coming back with a stick, asking me to throw it for him. I put my sketch book into my pocket, and ease my stiff limbs off the sand, struggling against gravity. Bloody Newton, I reflect; why did he have to think that up?

The dog is damp. I hope he doesn't start getting arthritis like me. He is quite old now, and Labradors have a tendency to have problems with their hind legs. He wags his tail, shaking his fawn coat and covering my bare feet with salt water and sand.

"One more throw, and then we'll go back." I chuck it as far as I can, and it disappears over some jagged rocks that tower up out of the sand.

When he brings it back, we'll walk up the long path to the car. I'm looking forward to driving back along the coast road to the warmth of my brother Paul's cottage, and a cup of tea with my girlfriend Peggy. We are staying there while we try to find somewhere to live. Peggy is on leave from the police, while she recovers from a bullet grazing her spine during a drugs raid that I was in charge of. She's doing brilliantly, but she gets tired from all the physio and just simply the business of walking. She'll be at the window, overlooking the harbour, reading something historical, I expect.

Paul will be practising for his gig tonight, which is in a local pub. His partner Andy will be cooking our supper. There might be cake or biscuits as well – warm from the oven. Andy is a great cook. And what am I doing? I'm waiting for a letter with the results of my tests for dementia, that's what I'm doing. The sea is the one thing that calms me down and helps me to stop worrying.

My mind is taken up with all this, so I don't see the dog until he's right at my feet, dropping something on the sand in front of me. It's not the stick I threw, it's small, square and a mottled brown colour – soggy with sea water. I nudge it gingerly with my foot.

"What's this you've found? Where's your stick?"

The dog wags his tail, and barks, expecting me to throw this for him to retrieve again, but I stoop down to have a closer look.

It's a leather wallet.

I pick it up. It's damp to touch, the leather is swollen and discoloured, so it's probably been on the sand for some time. Might even have been washed up by the tide. I walk in the direction of the towering rocks, the dog trotting beside me wagging his tail and hoping I'm going to chuck it for him to fetch again.

2

The rocks conceal the rest of the beach, and I walk round them to see if anyone's there.

As I expected, not a soul to be seen.

I open the wallet and a business card falls out. I bend down to pick it up and I can see the words 'True Ewe' printed on top of the soft-focus picture of an old-fashioned ice cream parlour. Turning it over, I can just make out something written on the back in pencil. The card is damp and wrinkled, but the name 'Brian O'Connell' is still decipherable, with a number written by it. The last time I encountered a man called Brian O'Connell, he clobbered me over the head and made off with millions of pounds worth of stolen paintings.

Me! Detective Inspector Arnold Rackham!

Painful memories of the last couple of months come rushing back: Peggy being shot by a terrorist; yours truly being nearly murdered by an evil old woman who had buried twenty victims in her garden; discovering that I'd been betrayed by my closest friend; finding out that my wife had been having an affair for decades.

I came here to get away from all this, and part of me says 'throw the wallet back in the sea, Arnold. Let someone else deal with it.'

But I don't – I can't.

My heart begins to thump as I sit down on a rock and look through the rest of the contents of the wallet.

Two cards, one debit and one credit, in the name of MR A M HUNT.

Four soggy £20 notes.

There are quite a lot of business cards stuck together, but I daren't try to peel them apart, in case they disintegrate. The information on them could be very interesting, especially if this is to do with the Brian I know.

A couple of cards come away from the rest, and fall in my lap. I pick them up carefully, and read:

Alan Hunt – Art Dealer
Chancery Lane
Hay-on-Wye
Herefordshire
UK

So Mr Hunt, the owner of this wallet, is an art dealer. Might just be the sort of person Brian would get in contact with, especially if Mr Hunt is a dodgy art dealer.

I turn the card over gently, and the other card stuck to the back reads:

Rigby Rogers – Gunsmith
Bright Street
Camden
NW1

So, an art dealer with an interest in guns? Unusual, I reflect. I breathe long and slow to calm my heart rate down. Have I just discovered a link to Brian and those stolen paintings? The ones that were lost due to my incompetence?

I have got a new job with a company that deals with art fraud, theft and insurance, but I don't start till next month, so I have a bit of time to follow this up – to make good, redeem myself. I should probably hand all this over to Grimwode and his pals in Counter-terrorism, but I don't feel like it – not after the way they treated me. And anyway, I'm still theoretically a policeman myself – at least for a couple of weeks.

What to do? What to do?

I carefully put the wallet and its contents in my coat pocket, ease myself up off the rock that I've been sitting on, and walk up the sand to find my shoes and socks. My feet are so cold I can hardly feel them as I stand up slowly to take a last look at the sea.

I breathe in as I watch the sea draw back – I breathe out as it comes whispering over the sand towards me. Then I turn and hobble up the path, the sticky feeling of damp grit returning to my feet, the dog leading the way. One damp wallet in my pocket.

"Merthyr? Isn't that a bit industrial?" I say, taking the soggy wallet out of my pocket. "Look what we found on the beach."

But Peggy's not interested – she's got the property pages in the *Brecon and Radnor Times* spread out in front of her on Paul's kitchen table. I place the wallet on the draining board, and put on the kettle.

"Not Merthyr Tydfil, Merthyr Cynog, silly."

"Where on earth is Merthyr Cynog?"

"Just north of Brecon. Lovely area. Really quiet... except for the military."

"Military?"

"Look, do you have to repeat everything I say?"

"Oh, sorry love. But look at this." I go over to pick up the wallet.

"So what do you think about this cottage? Come on, look." She points at a rental advert in the newspaper, I walk back over to the table, my mind still on my discovery.

"What about the er... military?"

"Oh they just practise up on Epynt, but it means there's less tourism and the rents are even lower."

I look down at the paper to see what appears to be the perfect Welsh cottage. Unspoilt and in beautiful surroundings.

"And…there's a job in restricted duties at Brecon police station. I saw it in the Pink Paper. I'm fit enough to do that now. Could ask for a transfer."

It comes back to me almost daily that I should have found that gun – the gun that was used to shoot Peggy, and injure her spine. I still feel it's my fault. And now here she is talking brightly about an admin job, when what she really wants to be doing is getting out there dealing directly with crime on the streets.

"Admin work is really important," she says, reading my mind, "and is becoming more so. Putting pieces together. Gathering intel."

"Well I've got some intel." The kettle's boiling, and I pour the hot water into two mugs with tea-bags, and leave them to brew. "Something the dog picked up on the beach."

Peggy pushes back the spread-out paper with a sigh. "So what do you think about this job I could apply for?"

"You're still on leave. You don't need to worry about a job yet, surely."

"I'm going stir-crazy sitting here doing nothing, eating your brother's food."

"We're contributing, and he wants us here."

"I know, but…"

"Well here's something to get your brain going." I place the damp wallet on the table in front of her. It looks bigger somehow, now it's inside the cottage.

"Someone's lost a wallet. Better take it in to the nearest police station. There's one in Haverfordwest."

"But," I turn, take the tea bags out, pour the milk into the mugs and bring them over to the table, "look what I found inside."

I sit down beside her, and place the business cards on the table by the wallet. Brian's name is just visible amidst the wrinkles.

8

"Brian O'Connell." She looks at me intently.

"And look."

Art Dealer and Gun Dealer cards go down.

"Shit! You really think it could be him?"

"Could be."

"We'd better get on to Commander Grimwode. Not our business anymore."

"Isn't it? I still feel involved. It was me that lost the paintings wasn't it? I mean, I feel connected to the whole thing."

"But your new job…"

"Hasn't started yet, I've got a few weeks left as a policeman."

"I'd have thought you'd learnt your lesson. That man's dangerous – he attacked you twice." That look she gives me – she's the grown-up here.

"Once a policeman always a policeman, isn't that what they say?" I feel a bit of a fraud as I say this. Another part of me never was a policeman. "But you're right, we should probably pass this on to Grimwode. It doesn't mean we can't have a look at it ourselves. Anyway, we should get all the stuff out of the wallet and let it dry before it disintegrates entirely."

"How do you think it came to be on the beach? Washed up, or just dropped?"

Images of a body thrown overboard and floating towards land come to my mind. "I don't know. It's very wet, isn't it? But not wet enough to have been out in the sea for long."

"Maybe we should go and have a look along the coast." She's getting interested now.

"Tide's come in so we can't get to most of the beaches, and it's getting dark. But we could have a look tomorrow. Best get this stuff dry and then get onto Grimwode." Something makes me not want to phone him straight away. I can just hear his sarcastic hard-edged voice saying 'Rackham, what do you want? I thought we'd seen the last of you and your half-baked theories.'

Peggy gets up slowly from her chair and reaches for her crutches. "I fancy a quick walk down to the harbour. You coming?"

"Hang on," I say, as she struggles into her coat, refusing my offer of help. "I'll just do this."

I spread the wallet contents out as best I can on the table, carefully prising the cards and papers apart a bit so they can dry, leave a note by them saying 'PLEASE LEAVE', and grab my coat. The dog wags his tail, and looks up at me from the warm mat in front of the Rayburn as if to say, 'You go out and enjoy yourselves, I'll just stay here and look after the cooker.'

Peggy is already out of the door and ahead of me, clanking along the path by the seawall on her crutches. I'm scared that the crutches will skid on the damp cobbles, and that she will fall – I imagine her head hitting the hard granite, and I shiver. It's got a lot colder since I got back, and the wind is getting up. It literally blows us down the path to the harbour.

"Storm coming. Should be fun tonight." I just catch her words as she walks ahead of me.

"I love you," I say, catching hold of her elbow and kissing her as she turns to face me. "I wish I could heal you."

"You are, silly, being with you is healing me."

Can I believe that? That my mere presence could heal her? But it's true that she is getting stronger and more mobile every day. Every day a step further away from that gun-shot wound. We do her physio exercises together, and quite honestly I think they do me as much good as they do her.

10

We walk on down. There's nobody about on this late afternoon in November. The lights are on in a few shops and cafes, though it won't be long before they close for the night. No cars queue and pile over the little harbour bridge. No grockles sit outside the big pub with its spreading chairs and tables. And the waves are getting bigger, the spray hitting our faces as we walk round the harbour.

We go up the cliff path on the other side of the little beach. I begin to worry about how we'll get down again, and I imagine Peggy's crutches slipping and her falling over the cliff, but I wouldn't dare stop her from doing this. She is so determined – scary even.

We pause to get our breath, and stare out at the sea, which is far below us now. The headland we are on is dark, and the waves are a deep green-purple with flecks of white whipped up by the strengthening wind.

"We should get straight on to Grimwode you know," Peggy shouts to the sea.

"Yes I know, but..." I don't want to face that sarcastic look. The steely angry voice. Does that man have any feeling? Any empathy? Yes, he's a good policeman – top of the force – but he misses things through his aggressive stance. Doesn't always see the subtlety.

"I mean, this is his stuff now, not ours. If it is Brian on that card, Grimwode needs to know as soon as possible. Anyway, what are we doing holding onto the wallet? We really should drive over to Haverfordwest and hand it in." Peggy has a tendency to do things by the book, compared to me with my old-fashioned-policeman ways.

"I agree about Grimwode, but handing it in to the local police would be a mistake. It could get left on some shelf and lost for ever. We have an intriguing riddle in our hands, and I'm not just letting go of it." Oh bloody hell, I'm sounding all poetic.

11

Peggy laughs, God bless her. "Arne, you should hear yourself. Like some kid who wants to play detective."

"But I am a detective." I wait for her to say 'was', but she doesn't – she turns and kisses me, and we carefully make our way down the cliff path back to the harbour.

"Fancy a pint before supper?" says Peggy. The old inn, which marks the beginning of our ascent back up the path to Paul's cottage, is open. We go in through the Victorian glass door, and find a table looking out onto the harbour. Little lights twinkle and reflect on the swelling waves as they sweep in and out of the bay. I'm thankful for the shelter of the cliffs that surround this haven. It will be getting very rough out along the coast.

"Horse riding," says Peggy.

"What?" I nurse my pint, sitting by Peggy and contemplating the wildness outside.

"I should try and find a stables. The physio says it would be very good for my back and balance."

"There must be a pony trekking place around here. Or maybe a…" I'm about to say a stables that works with people who've been disabled, but think better of it.

"I wonder if there's a Riding for the Disabled near here." She says it.

"Do you think you're eligible? I mean, you're…"

"The physio suggested it – they probably know. Anyway I could start there. They don't just plonk you on a horse. Apparently there's a lot more to it than that."

I look round the pub. We're virtually the only ones there, but I have this creepy feeling that someone's watching us.

"Freedom. That's what it gives you." I come out with this suddenly. I'm not thinking of horse riding, but of the feeling of freedom I felt as I left my home town and the local force, to come to Wales and have a break before taking up my new job. But ironically, as soon as something like this wallet appears, I find that all my instincts are crying out to get involved. I really don't want to let go of it and give it to Grimwode, but I know I should. Besides, I think sneakily, I can always do a bit of my own investigating on the side.

"You're thinking about that wallet again aren't you?" Peggy looks at me over her glass of lemonade.

"Yes, sorry… we were talking horses, but I'd better…" and before I have the chance to think about it, I get my mobile out and press on Grimwode's number. The signal is weak here, and I can hear the ring at his end is all wobbly as my signal struggles to get through.

"Yes?" Dick's voice sounds like a razor being sharpened.

"It's Rackham, I found a wallet. I think you'll be interested."

"A what-et? Is that you Rackham?"

"Yes it's me Dick. I've found something."

"I can't hear you, you're breaking up. Phone me back when you've got a better signal."

I look down at my phone. He's gone, but I am still determined to let him know that I've found something. I text him:

Found wallet on beach. Brian O'Connell's name on a card. Other things of interest. What do you want me to do? Rackham.

"Head back?" Peggy has finished her lemonade, and I swig down my beer, feeling that pleasant sensation of sugar and alcohol coursing through my veins. I help her up, she's got stiff from the walk, and we clank our way out of the pub and into the gale outside which is beginning to wail and gnash its teeth.

13

6.00pm 15th November

"Where's all that stuff I left on the table?" I don't believe it. Andy has come in and is cooking supper. His ingredients are all over the table and there are no signs of the soggy contents of the wallet.

"Oh that was yours was it? I needed the space so I cleared it away. Don't worry, I kept the newspaper. It's in the basket by the Rayburn."

"But the other stuff?"

"In the bin."

"But I left a note."

Andy shrugs and looks rather hurt – he's cooking our meal after all.

I look down under the table, and see my message "Oh there it is." I pick it up, and show it to Andy. "Must have got blown off when I went out of the door. It's very windy out there. Look, er, sorry. It was important stuff. Where's the wallet?"

"I put it up on the shelf out of harm's way. Did you drop it in a puddle?" He looks at me as if to say, 'you really do need looking after, you poor old codger'.

"Found it on the beach." I reach up for the wallet just as there's a knock on the door.

Andy goes over to open it, and I can hear my brother Paul coming down the stairs. "Who is it?" he shouts.

15

The door opens to reveal a short man with a lot of dark hair and a bushy beard. He's wearing oilskins and looks as if he's just come off a fishing boat.

"Hello?" Andy says.

"I've come for the wallet. Grimwode sent me. We need it straight away." He sounds like he's from the West Country.

Bloody hell, that was fast, I'm thinking. I only sent the text a few minutes ago.

"And you are?" I ask.

"Anti-terrorist." It doesn't sound like he's used to saying it.

"Can I see your ID?" I'm all policeman and suspicion now.

The man curses and starts to unzip his oilskin coat. On an impulse, I get my phone out and press 'Grimwode.' Paul comes through the door, followed by Peggy who's just been to the loo.

"What the..?" Paul is staring at the man. I look up to see he has a gun in his hand which is pointing straight at me.

"The wallet. Now. Put down the phone."

"Rackham, is that you?" I hear Grimwode's tones coming from my phone.

"Leave it." He puts his hand out. "The wallet."

"Here you are, here's the wallet," I say loudly and clearly for Grimwode's benefit as I hand it over. I hear his voice saying, "Rackham, what's going on?"

There's an explosion as the man shoots the phone, bits of plastic spraying all over the kitchen. He turns and goes, slamming the door. I start to follow him.

"Don't!" shouts Peggy.

We all freeze. Nobody wants to go out there – Peggy's right, no point in two people with gun injuries. I count to ten slowly, then go to the door, and open it carefully. Wind and spray come in, but as I look out, there is no-one on the path.

"Better phone Grimwode. Can I use your landline?" My voice is shaking. Last time I was confronted by a man with a gun I expected to die. That's what guns are for isn't it? Killing people.

"Have you got his new number?" I ask Peggy, who is wobbling over to the table to sit down.

"No, it was on your phone."

It's then I realise that the gunman may work out that most of the contents of the wallet are missing, and so is likely come back.

"I'd better find his number on my computer. This guy might come back." I dash into the sitting room and open up the lid of my laptop to find the screen has gone black. I jab at the space bar a few times – no life. Battery must be flat, and I can't remember where I put the lead.

"Peggy, do you know where my computer lead is?"

"No."

"Are you sure you haven't got his number?" It's useless. I know she hasn't.

"No. Call 999. They must have a response team somewhere near."

I pick up the phone and dial.

"Which service do you require?"

"Police. There's been a shooting incident."

"Sorry sir, I'll just put you through to the right department."

"Hello, hello…" The line goes blank.

"Police. How can we help you?" A woman's voice.

"There's been a shooting incident at Haven in Pembrokeshire. Can you send a rapid response team?"

"Who's this I'm talking to?"

"Detective Inspector Rackham. We need assistance urgently. We have been threatened by a man with a gun.

He has fired a shot already and may return at any moment."

I hear voices in the background: 'Rackham' is audible but the Welsh accent makes it difficult understand what they are saying.

She comes back on the line, and talks slowly as if I'm a dim recruit. "Please give your exact location. We will send someone round as soon as possible."

I give her our address. "This is urgent. How soon can you..?"

"Don't leave the house." The female operator sounds like she's reading from a card. "Lock all doors and windows and keep away from them."

"Yes I know. I'm a ..."

"Our armed response team will be with you as soon as possible."

"Now would be good!" I can't help feeling frustrated with what seems to be a pleasant robot at the other end of the line.

"As soon as possible." She repeats. "Don't..."

I put the phone down

"Lock all doors and windows," I shout as I go back into the kitchen and lock and bolt the front door. "Keep away... what's the matter with Paul?"

Andy has his arm round Paul and is dabbing his face with a cloth.

"Bit of your phone caught me in the cheek. It's not as bad as it looks." Blood is pouring down his face and dripping onto the kitchen floor. Andy is in tears. I feel so fucking responsible.

For a moment I wonder how someone cottoned onto the fact that I had the wallet so quickly. Has my phone been tapped?

An armed response unit could take ages to get here. I realise that I need to find the lead for my computer so I can get straight on to Grimwode.

"Anyone seen my computer lead?"

"Try the bedroom," Peggy shouts.

I run up to the bedroom, search round the bed – nothing there. No sign of it in the sitting room, so I start searching frantically round the kitchen, pulling open drawers, moving pots from in front of electricity sockets, inadvertently knocking a tin of biscuits onto the floor...

There's a bang on the door. Someone outside rattles the handle.

We all go very silent, which is pointless as he must know we are in here, and will try to break in anyway.

"You have taken things out of the wallet. Return them to us and nobody will be harmed." It's that West Country accent again. I can hear someone else out there.

"Move it. They'll have called police." A woman's voice. Definitely not an English accent – probably Scandinavian.

"I'm counting to three, then I'm going to shoot out the lock," he shouts.

"One, two, three..." There's a report from outside and a bullet whizzes through the door, hitting a table leg. The dog, who has taken no part in this, leaps up and starts barking at the door.

There's another report, and the door lock disintegrates in a shower of old metal, but the door remains bolted top and bottom. Nothing like an old-fashioned bolt to keep a gunman at bay.

He must have guessed because the next bullet just misses the top bolt and buries itself in the ceiling. The dog continues to bark.

But over his barking we hear a blessed sound. A siren.

"Bugger! We go." The woman speaks. The man launches himself at the door in a last attempt to get in, but to no avail. Big, thick, old-fashioned oak door. I hope it bruises his shoulder. There's more cursing, and then the welcome sound of retreating footsteps.

We pause. The dog stops barking and stands, legs tense and quivering.

From the silence inside we can hear shouts. Car doors slam. More shouting.

"Police. Get down. Down on the ground." They sound really aggressive and I imagine our assailants lying on the ground, police carbines pointed close range at their heads.

There're more shouts of 'police!' Then the sound of an argument. They're talking to our attackers? They should be bound hands and feet and taken off to be interrogated. But…

I hear footsteps approaching the door.

"Open the door! Police!" Then a sound of shuffling, and what I guess is the click of safety catches coming off.

I step forward, warning the others to keep back. The dog barks. I slide back the bolts and wrench the door open, the remaining bit of lock falling to the floor.

"Down. On the floor." Two helmeted policemen clad in body armour rush straight at me.

"I'm police!" I shout above the dog whose barking has reached new heights.

More of them rush in, telling everyone to get down, and then from my kneeling position I see a man I recognise – his clothes are soaking wet, his face is grimy and he's got sand all over his hands and knees.

"That one's Rackham," he shouts to the storm troopers who are storming through the kitchen. His tall gangly frame towers above the others, his Adam's apple – which is very prominent – quivers.

"They've gone." I shout from my kneeling position. "It's just us here. My brother, his friend, and Detective Sergeant McDonald. They left when they heard you coming."

I'm too late to stop the rampage through the house, but I try to calm the dog by catching his collar and stroking him. Paul and Andy look terrified, and Peggy is flat on the floor, having slipped as she tried to get down too fast.

A couple more plainclothes come in through the door, guns in their hands. They both look a bit damp and sandy like 'Adam's apple', and thoroughly disgruntled.

"Who called in the fucking cavalry?" 'Adam's apple' hisses at me.

"I did. I wasn't expecting…"

"Grimwode heard a gunshot before his phone went dead. Sent us…"

"But you're in London. How'd you get here so quick?"

"Something local's going on. We were just up the coast."

"So you didn't see anyone?"

"No. Just sand." He spits onto the floor. "We turned up at the same time as the rapid response team. They thought we were your assailants."

I stand up and walk over to Peggy. "Are you alright?" She quite clearly isn't. Pain shows in her face.

"Something in my back."

"Can you move?"

Wincing, she shifts and tries to get up using her hands and knees. Two paramedics appear at the door and go straight to Paul, whose face is still bleeding.

"Over here!" I shout. "She has a back injury."

One comes over and we carefully lie Peggy down on her side. The storm troopers reappear. "All clear sir," one says to 'Adam's apple', who has clearly taken charge. The dog is sniffing the men's shoes. All friends now.

21

We get a cushion and a rug for Peggy, and I pull myself away from her to talk to 'Adam's apple', who finally introduces himself as Inspector Dawson. I must have heard his name before, but I can never remember names at the best of times.

7.00pm 15ᵗʰ November

Sitting at the table peeling bacon packets and cheesy cellophane off disintegrating pieces of paper is not the easiest of jobs at the best of times. The wallet's gone, with the two business cards, and the 'True Ewe' card with Brian's name and phone number on the back. Also missing, are the bank cards and the soggy £20 notes. I do a sketch of the two business cards on a piece of paper for Dawson. It's my best way of remembering them, and it's all there. But no chance of finding out what that number was written next to Brian's name.

"True Ewe's very well known locally – great ice cream." There's a misty look in Dawson's eyes that makes me think he might actually be human – so ice cream is his poison.

"They do good coffee as well," he adds.

Well, well, I think. It might be worth a visit.

"So you know Hay?" I ask.

"It's my home town."

"But what are you doing here now? I thought you lot were still in Hertfordshire." I'm getting chummy. Things are warming up.

Dawson taps his long thin nose by way of an answer. "We'd better get this lot sorted. We'll take it off to forensics. We need you to come in and see if you can identify the gunman. Better do it at Haverfordwest."

23

So that's it. Back to business. No 'thank yous' for my discovery, my drawings, nearly getting killed etc.. I'm *so* looking forward to leaving the police force. Peggy's in the next room on the sofa. She's in pain, but the paramedic said he couldn't find anything wrong. Just gave her painkillers and told her to rest.

"I'm just going to Haverfordwest to try and identify the gunman. Are you going to be OK?"

She shakes her head. "I'm coming too. I saw him as well, remember? Paul needs to calm Andy down. Anyway, they don't need to come – we should be able to identify him if he's on their records."

Paul and Andy are upstairs with a police liaison officer, 'getting help'. We have two armed officers outside the front door. The rest of the squad have gone, and there's just Dawson, and his two officers from Counter-terrorism who are sorting through the contents of Paul and Andy's rubbish bin.

"Sergeant McDonald wishes to come too," I say to Dawson, who just shrugs and looks down at the detritus on the kitchen table.

"Come on, let's go. We've got all we can from here." He says this to his two acolytes as though I don't exist.

I help Peggy up from the sofa.

"I think the pills are starting to kick in," she says, wincing as she stands up.

I help her carefully out of the door and down the cobbled path. Dawson and co. don't bother to wait for us and are in their car out of the storm, the engine revving impatiently as we get to them. There's just room for us to squeeze in on the back seat. I pull the door closed and we're off before Peggy and I have got our seatbelts on. Still, I think we're better off than the two officers standing outside Paul's front door in the wind and rain.

"Oh fuck it!" Peggy finally explodes.

We've been sitting looking at photos for nearly two hours. We've had a cup of tea and we're starving. "We're not getting anywhere. These men don't look anything like the man who so kindly put bullets into Paul's kitchen table."

"We could look at another database." The Welsh female officer is gentle and slow and deliberate. At this rate we'll miss breakfast as well.

"I could... draw him." I hesitate.

"Yes you could." Peggy turns to the poor officer. "Arne...er...Inspector Rackham is a very experienced artist. Why don't we get him to draw the gunman? Save us being here all bloody night."

I feel like the talented little boy being wheeled out to play '*Für Elise*' in front of ancient relatives.

"OK," I say. "I'll do a front view and guess at a side view." He never turned conveniently to give me a profile, but I have a good idea how he would look.

"But..?" The poor woman is obsessed with procedure.

"No buts. Watch." Peggy's need for food has pushed her into a different personality phase, or maybe it's her back pain – a well-known cause of bad temper.

I am given a pen and paper. Not my favourite paper – too skiddy – and the pen's a bit thin. But I bring him to

25

life. His jutting-out hair. His bristly beard. His earring, and the bullish look on his broad face. All dark.

Viewed from the side, I think he will have a flat back to his head and a snub nose. His ears are quite big, and his earring is thick gold – a pirate by all accounts. 'Ah, Jim-lad!'

"There. That should help." I give the drawing to the officer who looks at it as if a miracle has just occurred.

"Right I…"

"We'll be going now. That should give you what you need." Peggy is firm. She's had enough and is slowly and cautiously getting out of her chair. I imagine the officer diligently working through the night, looking down at my drawings, up at the screen. Down, up, down, up. I don't think she'll find him.

Peggy clanks out of the room, cursing with the pain, and I follow her, feeling guilty that I brought all this down on our heads.

"If only you'd just brought the wallet straight here."

"I know, I know. Sorry. How's your back?"

"It will get better." She winces as she turns a corner in the corridor. A dark tall figure is coming straight towards us. I imagine the long talons concealed beneath his long flapping coat, the sharp pointed teeth, the…

"Ah, Rackham."

"Dick er… sir."

He turns to the minion who has been following. "I need a room. Inspector Rackham and I need to have a discussion."

"Peggy… Sergeant McDonald had a fall. She's in pain." I don't want her to be stuck here all night.

"Won't take long." Dick Grimwode's interviews with me never do.

The minion leads us to a vacant interview room. I look at the one-way mirror and take the seat reserved for suspects. Peggy eases herself down beside me in the chair usually reserved for a suspect's solicitor.

"Dawson told me you found Brian O'Connell's name on a card in the wallet that you failed to give to us." Always direct and to the point, Grimwode.

"Yes I…"

"And you drew the other two cards by memory. Shame you couldn't draw that number by O'Connell's name."

"No I…"

"Don't remember it?" His voice is so crisp and hard I can feel it going right through me.

"Seems to me that every time you come into contact with anything to do with O'Connell, you make a mess of it and he disappears."

"Yes, sir."

"You're still in the police force, Rackham. You haven't worked out your month's notice yet. I want you to think about this very carefully. Anything you remember, anything you come across comes straight to us. Right? I don't want you going AWOL again, picking up clues like some bloody old bloodhound. Have you got that?"

"Yes, sir. I have drawn a picture of the man who took the…"

"More drawings? Him and his bloody drawings," Grimwode mutters to himself.

"Sir?" It's Peggy. She's going to come to my defence.

"Yes, McDonald."

"I might be able to help. There's a vacancy in admin at Brecon." She's not coming to my defence.

"But you don't look up to it at the moment, McDonald. You should make use of your leave. Look after Rackham. Keep him out of trouble. I don't want him getting in the way."

"Dick!" I am coming to Peggy's defence. I won't have her being treated like that.

27

"What?"

"You seem to have forgotten…"

"Sir!"

"What?"

"Sir to you."

"… you seem to have forgotten that I discovered all that art concealed in The Avenues, that you offered me a…"

"Jones, we've finished." He gets up and goes to the door. Interview over. Jones opens it for him, and he's gone. I look at Peggy, she has tears in her eyes – whether from pain or frustration I can't tell.

"Constable? Can you get a car for Detective Sergeant McDonald and myself – to take us home?"

Constable Jones looks at me and smiles. "No cars available sir. Get you a taxi sir?"

How does he know there are no cars available?

9.00am 16th November

Peggy's asleep beside me – the painkillers finally kicked in at 1.00am, after a spoilt meal of congealed pasta and tepid tomato sauce.

I hear sounds of life coming up from the kitchen. I suspect that Paul and Andy are both a bit pissed off with me for bringing this curse down upon their heads. I get quietly out of bed and look out of the window. Just below me I can see the top of a policeman's helmet, the end of his gun barrel glinting in the morning sun.

After the storm, everything looks fresh and washed. The poor bugger who had to stand out there in the rain last night has been replaced, and the smell of salt and fresh air reaches me through the window.

I should go down. Give a hand with things. I've been lying in bed too long thinking about what to do next: look at that cottage near Brecon and get out of Paul's hair. I just hope that there was no permanent damage to Peggy's back last night. She was confident it would wear off. We should go and check with her consultant, but Luton and Dunstable Hospital seems a long way away.

I creep out of our room and down the stairs to find a man in overalls checking round the kitchen for missing bullets, fingerprints, DNA, anything our assailant might have left behind. The damage to the table, ceiling and door are all plain to see, but every scrap of my exploded mobile phone has been taken away – for what? I wonder. The only evidence on it will be my attempts to contact Grimwode. The kitchen bin has gone too – its smelly damp contents being examined in some police laboratory, no doubt.

"Morning, sir. We've nearly finished. Be out of your hair." His tired face gives me the impression he's been up all night. It will be his bed he'll be wanting.

"Er… thanks." I don't feel like a Detective Inspector in my dressing gown. "Like a cup of tea?"

"No thank you, sir. You help yourself."

So they've taken over. I have their permission to make a cup of tea.

"I will, er…"

"Gray, sir."

"Thank you er… Gray."

I fill the kettle, find a tin of tea bags, hoping that I'm going to get caffeine and not one of Paul's healthy alternatives. While that stews, I go to the window and gaze at the peaceful bay just visible past the armed policeman's shoulders. My dog, where's my dog? They haven't taken him away for DNA inspection, or an interview. My mind imagines Grimwode asking him questions: '… and what did the gunman smell like?' 'Woof, woof, growl, woof.' The thought makes me smile.

"Mr Rackham's out walking your dog sir." He picks up my thought.

I look down, and there, wedged under the skirting board at the bottom of the window seat is something small and black.

"Er… Gray?"

"Sir?"

I crouch down and point at the floor. My fresh eyes have picked out something he's missed. He gets a plastic bag and some tweezers and picks out a button. Could be anybody's, but my mind goes back to the gunman cursing as he tried to get his gun out.

30

"Could have come out of the suspect's pocket as he pulled his gun out. He had difficulty, I remember, though I was looking at my mobile phone at the time."

"Thank you, sir."

"Better check with Mr Rackham, to make sure it's not one of his or … er, Andy's."

"Yes, sir."

There's a scuffling sound at the door, and the dog enters followed by Paul. The dog is holding a woman's court shoe in his mouth.

"Couldn't get him to give it to me," Paul says ruefully.

"Drop," I command.

The dog gives me the shoe. It's dripping wet with a small strand of seaweed inside. Silver. Low heel. Size five I'd guess. Betty's size. Where's Betty now? I wonder.

"Sir? May I?" Gray is ready with his bag. I have one finger in the heel of the shoe to avoid any further contamination, though the sea and the dog's saliva will probably have wiped any evidence as to the owner away.

"I don't suppose it's connected. Where did you find it?" I turn to Paul.

"Down in the next bay. I threw a stick and he came back with the shoe."

Obviously a new method of clue collection – throw a stick for the dog and see what he comes back with.

"Lots of bits and pieces must have been washed up after that storm. Could have come from anywhere. Not the kind of shoe you'd wear on a small boat." Though how did it get into the sea I wonder?

Gray's mobile goes off. His expression changes as he listens – his tired look vanishes and a keenness takes over. He's not going to get to bed very soon, if at all.

"Excuse me, sir," he beckons me in to the sitting room. Closes the door on poor Paul. "They've found a body, sir,"

31

he says in a low voice. "Washed up on the same beach you found the wallet."

"Man or woman?"

"Woman, sir. Commander Grimwode thinks you might know her, sir."

It hits me like a sledgehammer: that could be Betty's shoe, and she got herself involved with Brian. What has happened out in that cold Irish Sea?

10.05am 16th November

We walk down the stony path, across the boulders, to the long sandy beach which extends a long way beneath multicoloured cliffs. It's my favourite beach in all the world. So many times spent here with my brother Paul, and on family holidays before he was old enough to buy his cottage in a neighbouring village. Betty never liked it, and would make her excuses, leaving me to go off and visit Paul on my own. Now I am expecting to see her body washed up on this very beach. Maybe she had some premonition that she would end up dead here, but actually I suspect she just didn't like cold Welsh beaches. She preferred sun-kissed Mediterranean sand.

I don't know what I feel, as I walk slowly towards the group of people huddled round a small dark mound. Do I wish her dead? Would that be a fitting end to her years of lies? Do I want to be free to have my true relationship with Peggy? It would be so convenient from the financial point of view. But in reality, it's a terrible way for things to finish between us. No resolution – just the savage scythe of the Grim Reaper. I hate myself for seeing it as convenient – her death. Suddenly, the early years of our marriage come back to me – the hopes, the love. I did love her then. It might be gone now, but I still feel the pain of her rejection, and my longing. No, I want to say goodbye properly.

Through the mist of tears I'm trying to keep back, I see a tall gangly figure detach itself from the group and stride towards me. I recognise the bony features of Dawson – lover of ice cream.

"Commander Grimwode's had to go, but he thinks you will recognise her. She's been shot in the head. Quite a mess." Dawson doesn't seem to care that it's my wife we're talking about. No empathy at all.

As we approach the body, a doubt begins to fill my mind. The figure on the sand looks too tall, too thin. Maybe it's just the perspective – squashed on to the sand by the weight of death. The back of her head is a mess of red – I feel sick as I slowly walk round her body and stoop down to look at what's left of her face. Nails come into my mind, and I look down to her hands and see immaculate fingernails, painted red.

I let out a long breath. It's not Betty. It's her solicitor. I'd swear to it. I can see why Grimwode wanted me to take a look. She's almost unrecognisable but still has that cold, calculating look in the half of her face that remains.

Mrs Braithwaite, I presume. I wonder where Betty is.

"Yes, she was my wife's solicitor," I say to Dawson.

"Braithwaite. We thought it must be. Your wife went off with her, didn't she, last time she was seen?"

We walk away from the gruesome pile, the sea breeze is in my face, and I am strangely happy. There's still a chance to sort things out with Betty – come to some conclusion. But she must be mixed up with this. And there's the shoe.

"We may have picked up one of my wife's shoes. My dog found it on a beach a couple of miles north of here. Gray's got it. There might still be some DNA on it."

"We'll take it back to Haverfordwest and get it tested," Dawson says, looking out to sea, as though it's of no real interest.

Poor Haverfordwest, I reflect. I know what it's like to be invaded by Grimwode and his bunch from Counter-terrorism. I wonder if they'll get the local murder squad moving in as well. There's probably a guy just like me being shoved out of his office, even as we speak.

I need to get away from them. All these police ferreting around this dead body – ferreting around my life. I feel the urge to walk to the other end of the mile-long beach, and without a word, I stride off, feeling the sea breeze on my face. Walk, walk, fast – the sand kicks up behind my heels. Round the walls of jagged rock, pushed up into crazy angles, millions of years ago, as the world thrust itself into shape.

The sea calls me. I must go to it. I must find something out there. The skies swoop, the sands whirl, and I feel my feet sinking into damper sand as I walk to the edge. I walk on, feeling the cold wet creep up my ankles, my calves, my knees.

Stop. What is this I'm surrounded by? Why is it so cold? Why does it keep moving? The swooshing sound around me makes no sense. I feel panic somewhere in my chest. Move, move, my body says. But I am rooted like a rock in this swirling cold. Just let it be, a voice says in my head. Stay here – feel nothing. But another voice breaks in from outside my cocoon:

"Arne! Arne! What are you doing?" There's a splashing sound, and something large and furry pushes at my legs. I turn then, to see this animal. Fawn wet face. Dark eyes looking up at me.

"Arne! Please come out!" There are two people on the edge of the... sea. The sea. That's it, I'm in the sea.

"Arne, are you OK?" The voice sounds urgent, worried. There's a woman crying. I look back out to sea. Why did I need to go out to sea?

More splashing, and a firm hand takes my arm. I turn and see my brother's face.

"Come on," he says. "Come home."

And I splash through the gentle waves to the edge of the sea, and to a woman who is crying. She has crutches so she cannot reach out to me.

"Arne…"

"I'm sorry." At that moment I don't know who she is, but by some instinct I reach out and hug her, and we stand – the earth stands still with us. I feel my brother's hand on my back, and a wet doggy nose at my knee, and I come back to Paul, the dog, and at last Peggy – the woman I love.

"It wasn't Betty. It was her solicitor. Shot through the head. Almost unrecognizable." I'm still shivering, and clutching the hot chocolate that Paul has made for me. Peggy sits opposite me at the kitchen table. Her pale face shows relief. It's the first thing I've been able to say since Paul pulled me out of the sea.

"Why did you go out and stand in the sea like that? We saw you as we came down the path. You just stood still, looking out to sea. At first I thought you'd found something, but you just stood there like a statue. You didn't even seem to hear us calling. It was only when the dog touched you…"

"Sorry, sorry, it's…"

"It was one of your absences, wasn't it? Arne. Talk to me. They've started again haven't they?" She tugs at my arm.

"I just don't know how it happened. I had to get away from Dawson and everybody crawling all over that body. The sea called me…"

"The sea called you?" She looks down at the table in front of her, and takes her hand away from my arm. With her forefinger she starts to trace a line in the grain of the oak. It comes towards me, and then swerves off to the side. I don't know what to say, neither does she.

Silence.

37

The phone rings. "I'll get it," says Paul, and goes out into the sitting room. The ringing stops and we can just hear Paul talking, then pausing, then talking again. No audible words – just a murmur.

My eyes meet Peggy's, and she tries to smile.

"A letter came for you this morning," she says. "It's on the Welsh dresser."

"A letter?" My mind immediately goes to the dementia specialist in America looking at my brain scan.

"I think it's to do with your cottage. It's from the estate agents."

"What?" Mundane life comes back to me, and I welcome it. "Oh... must be to do with renting it out." Betty's cottage next door will not be for rent. Probably be swarming with my colleagues, now that her solicitor has made such a dramatic reappearance.

Shakily, I put my mug down, go to the Welsh dresser and open the letter.

Dear Mr Rackham,

21 Gravel Lane

We would like to meet you at the property at your earliest convenience to discuss the requirements for renting it out.

Please contact Julie on ....678450.

Kind regards

Michael J Creaser FRICS

'Earliest convenience'? 'Kind regards'? This is the language of my home town. So genteel, but concealing so much. I wonder what I will get in rent to support my new life with Peggy.

Paul comes in from the sitting room.

"I had someone called Inspector Dawson on the phone," he says. "Was that one of the guys from yesterday?"

"Yes, he…"

"I said you weren't well. Thought you and Peg needed a bit of time to talk." The dog wags his tail, and it thumps against the bullet-scarred table leg.

"Er… I'm much better now, thanks. I've just got a letter," I say, trying to return to normality. "Need to go home and sort out renting my cottage. Will you be OK?"

"We'll be alright, but I'm a bit worried about Andy. He's still really freaked out by the attack last night – they're offering counselling but he doesn't want it. I've suggested we go away for a few days. This guy Dawson said we need to be protected, but I don't want to stay here."

"Sorry, Paul. I've brought this all down on your heads. Wish I'd never found that bloody wallet." No I don't. I want to know. I want to know lots.

"Apparently there's a safe house up north that's in a beautiful spot. We could do some walking. Calm down. Dawson suggested it." Good old Dawson. He does seem to understand the good things in life – my mind flashes back to the ice cream parlour in Hay.

"Oh, and one other thing." The way he says this suggests it is *the* thing. "He wants us all to go down to Haverfordwest. To sort out our security after the attack, he said."

1.30pm 16th November

"We think they must be tailing you. It's certainly a possibility, so we want to tag you so we can keep your movements monitored." This all sounds very plausible and interesting, but I wouldn't be at all surprised if our terrorist friends, if that's what they are, might have thought of that. I stick my leg out, expecting the usual parole tag.

"We're going to give you an upgraded tag with a better range." This officer may well be my junior, but he doesn't call me 'sir'.

"Sergeant?" I take a guess.

"Morris," he replies. I guess that's his surname.

"Sergeant Morris, I am still an inspector in the police force, and would normally expect to be called 'sir'."

He looks at me, his mouth half open in disbelief. He's tall and thin and wears glasses with thick black frames. Short hair slicked back – geeky. Probably their IT and gizmo specialist. I doubt if he spends much time out on the field.

"Here's your tag," he says, handing me a mobile phone. "Sir, it's in this mobile phone for you, sir, to replace the one that was destroyed by a bullet, sir." He's really pushing the 'sir' thing now, and I'm regretting bringing it up. After all I can only hold on to that privilege for a couple of weeks, and then I will be 'sir' because I'm a member of the public.

41

"And, sir..?"

"Look Morris…"

"Sir?"

"Let's drop the 'sir' thing. Sorry I mentioned it. Doesn't suit your style."

The geek smiles. He's won, and I wonder about him. Not so skinny and pathetic I suspect.

"OK, now I have to ask you," he says. "Have you recently used a firearm?"

"No. I did a course when I was in the Met, but that was twenty-five years ago."

"Could you use one now?"

"What do you mean?"

"I mean, how would you feel about using one?"

"I don't know, I… I might have lost the knack." I don't like the sound of where this is heading.

"I think we should take a quick look to check how you are now."

What? Are they training me up to be a James Bond? "But I…"

"There's a good range here. I'll show you. It won't take long."

And we're off. And I'm wondering what's happening to the others who are with Dawson.

He leaps down the stairs ahead of me as I creak along behind, my arthritic knees crunching and grinding with each step.

"Down here." He turns at the well at the bottom of the stairs, and smiles up at me.

"OK, Morris, here I am. What now?" I am expecting crowds of keen marksmen practising in ranks, volleys of deadly steel hitting paper targets – but it is silent except for the sound of Morris's keys as he unlocks the entrance to the firing range. He pulls back a thick, armoured door, and switches on the lights. We are alone.

42

"Here we are. No-one on duty, so we can see what you can do without anyone looking over your shoulder."

But you're looking over my shoulder, I reflect as he unlocks a steel cupboard and brings out a couple of automatic handguns.

"You use Glocks now, don't you?" I say.

"Yes, Glock 17s."

The gun feels like it's made of plastic. It could almost be a toy – so different from the pistols I fired twenty-five years ago. He gets out some magazines, and a couple of pairs of ear defenders. "Right let's try it."

We go up to the counter. He stands by me as I put in the magazine and don the ear defenders.

"Where's the safety catch?" I ask, wondering how I will get the gun to work in the first place.

"It's a lever set inside the trigger. Just pull the trigger firmly and it will fire."

I reflect how in the past one had to flick a lever, or cock the gun in order to get it to fire. Now you just press the trigger and, blam! out comes a bit of metal death. I take aim at the target and fire. The trigger feels weird and the recoil takes me by surprise – I don't know where the bullet went. I turn to Morris and shrug. "Too long ago."

"Let's start by getting used to it. The grip on the Glock makes it aim higher than other handguns and it's a lot lighter. Lean on the counter and use both hands. Remember to line up with both sights but once you've fixed on the target, keep your eyes on the front sight."

I let off a few rounds and hit the target surprisingly easily. One bullseye.

"See? You've still got the eye."

What does he mean by still?

"Now both hands but no other support."

I feel the recoil more then. One wild shot, but then I adjust my stance – bend knees, both arms straight, and I start hitting the target. This feels horribly familiar. I did this a lot all those years ago. Funny how I forgot, but then I wanted to forget.

"Good shooting." Morris hands me another magazine. "Now try putting your right foot forward a bit, so you turn slightly side on. Keep your arm straight and support it with your other hand. No, not like that, you'll take your thumb off."

I adjust the thumb of my left hand, feeling a complete novice and wondering what the point of all this is, but when I fire it feels easier to aim.

"Now that is good," he says after I hit the target a few more times. "I think we need a challenge. I'll just set up a new target for you, and one for me." Morris unlocks the door to the range. "Better clean this lot up after." There're quite a few bullets lying about on the floor in there. Is this just a waste of metal? He takes down my shattered paper body target with its bullseye where the heart would be, and puts up another one.

"OK. Let's do six shots. Fire at will." He's at his counter, I'm at mine. He lets off six rounds so quickly, I've only got a couple in. I glance at his target. All very close to the bull's-eye. I fire off three more – one hits the bullseye, and I'm just taking aim to hit it again when I hear a click behind me, the shot goes wild and I hit the target in the head.

I turn round to see Peggy. "I didn't know you could do that. Bloody hell, Arne, you're lethal. The last one in the head."

In the head. Shit!

"He got top marks in the Met. I checked," Morris says to Peggy, as he takes off his ear defenders. "Not bad. A bit slow, but you got a couple of bullseyes. That one in the head… might be the unfamiliar grip." He looks at Peggy, but Peggy's looking at me. We're both thinking: what

44

happens if I have a gun when I have one of my episodes? I really could be lethal.

"We want you to carry a gun for now."

"But…" I can't think of an excuse.

"Grimwode's orders. Sir!" Morris grins and hands me the gun, with some magazines and a holster. "I'll sign it out for you."

8.30am 17th November

"You take the gun," I say.

"I don't want the gun," says Peggy.

"I can't carry it," I say. "It's too dangerous."

We're in the car about to set out for Hertfordshire to sort out my cottage. There are two bullet-proof vests on the back seat, and this bloody gun in its holster.

"Alright," Peggy snaps. "I'll take it. But you're the one who knows how to use it, if we…"

"Get into trouble. Well, we'll just have to stick together." I grip her arm and lean over and kiss her on the cheek. It's then I see the tears. Guns and Peggy just don't go together. A gun has shattered her life. She can only walk with crutches now, she was an athlete before she was shot.

She shrugs me off, and starts the engine. The radio comes on, and as we drive away into the mountains we hear the news that a young female politician has been shot dead. I resist the temptation to get Peggy to stop the car and throw the gun into the bushes. We can't do that – anyone could pick it up, and we can't give it back without telling them all about my memory episodes. So we're stuck with it. I just hope we never need it.

"Shall we go via Hay-on-Wye? There's a really good ice cream parlour there." I want to lighten our mood. Peggy's been silent since we heard the news.

"Ice cream? What for?"

"It's meant to be really good. Dawson told me. And it's sort of on our route."

"It's to do with that card, isn't it? The one with Brian O'Connell's name on the back."

"Yes, and…"

"Have they asked you to investigate it?"

"No, but…"

"So why are you taking us straight into trouble? They're treating us like decoys as it is."

"No. Come on. We'll just have an ice-cream, and then carry on. I just want to sit there, and soak it all in. I'm not going to start asking questions, showing photos and that sort of thing. Honestly, it will be fun. Anyway," I turn on her with mock accusation, "you love ice cream."

It turns out to be market day and parking in Hay isn't that easy. The car park, which slopes down like an amphitheatre to the hills beyond, seems full, so we have to trawl around slowly looking for a space. The dog is keen to get out, and in the end Peggy lets us out while she carries on her search, and I take the dog down to the grassy edge to relieve himself. Dear old dog, who found the wallet that caused all this upsurge of trouble, how I love you. I take his head in both my hands and look into his trusting eyes. Silly old dog. He wags his tail, and we go off to find Peggy with her lethal car-load.

She's had to park right down the bottom, and she's just ferreting in her bag for some change. The gun and holster are in her way.

"What are we going to do with this? We can't leave it in the car. And do we need to put these on?" She points to the bullet-proof vests.

"They're not going to take pot-shots at us in a place like Hay. And anyway, why would they? They want

48

information, and dead people aren't very good at giving that."

"Then why did Grimwode want us to have all this clobber? He must be expecting something."

I wave my arms about in a futile gesture. She's right, and I know it, but putting on a bullet-proof vest in the middle of a car park without being noticed is a bit of a trick. In the end we take it in turns to struggle into them on the back seat of the car.

"The gun," says Peggy, reaching back into the car.

"Oh God, I forgot to strap the holster on. Here, give it to me, I'm not taking my coat off again – I'll put it in my pocket. I won't have one of my things with you here." Suddenly I want to hug her so hard that I'll probably break something. I put the gun in my coat pocket, and put my arms around her. It's odd hugging her with these vests on. Along with her crutches, they get in the way, but we stay there for a bit while the dog stands by, wagging his tail. Then we disengage like two knights in armour and walk stiffly up the car park and into the town.

We walk past charming little shops – I notice one called 'The Thoughtful Gardener', and it reminds me of my brother's song:

But come the autumn they will die
And I will have the chance to dig them out
And put in bulbs, and watch them grow
When spring comes round again.'

I'm so taken up with this that I turn and wander into the shop before I realise that I have no garden at the moment.

"Hello." He has a friendly face, quite tall and dark.

"I… I…"

"Arne, what are you doing?"

49

The dog wags his tail, he likes this man, and I realise there are lots of things stacked in this tiny shop: soaps, socks, candles, and bulbs. But the dog will knock something over with his tail, so I decide to make an exit.

"Lovely socks," I say pointing to the colourful socks stacked by the door. "I'll come back when I've got a garden... to garden."

The man nods sagely, and I join Peggy outside.

"I didn't know what you were doing," she says to me in a fierce whisper. "I thought you might..."

So it was all about daft Arnold carrying a gun. "No. I was reminded of that song of Paul's. You know, about gardening. Forgot I've got nowhere to garden, now that I'm renting out my cottage."

"Where's this ice cream parlour?" Peggy's getting tired, though she won't say it.

"I think it's by the market square." We pass a number of small shops stacked with second-hand books, up a narrow alleyway, along a narrow pavement which is hard for Peggy to negotiate – especially as cars brush by us, unheeding.

Peggy sees it first. "There it is. It's like a real old-fashioned shop."

She clanks stiffly up the steps in front of me, and finds a seat in a little bay just by the door. "Find me something interesting. Not chocolate. Oh, and a decaf latte. Large." I can see she's having trouble sitting down. The stiff vest doesn't help with her injured back. The dog sits happily by her feet.

A cheerful woman in her fifties greets me behind the counter, and I choose ginger and pecan ice cream for Peggy, and chocolate for me.

Returning to our table, I nearly spill the coffees as I bend down, but I manage to sit by her, looking out of the window. It's then that I notice a curious effect. There's a tall mirror on the wall next to the window, put there to give the impression of space. But as I look in it I can see the faces of people as they walk past the parlour on the pavement outside without them noticing, or, if they're going in the opposite direction, I can see their backs as they walk right up the hill. A perfect place for a policeman who wants to keep an eye on what's going on outside.

Eating an ice cream in a bullet-proof vest with a gun in my pocket feels very strange. On the one hand I am having the most innocent of experiences – eating an ice cream; on the other the I am armed to the hilt, ready for a shootout with a terrorist. Bizarre.

" Great ice cream, and they know how to do coffee." Peggy is smiling at last.

"How's your back?"

"Nearly back to normal."

"You mean?"

"Before a load of armed police made me sit on the floor." She laughs. I wouldn't have laughed, but she's Peggy, and she's tough.

"Listen." I put my hand on her arm. "About that shop just now, I realised I wanted to find somewhere to live – with a garden, you know. And um, well actually I need somewhere, er... with... you. That place in Merthyr..."

"Cynog," she gives me a straight look. "You know Arne, you're such a..." she prods me in the ribs, and then winces as her finger comes up against the hard bullet-proof vest. We both get a fit of the giggles.

"So?" I manage to say with a straight face.

"Yes, we could look at it when we get back. My flat above the sweetshop has been rented out already. Hannah organised it." Good old Hannah. Fab cellist and a great friend – to Peggy, to the dog, and almost to me.

"I've never seen your flat. What's it like?"

"Tiny. Tight winding stairs. I'd never get up there now."

I get distracted by a face that appears in the mirror. It looks so harsh and spiteful, ferret-like. It's a woman's face, middle-aged – thin and bitter. She turns – she can't have seen me looking at her in the mirror – and the next thing she's coming through the door.

"Lemon sorbet." She has an Eastern European accent, and I notice the absence of 'please'. But also there's something about her voice. "Espresso. Yes." The coffee machine hisses gently.

"Arne, what?"

"Oh, sorry. Just thinking."

"Would you mind?" The woman is standing by our table. Looking past her, I can see all the other tables are taken. Her face is smiling – completely transformed. I wouldn't have recognised her from the woman I saw in the mirror.

Peggy looks at me, and I can see she's thinking she'd like us to be on our own, but silly old gallant me has to say, "be my guest."

The woman puts down her coffee and goes back for her sorbet.

"Arne, I thought we were…" Peggy whispers.

"Shh, she's coming back… I recognise her voice from somewhere."

She comes back and sits at our table. She smiles at both of us. "So… you tourists?"

"Came here for the ice cream. Delicious, isn't it?" I realise, too late, that she is eating a sorbet. Odd combination of sour tastes – lemon and espresso.

"Yes. But I like books." She looks at us both again. We are obviously going to have to talk to this woman. End of our tête-à-tête.

52

"We're just passing through…" I feel a kick from under the table.

"Hay-on-Wye is book capital. Yes? You must like books."

I see Peggy wolfing down her ice cream. She wants to get out.

"Gosh, yes." I haven't a clue what to say, or why Peggy's trying to attract my attention.

"But you, you are here for something else, yes?" She looks at me with suddenly piercing eyes, and for a fleeting moment I catch a glimpse of the ferret-like face I saw in the mirror.

"Ice cream…" I choke on a bit of wafer.

"Is long way to come for ice cream." She doesn't smile.

What's it got to do with her? I look over at Peggy, whose face has gone rigid.

"No, we're on our way… and have you come for the books?"

"Books? Books…" she seems to savour the word, as though checking it for poison. "Yes, maybe. But I'm looking for someone… like you…"

"We're not looking for anyone, we're just…"

Peggy is getting up. "I think we should go." The clatter of her crutches breaks the spell.

I dump my half-finished ice cream in what's left of my cappuccino and get up.

"Sorry, I hope you find… what you're looking for." I join Peggy and we creak and clunk our way out of the door.

"What a peculiar woman. But what's got into you?" I ask as we walk up the street and past more bookshops.

"Her voice. Didn't you recognise it? It's her. The woman who was with the gunman outside Paul's house. I'm sure of it."

"Shit, that means we've been followed…"

I look around me. Up and down the street. No lurking gangsters, just happy – and mainly elderly, book-shoppers carrying on with their normal activities – going into bookshops.

"Better call Grimwode." I get my new phone out – his name doesn't come up, and I'm not used to the phone. Can't work out how the contacts work.

"Here give it to me." Peggy takes it and holds it away from her, precariously balancing with one crutch.

"There, found…" A man rushes past us grabbing the phone as he goes and pushing Peggy off balance. I catch hold of her, the dog gets tangled between my legs, and we fall over onto a book display that some shop owner – trusting both the weather and people in general – has put up outside his shop. Paperbacks fly everywhere, and Peggy has fallen right on top of me. Beside me on the pavement Raymond Chandler keeps company with Ngaio Marsh.

"You OK?" I shout in Peggy's ear, as the dog, who has immediately got onto his four feet, sticks his nose in mine.

"No need to shout." She pushes an elbow into my stomach in an effort to get up.

"What happened?" The bookshop keeper is looking down at us.

"Someone stole my phone and pushed my… companion over."

He sees the crutches, and bends down to help Peggy up off my lap. "Happens a lot around here. You wouldn't think it, would you? Lots of tourists with their mobiles out and their guard down. Easy picking. People should be more vigilant, don't you think?"

I pick myself up and help the shopkeeper get Peggy back on her feet.

"We'd better check the ice cream parlour."

The shopkeeper shrugs and gives me a 'some people' look, then bends down to re-stack his display muttering under his breath.

"Are you OK?" I ask Peggy.

"Yes, thanks for the soft landing. Do you think that was a bit of bad luck, or one of our friends?"

"Bit of a coincidence. Let's see if our charming lady is still there." I don't know what I'll do if she is. Arrest her at gunpoint?

We find a queue has built up round the door. In spite of the cold November wind, people here are keen for their ice cream fix.

"Stay here. I'd better try."

" 'scuse me," I say. Leaving the dog at the door, I push my way past unwilling customers, narrowly avoiding pushing over an octogenarian lady with two toddlers in tow. Our window table has been taken over by a young family, the children are looking at my forlorn ice cream in cappuccino with disgust. I look up and down the long café, but there is no sign of our inquisitive lady.

1.00pm 17th November

"Yes D… er, sir, Sergeant McDonald is sure she recognised her voice."

We're on Peggy's phone, seated in the corner of a tapas bar. The Spanish music is loud enough to stop anyone hearing our conversation.

"And you've managed to get your mobile stolen already. Still got your gun I suppose?"

"Yes, sir."

"Well, the silver lining is… what?" Grimwode's voice goes even sharper, but fades as he turns away from his phone. "No, the phone…" There's a pause, and some mumbled conversation.

"Now listen Rackham, because the phone has a tracker on it, we know where it is, and will keep an eye on where it goes. I gave you a firearm so that you would be able to protect yourself, and Sergeant McDonald. We can't babysit you, we haven't got the manpower. Just try and keep out of trouble, but inform us IMMEDIATELY of any further contacts with our friends. Do you understand?"

I understand. This still being in the force, is like a lead weight in my stomach, not unconnected to the weight in my pocket.

"Yes, sir." We are the decoy ducks, though what anyone thinks they're going to find out from us, I can't imagine.

"What are you doing now?"

"Having lunch sir…"

"He's having lunch," Grimwode's voice goes all faint and edgy again. "Sounds like he's on the Costa Brava."

"And after your… lunch?"

"Driving back to sort out my house, sir."

"Good. Now Brown will be in your, herm … wife's next door. Don't interfere."

The phone goes dead. That's it. A typical conversation with my old colleague Dick Grimwode. There was a time when we were equals. Worked together. Now he's a commander and I'm a retiring inspector, and I can't wait to get away from him.

"Well, at least we managed to contact him. Thanks for trawling through all your police connections."

Peggy looks amused, and is scratching the dog behind his ears. Something he loves. "Friendly, was he?"

"Usual."

"Usual? Look, I'm sorry I lost your phone. Stupidest thing to hand it to a passing chancer. Do you think it was them?"

"I hope so. Dick's mob won't be pleased if they end up wasting their time following some kid."

"It happened so fast. I didn't see him."

"It was a him." I got an impression of someone young, medium height, hoody, jeans, pumps. Good old visual memory. I get my small sketchbook out and draw the thief. No face. No use, in fact, but…

"Hey, Arne, is that what he looked like?"

"Yes. Is your back alright?"

"Don't keep asking. It's fine. Right?"

I've touched another nerve. She's frustrated with herself. It isn't so long ago that she'd have given chase and caught the thief, but then it was doing precisely that…

"Here's our food." A young waitress appears with small dishes of chorizo, potatoes, olives, sardines, goats' cheese salad, and houmous.

"Another glass of Tempranillo, please," I ask.

Peggy looks at me.

"Well, I'm not driving."

"But…" she looks down at my coat pocket.

"Oh, I'll be OK." Drunk in charge of a firearm.

The wine is good, very good. So is our food. It's funny how these little dishes fill you up. Not like your meat-and-two-veg, but definitely sustaining, and rather more interesting.

"That goats' cheese on mushrooms is really nice." Peggy is all bright again. Trying to cheer us up. But goats' cheese? I tend to avoid that sort of thing like the plague, but Peggy's always a bit alternative when it comes to food.

"Go on, try some."

"Mmm mm m…" My mouth is full of chorizo and potato.

"Oh, you're such an old fogey when it comes to food." She smiles at me in a 'silly old bear' kind of way, and I take a spoonful of goaty stuff and plonk it on my plate. I cautiously take a little bit on my fork, pop it into my mouth, and bite on rich, creamy, savoury food – the juices of the mushroom mingling sumptuously with the crusty cheese.

"Mmm mm m…."

"You like?"

"Mmm mm m."

It this moment we are joined by a dark-haired lady of indeterminate age. If she was Jewish she'd look like Maureen Lipman, but she's Spanish.

"Alright, loves?" She's not Spanish.

59

"Really nice." Peggy wheels out the posh accent. We're good middle-class citizens savouring the delights of Hay-on-Wye, not gun-toting police in bullet-proof vests.

"Good, ain't it? All to your satisfaction?" She gives us a big smile, and moves on to check the next table.

"I could sit here all day," I say taking a swig of my second glass of wine. The image of retirement crosses my mind. Sipping retsina on a Greek island. The warm Mediterranean at my feet.

"But… we must get going. It'll be dark by the time we get home."

Home? What is my home? That little cottage where I avoided life – just the dog for company. Now Peggy will be there. Will she transform it? For a night maybe, then we'll leave it, and some other person, or people, will come and live there, making it their home. It's an odd feeling, and not an altogether pleasant one.

The dog shifts uneasily under the table, Peggy gets hold of her crutches, I swig down the rest of my wine. Time to pay the bill and go.

Walking through the narrow hilly streets, we keep an eye out for the lady we met in the ice cream parlour. The shops are cluttered with people and books. Such an easy place to appear and disappear at will.

Down through the car park. Let the dog relieve himself in the bushes. We get into the car to find we're still wearing our bullet-proof vests.

"I can't wear this all the way home," Peggy moans. With a sigh, she takes off her coat and jumper, and I help her out of it, then do the same for me. It's all a bit of a struggle, but I feel like an emerging butterfly afterwards. After a discussion in which Peggy refuses to take the gun back, I leave it in my coat pocket, and we're off – taking the scenic route.

We drive down narrow lanes, sometimes having to stop, or reverse, sometimes having stunning views of the Black Mountains. I doze beside Peggy as she drives – the wine is having its effect, but from time to time I check the wing mirror. It's a habit of mine when I'm not the driver – I like to know what's going on around me. There always seems to be a car behind us. Not too close, so I can't read the number plate. Silver grey. Could be a VW or a Seat. I look and look…

"Not far to go. You've had a good sleep. I suppose it's all that wine." Peggy's cheery voice wakes me up. My neck is stiff and my head hurts from where it rested against the car window.

"Oh, sorry. Must have dozed off. There was a car following us… I thought."

"There've been loads of cars following us. I don't think any particular one…"

"A silver grey VW."

"I've seen plenty of those in my mirror these last two hours. Had to do something while you dozed away. Great company you've been, so I kept a watch on what was behind us, just in case."

"Where are we?" I decide to change tack.

"Aylesbury. This lane system is a bit ambiguous."

Somebody cuts in on us, and Peggy has to brake hard. There's a furious hooting behind us. "Idiot. Nearly went into the back of us. I've a good mind to pull him over for driving too close."

"It's a her not a him." I say, as the woman behind us pulls out and undertakes us in her smart silver Audi, giving us the finger as she passes.

"Now we're in the wrong lane." Peggy slows right down and indicates, to wait for a space in the lane to the right, which brings on another spate of hooting from behind us – this time, from a large white van.

61

"Right. That's it." She puts on her hazard lights and stops. Getting out without her crutches, she limps towards the van behind, supporting herself with the side of our car and brandishing her warrant card. I don't hear what she says. I almost can't bear to look, but peeking in the mirror I see a man get out from the driver's side. He's big, he's young, he looks tough, and he has no hair. He's shouting something at Peggy and pointing his finger at her. Somewhere back in the queue someone leans on their horn. That's enough, I think. Time for action. I get out of our car, and find that one of my legs has gone to sleep.

"Get back in the car, sir," I say, keeping my balance by leaning against the side. "Threatening the police is a serious offence. I don't want to have to arrest you."

He's a head taller than me, and I wonder whether my gun would have come in useful. An image of American-style arrest with the man pushed against the side of his car, with my gun pressed to his head, passes through my mind, and I dismiss the thought.

The man backs away, grumbling. "She can't fucking drive for toffee, that one."

"Don't make it any worse," I say to anyone who wants to hear. The dog starts to bark from the back of our car. Time to go.

6.00pm 17th November

"We can't possibly go out again." Peggy is outraged at my profligate attitude to food.

"We've got nothing to eat. You must be starving after all that driving." And taking on the incredible-hulk-van-driver in Aylesbury, I reflect, privately.

Finally, we're back at my cottage. It feels cold and damp, and not at all homely. There are no sardines in the cupboard, there is no beer in the cellar, and it's not a 'capital little house.' The dog likes it though. He goes around sniffing everything and wagging his tail. It's 'home' to him. For me, it's like the memory of a different life. One that I'm trying to leave behind, but it keeps coming back to haunt me.

"I'm knackered," Peggy says from the armchair. "I don't want to go out again. Can't we just order a take-away?"

There's the sound of someone banging on the wall from next door. I don't know what Sergeant Brown and his Merry Men from Counter-terrorism are doing in there, but they sound like they're taking the whole place apart – the diminutive Brown, who always looks so worried, but comes up trumps when you're in a tight spot. Looks like a puff of wind would blow him over, but carries a gun and is capable of standing up to the fiercest of people – even women.

A drill starts up. I thought it would be forensics pottering around dusting this, and taking samples of that, but it sounds as if they're taking samples of the brickwork. A particularly heavy thump from next door causes some dust and old plaster to sprinkle down on the floor in front of me, and I look up at my ceiling with some trepidation, to see the light swinging to and fro.

"Look, I can't stand this. Can't we just go down to the pub? The specials are really cheap, cheaper than a take-away, and we won't have to put up with an earthquake next door."

I see her smile. "You win. Just watch you don't have too many, and be careful what you say. We don't want a repeat of what happened after the last time we went to a pub."

I help her up, which is a good excuse for a hug. We do good hugs, hugs like I never had before in my life.

I look at Peggy as she puts her coat on – slim, beautiful, in her thirties, as she pulls the hood of her duffel coat over her long brown hair, and I wonder – not for the first time – what she sees in an old copper in his late fifties.

"Peggy?" I ask, as I put my own coat on and find the dog's lead. " Why do you love me?"

She looks at me – her eyes searching my eyes. "What sort of question is that?"

"Well, here I am in my fifties, near retirement, losing my marbles, and you, so much younger, and so... beautiful. You could have had any man you wanted..."

"No I couldn't. It doesn't work like that. Anyway, it's not about age, or how beautiful you are. We just happened."

She gets her crutches, which are propped up by the door, I put the dog's lead on, and we go out into the evening air.

64

"Those years of working with you…" she continues. "I got so close to you, felt I could trust you. I don't find it all that easy to trust people. We see so much of the harm that people do to each other – particularly men."

"So I'm safe – a harmless old copper."

"Stop running yourself down. Anyway, you've got a gun – not so harmless," she says with a laugh.

I feel in my pocket to check it's there. My heart lurches as I feel its hard cold shape. "Yes, all safe and sound." I laugh too, though it feels a bit hollow.

"You know I was adopted by an older couple. They were very kind, but I never quite felt they were Mum and Dad, though I called them that. Anyway, it was just them and me, and then… Dad died." She stops and looks down at the pavement. I take her arm, and look into her face. I see two tears running down the side of her cheeks.

"Am I a father figure?"

"No." The sad moment is broken, and she laughs. "All those talks we would have about your problems and worries about your marriage. You were like a boy, and I was your mum. You came to me with your problems. You still do."

"So what am I? Just safe?"

"That counts for a lot in my world. But you're not just safe. I love you because… because you're you. Interesting, funny, loveable, and yes, I trust you. I've never known anyone so trustworthy." She gives me a hug as best she can with crutches and dog to contend with, and we walk on down towards the pub.

"But you trust Hannah, don't you?" I always feel a bit envious of Hannah – Peggy's close friend who seems to be good at everything, especially playing the cello.

"She's a woman, and it's different."

"Tell me."

Peggy takes a deep breath. "After... Dad died... you know it's funny, I can't call him John, even though I didn't think of him as my dad."

"Were you close?"

"You know we were. I've told you before."

"Sorry..."

"You say sorry so much. You shouldn't, but it's one of the things I love about you."

"And your mum was Annie, wasn't she?"

"Yes. So Mum and I were on our own. Not much money. You know we lived in that village close to here. Mum and I managed, and then she had a breakdown. Started behaving strangely – running from room to room wringing her hands and singing. Then I'd stop her and get her to sit down and make her a cup of tea. I was only young – early teens – and my whole world was collapsing."

"So, Hannah?"

"Her family rescued us. They were the posh house up the road, and I used to meet Hannah when I went running before Mum broke. Hannah ran too, and we would talk sometimes when we stopped. So when I hadn't turned up for my usual run she was straight round to check I was OK, and she saw Mum in one of her singing moods. She was so much older than me, and she took charge. She helped me get Mum sectioned, and we got Mum into a psychiatric hospital to get treatment. Hannah and her family took me in while Mum was in hospital. Hannah was a struggling musician, and lived at home. But her parents..."

"They sound rich, and generous."

"They were. Her dad had been something big in the Civil Service and had a good pension, and her mum had inherited."

"So your mum, Annie?"

"She never really recovered. Went in and out of hospital."

"God, that must have been hard."

"If it hadn't been for Hannah and her family, I would have been taken into care until I was sixteen."

"All this about you." I wonder how we'd never managed to have this conversation before. "All this stuff I never knew."

"You've had so much to deal with…"

"But I should have asked."

"Think, Arne. Think back over what has happened during the last couple of months. There's been no time. Anyway, you opened this can of worms by asking me why I loved you."

"We have more in common than I thought. My dad was in and out of hospital with alcoholism…"

"Your brother died…"

"And so we both had a pretty unsafe and shaky start to life."

"Explains a lot." Peggy grabs my arm and stops, looking up into my face.

"Keeping people safe, you mean," I say.

"Keeping people safe."

"Well, here's a safe place," I pronounce as we find ourselves at the pub door.

"Not so safe if you're an alcoholic."

"True," I say, wondering if Peggy thinks I drink too much.

The pub is almost empty, but the specials board is proclaiming steak and chips for £7.50, or £8.50 with a pint. Too good to be true. We find the only sofa, which is in a corner behind a low table, and I go up to the bar to order our food. It's then that I realise why it seems so empty. No Charles propping up the bar. My friend Charles, who, all the time, was leading me up the garden

67

path. He's in custody now, helping Grimwode and co. with their enquiries, but I miss his large cheerful form in his habitual corner by the bar. Can't help it. A bit of my old life that I liked, once.

The bar's the same as it always was. The bottles arranged on the shelf behind are the same. Some of them are very dusty – strange liqueurs from distant lands that no-one wants to try.

"Hello." A cheerful voice from behind the bar wakes me from my reverie. Long dark brown hair frames a pretty, cherubic face. The girl looks too young to serve alcohol, but perhaps I'm just getting to that stage in life where I can't tell age any more.

"You're new here, aren't you?" I say by way of conversation.

"My dad's the landlord. Gap year." She shrugs her shoulders and smiles a lovely smile. "Hey, aren't you that policeman who solved all those crimes?"

I nod and smile. Fame at last.

"Dad said he knew that... that Charles Hamilton was up to something. Surprised you didn't catch him earlier, he said. Still, he was a good friend of yours, wasn't he?"

Oh dear, now my smile feels false. My glory shattered at a stroke.

"Can I have a steak and chips and a pint, and the mushroom risotto with a tonic water?"

"Ice and lemon?"

I'm confused for a moment – ice and lemon with beer? But it's for the tonic, and I realise that I still don't know whether Peggy likes ice and lemon. I decide for her. "Yes, please." More for my money.

"You should talk to my dad. He knows a lot about people in this town." So did Charles, I reflect ruefully.

"Thanks. I'd er... love to." I pick up our drinks, and return to the sofa and Peggy. The dog gets up and greets me, and I wonder if he's done enough business today. He's looking a bit cross-legged.

"Ice and lemon?"

"Oh thanks. Actually, I don't usually have it. But..." She gives me a gentle smile. Poor old Arnold and his memory, it says.

"Sorry. I haven't quite got the hang of what you like, have I?"

"I like you," she says, putting her hand on my knee.

"Look, the dog needs a wee. Will you be OK if I take him out for a quick run on the common? Five minutes?"

"You go, I'll wait for the food. Don't be too long – it'll get cold." She takes a sip of her tonic, and involuntarily wrinkles up her nose. I wonder if she'll go back to the bar and change it for one without ice and lemon.

I slip out into the cold night air. A dry November night with the lights of the town twinkling in the distance. I let the dog off the lead, and he makes for some bushes that border the old cricket pitch. I follow him, partly to check what kind of relief he is finding in the bushes. Don't want any unsuspecting person treading in something he's left behind.

I just duck down to inspect the ground where he's been, and the branch behind me explodes, wood splintering everywhere, and I have that same feeling that I had in Paul's kitchen.

Somebody's taking pot-shots at me.

I dive onto the ground and fish out my gun ready to protect myself. Everything is going in slow-motion, my thinking is racing at super-speed. He must be using a silencer, and he will be coming towards me to find out if he hit me. It's too dark to see anything clearly, and I listen carefully to the sounds around me. The dog is oblivious of this threat, and I will just have to trust he will keep out of the way. I don't want to move. I want the gunman to think

69

he's got me, and to come into range so I can disarm him somehow or other. I haven't got a plan – I'm just guessing and hoping.

I hear a rustle from the bushes opposite, and I can just make out a figure walking in a slightly bent way, looking from left to right. He's lost the orientation of where his shot went, and as he gets closer he turns to the right as he hears the dog moving about in the bushes. Shit, he'll shoot the dog before he realises it's not me. I see the silhouette of his gun raised to fire, and I take aim and shoot it out of his hand. The noise surprises us both, and he stares at me in disbelief as I clamber up out of the bushes.

"Put your hands up," I say, realising too late that I should have told him to get down on the ground in true aggressive armed police fashion.

He doesn't put his hands up, he runs for it. I don't want to kill him so I aim for his legs. For some reason, tears come to my eyes, and all I succeed in doing is hitting his shoe, which goes spinning off as he plunges back into the bushes.

"Stop where you are. We're armed. Put the gun down and lie on the ground." Somebody's saying it for me, and for a moment I think they're shouting at my assailant, but as I turn I see lights aimed at me. I drop the gun.

"On the ground." I recognise that voice.

"He's getting away!" I shout as I sink to the ground.

"Who's getting away?" It's Sergeant Brown. Last time I looked, we were working together looking for stolen paintings. Now he's got a gun to my head.

"Brown! It's Rackham, for God's sake!" I turn and look at him. Our eyes meet.

He gives a sharp intake of breath, and removes his gun from my head. "What's going on, sir?"

"Man took a pot-shot at me. I shot his weapon out of his hand. He's run off in that direction, and he's lost a shoe." I pick up my gun.

"We'll take care of this, sir." Brown and two other plainclothes dash off into the undergrowth. I doubt they'll catch him now, in spite of the lack of a shoe. I hear a siren. There're more police appearing, called by Brown no doubt. The dog, oblivious of all the trouble comes up to me wagging his tail. He's done his business somewhere, but I'll never find out where. I go over to the gun lying on the ground. It looks a bit mangled, the silencer sticking up at right-angles like a fuck-off finger. I have no idea what kind it is – not my department – but Brown reappears from the bushes and stoops down with a bag and picks it up.

"You alright, sir? We can deal with this."

"Thank you, Sergeant, I'll be in the pub." Actually, I feel very strange. Elated, but with fear pumping adrenaline round my veins in large quantities. Somebody tried to kill me and I'm not sure why.

Peggy's standing by the door of the pub, looking at her mobile phone, when I arrive with the dog and one of Brown's minions in tow.

"Arnold, what's going on? I heard shots. I've just tried Grimwode." She never calls me Arnold. She's scared.

I shrug my shoulders. I can't speak. I sit down at our table, leaving Brown's man by the door, and down my pint in one. My cooling plate of steak and chips doesn't look very inviting.

"Who was it? Was that you shooting?" Peggy says, as she sits down shakily in her chair.

I nod. Still can't speak.

"You're not hurt are you? Tell me what happened!" Peggy is gripping my arm, looking for signs of blood. The

71

dog stands by, wagging his tail. He didn't know how close he came to death.

"Here's a pint on the house. Looks like you need it after what happened out there." A small chubby hand puts it down on the table in front of me, and I look up to see the landlord.

"I guess that's one of yours by my door. It's not every day I get that kind of protection. That was to do with you – all that shooting? Saw the flashes from upstairs."

"Thanks." I manage to get it out.

"Thank you," Peggy says to the man. "Would it be OK if Inspector Rackham and I have a word on our own?" If it wasn't for the slight shake in her voice, I would have thought she was talking about buying a domestic appliance in a shop.

"My daughter told me you were here. Good to see you back. Maybe we'll have a chat another time." He moves off, totally unfazed, as though shootings and armed police inside his pub were commonplace.

"So, tell me." Peggy looks into my eyes, and I begin to laugh. The spectacle of Brown looking into my face comes back.

I take a swig at my new beer, pick up a tepid chip. "Someone took a pot-shot at me. Thank God I had the gun. I disarmed him – it was all so dark he couldn't see me. Looked like he was going to shoot the dog thinking it was me. Oh, and I shot his shoe off. I was going to go after him, but Brown and his men must have heard the shots from Betty's cottage, because they came running down and tried to arrest me. It was so funny when Brown saw my face." I crack up again. Take another swig, another cold chip. "The man has probably got away. Not that I could have caught him anyway. I should have sounded more aggressive when I had him in front of me. Would you believe it, I said 'hands up' like some bloody cowboy

72

film, and he legged it." The laughter takes over again. Another swig. Another chip. "What's amazing is all these police around. It's like a police state here. How did they get here so quickly?"

"Arne, Arne listen to me." Peggy grabs my arm again. "Look at me."

"I…"

"No, stop talking and have some food. I'm so glad you're here. Safe. There's obviously something going on that Grimwode knows about. That's why he insisted you have a gun. And the vests as well. He knows something we don't. Could it be to do with..?" She looks me in the face, and I think I know what she's thinking.

I tuck into the steak. It's a bit overcooked, but it's doing the business, and I start to feel closer to normal. But now I wonder what that thing is that Grimwode thinks I know. That thing in the report that I lost, back in September.

10.15am 18th November

"Good shooting, Rackham. It's a shame you didn't immobilise him. Now we've lost him." Grimwode has come down to my home town, and is sitting in my old office twiddling one of my pens. I am slumped in a chair opposite, feeling like death warmed up.

"I couldn't do it, D… sir. Not after… what happened in the Met."

"What happened?" He looks puzzled for a moment, then nods. "Ah yes. Anyway it seems like you did a good job disarming him."

"Thank you, sir." Actually, I was protecting my dog – a very forceful motivation.

"Anyway," Grimwode grunts. "We've got the gun, and a size 8 shoe. There'll be some DNA with any luck, and we're still working on the gun."

"I'm glad you armed me. Had no idea I was a target."

Grimwode leans across my desk and looks at me. He seems about to say something, then changes his mind. He gets up and prowls around behind the desk.

"We won't be able to protect you for ever. Once you've left the force…" He shrugs his shoulders. "You know, you could have been a good policeman. Instead you opted for the easy life, and look where that got you."

So it's going to be a lecture on my failings.

"By the way, that report I gave you. You know, the one after your bungled raid. I'd like it back before you retire. In fact, the sooner the better."

He sits down and starts to read some papers on the desk. "Goodbye, Rackham." He doesn't look up.

11.00am 18th November

"He wants the report back. You know, the one that got stolen when they poisoned the dog."

We're sitting in my kitchen. Peggy has made us coffee in the machine that Betty gave me. It tastes good this morning – much better than I could have made.

"You didn't tell him?" Peggy gives me a look.

"I couldn't. I'd get into so much trouble. I…"

"But you're retiring the week after next."

"I don't know what they'd do to my pension if they found out."

"Who are *they*? I think you're being paranoid." She pauses and shifts in her chair. "Listen, Arnold." This is a bad sign, her using my full name again – she's going to give me a lecture. "I think you should have told them about losing the report, and about your episodes. You should have been open with them. The police look after their own, you know. They won't just chuck you out on the street. In fact you're lucky because you're so close to retirement age, and you'll get a better deal than I will in twenty years time."

"But I'm afraid I'll lose out big time…"

"Look, Arne, have you actually tried to find out? Have you looked into it?"

"No I…"

"All that time when I was covering up for you. I was in loads of pain, and I didn't want to cause you any. But now

77

I'm beginning to wonder whether we did the right thing. Grimwode needs to know that you lost that report."

"I can't. It's too late now. I could be prosecuted. And… I just can't do it." I look at her, pleading.

"Well, if you can't tell him the truth, why don't you just say you destroyed it – burnt it in the fire."

"I can't just lie like that. He'll know."

"But you're lying anyway."

I put my head in my hands. Through my fingers I see light chasing shadows. She's right. Grimwode needs to know. For all our sakes.

"I'll tell him."

"Tell him what?"

"The truth."

Peggy looks hard at me, trying to catch my eyes.

"You really would?"

I nod. "You're right," I say.

"Hope so."

I don my bullet-proof vest on Peggy's insistence. Holster strapped on an' all.

"They won't try again," I say petulantly.

"You don't know that. I wish you'd take the car. And remember you've got the estate agent coming at one."

How mundane. I long for that normal life, but for now I'm stuck in a high-anxiety existence, wondering where this will all end up.

"I need to walk, just to prepare myself."

"He's a human being, Arnold."

Arnold again. "Is he?"

Down the garden to the common. Through the shrubs and trees towards the town. *My* town it was, once. Now I don't want it. The place is spoiled for me. There are ghosts everywhere, my friends were imaginary, and sourness takes the place of comfort.

Down, down into the town. A favourite lunchtime pub on my right. Up the hill towards the station. I find myself thinking of Lilly, that poor girl who was trapped in this town for a night, and then in a mental institution for years. This cruel town, full of rich people. Uncaring. Unseeing.

Shaky legs take me off to the left, past the Congregational Chapel, up to the Library, and over to the Police Station. This was mine once. Not since September though.

I say hello to Claire at the front desk and walk straight to my office, where I expect to find Grimwode.

"Sir?" Claire calls from the desk.

I can't stop now. I knock on the door.

"Come." The voice sounds strangely high, maybe I am hearing everything differently in my altered state of truthfulness.

I walk in, to find three officers, their jackets off, exposing holsters and bullet-proof vests. And sitting in my old chair facing me, a completely unfamiliar woman. She's in her fifties. Short grey hair. Square face with regular features that would be attractive, if it weren't for a feeling of 'danger – keep off' that emanates from her eyes.

"Yes?" She sounds annoyed.

"I… I came to see Grimwode. I…"

"Commander Grimwode is not here. You are?"

"Inspector Rackham… ma'am. I…"

"Ah, I have heard about you, Rackham." She lets out a sigh, stands up, and puts both her fists on the desk. "John, Matt, Alan, could you give us a moment, please." Her three acolytes trail out of the room without even looking at me.

"Sit." She indicates the chair that I only recently vacated.

Momentarily confused, I look round for the dog, and then realise she means me.

"You…" she shifts the papers on her desk, "will have read in the report following the shooting of Sergeant Peggy McDonald, that this terrorist cell poses a significant threat to our national security."

I nod, trying to catch a peek of her papers. A copy of the report that I lost is sitting there, teasing me, on the desk.

"It seems that they have become more active. They attacked you in Wales. We suspect they are behind the killing of the woman you identified as er…"

"Mrs Braithwaite," I pipe up.

She fixes me with a particularly old-fashioned stare, "and they had a go at you last night. Do you have any ideas as to why they are taking the trouble to eliminate you?"

No, but I am now wondering if she does. But I daren't ask. Instead I say, "it could be to do with the paintings, and the wallet I found with the art dealer and Brian… O'Connell's name inside."

"Oh yes, lost and found, lost and found. Anyway you are obviously a nuisance to them." Even more of a nuisance than I am to you, I reflect.

"Er…"

"Jackson."

"Jackson?"

"Jackson. My name is Jackson. You may call me that. You were saying?"

"I would've thought that they would want to see what I was up to. What I knew. Whether I knew where the paintings are that I er…"

"…lost. No, I think they know where they are. We are waiting for Mr O'Connell to turn up… probably dead."

Stupid man. "So what…?"

"They must think you pose a threat to them in some way. You're obviously pressing some buttons. We want you to continue to do what you're doing. Snooping around. Playing the detective. You haven't got long to go, Rackham. Will you do that for us?" It's not a request, it's an order.

"And after?" I really want to know.

"When you're retired, you mean?"

"Yes."

"You'll be on your own. But for now you're armed and you've got protection. You are wearing…?"

"Yes."

"We'll cover your back."

"Er… thanks." But it's my head I'm worried about. I don't have a bullet-proof head, and they seem to like shooting people in the head.

Also, I wonder what will happen if my head goes AWOL.

1.30pm 18th November

"Jackson. She's called Jackson. I think she must be MI5 – certainly not one of Grimwode's lot. Wants me to go around pretending I know something, so that our friends can keep taking pot-shots at me."

Peggy hisses through her teeth. "Did you tell her you lost the report?"

"No, I…"

"So they still don't know."

"No."

The estate agent has been and gone. Sniffed round my cottage. Sniffed at the dog. Sniffed at Brown and his men next door.

"We'll come back to you with a figure," said the black-suited young lady, still wearing her poppy in her lapel. "We'll look after everything for you."

I have been through the form with all the stuff about contents, heating, drainage, cooker etc. I will have to clear out my personal possessions before they can let the cottage.

"Do you want to hire someone to spring clean?" the agent sniffed. "Or would you like us to organise that? Oh, and the garden."

"What about the garden?" She was really beginning to get up my nose.

"Lawn mowed. Beds weeded. Regular upkeep," she sniffed, looking out at my long thin patch of concrete and mud – the weedy patches of grass struggling in the cold November air.

"Shouldn't take me long." Better make sure there are no dog poos left.

"No, I mean do you want someone to look after it, or shall we leave it to the tenants?"

I began to see my profit on the rent being knocked on the head as the agent notched up more and more costs. 'Leave it to us' equals 'we'll take your profit and give it to our friends'.

"I'll look after all that," I said. And as a generous afterthought: "The tenants can take care of the garden."

The agent sniffed one more time, and took her leave before I could knock her profit down any further.

"Look Peggy, I want to find Dick Grimwode and tell him in person." Somehow that feels the right way to do it. Put my head in the lion's mouth.

"Where is he?"

"I don't know – she didn't say. Brown might know. Anyway, you've got a number for him on your phone."

"I don't have his personal number. He phoned me back from an office."

"Well, let's try that…"

Peggy gets her mobile and starts rifling through her calls, while I sit looking out at my bleak garden wondering how on earth I'm going to make it look like anything.

"Ah… oh, 'caller withheld'. What now?"

"Cup of tea, then I'll tackle the house. Try and nab Brown when he's not deconstructing next door." It's my house, and I can't even go in there. They'll have found the mess I made of Betty's bedroom. A good reason to leave well alone.

I make tea, insisting that Peggy puts her feet up, and set to, starting with the kitchen.

I clear out the cupboards: not much there. A tin of baked beans, tinned sardines in tomato juice, UHT milk, very old biscuits, a bottle of soy sauce all sticky on the outside – not much left inside.

I'm leaving my crockery and cutlery – it's a furnished letting, but I stick all I can in the dishwasher and wash up the rest. Hoover, mop, cobweb spot. I draw the line at doing the windows. Old Jack does the outside every now and then.

More tea, then the sitting room. Hardly anything there. Just my collection of folk CDs and all Paul's albums. A few vinyl records with nothing to play them on. Dust shelves – bloody hell, when did I last do that? How come dust can get so greasy? Scrub, dust, hoover. The dog sits in a corner looking at me as if to say, 'what's my part in all this?' Dear old dog – new life coming up.

I hear Peggy moving about upstairs. "We'll have to get this lot packed."

I go up to find she's stripped the bed and put everything into neat piles. "You shouldn't…"

"What am I supposed to do? Sit around all day?" She looks tired and fed up.

"Where are we staying tonight? Could you book something?"

"What about the Red House Hotel?" she says, showing an unusual lack of thriftiness. "I've always wondered what that would be like to stay in."

"I thought more The Engineer. A last night in my local." And a damn sight cheaper.

She gives me a withering look: "I'll see what's available."

I do the bathroom, the bedroom, then enter my studio-that-was. I've been dreading this. The place where I drew,

85

and painted, and escaped to. My inner sanctum. Now I will turn it into 'bedroom two, 8ft 6 by 9ft.' Not a big space, but mine. Once.

Piles of unfinished sketches that I can't throw away. Peaceful paintings of my town that nobody wants to buy. My easel. My brushes. My collection of oil paints, water colours, pencils, charcoal. Half-finished sketch pads and bits of canvas. And sitting in a corner, facing the wall, the last painting that I ever did.

I pick it up and look at it. A peaceful landscape – it's the view from my window. Very accurate and meticulous. A safe place – or so I thought then. My past life in a nutshell. One corner remains unfinished – the careful sketch lines to be filled in with detailed brushstrokes. Almost painting by numbers. Bizarrely, it's the area of the common where I nearly had my head blown off last night. What a different world – I can never go back there now. Not sure I'd want to – I think I prefer living a precarious life to being half-dead.

As I pack the materials up into a couple of boxes, I wonder if I'll ever use them again.

"They can do an executive room on the first floor. There's a spa." Peggy's voice comes up from downstairs. "They can do a deal if I go online."

"Sounds lovely." No it doesn't – I feel my nice pub evening slipping away. A faceless hotel room with all modern conveniences but no atmosphere. The air con and generic hum keeping me awake. Then, with a shock, I remember that Peggy could do with a lift, a spa, and easy access. The pub stairs might even have been beyond her stubborn insistence to get around on crutches whatever the challenge.

"They're not doing food tonight though."

"The pub will be OK won't it?" A bit of a pub evening after all.

"Suppose so…" she doesn't sound keen. Maybe the events of yesterday have put her off the pub for now.

"Lightning doesn't strike in the same place twice," I say by way of reassurance. Then another thought comes to me. "And the dog? Is that going to be OK?"

"He counts as an assistance dog, doesn't he? You've still got the letter. I'll check with them after I've booked, but it doesn't say no pets anywhere. They should make that clear if …" she stops, and I hear the clatter of her crutches as she moves about downstairs.

Having packed my few possessions together into boxes and suitcases, I start taking them downstairs ready to take out – fortunately, I had the wisdom to hire a white van for the week. Strictly speaking, I have been advised not to drive in case I have another episode – but it's not a legal requirement, and needs must.

I thought I had no possessions, but now there's a pile of stuff in the sitting room that tells me otherwise. I start taking things out and stacking them in the van, and it's on one of these trips that I bump into Brown, who's going out to his car.

"Ah, Brown. Just the man I wanted to speak to." I can't resist pulling rank – he: Sergeant, me: Inspector. "I need to talk to Commander Grimwode. Have you got a contact for him?"

He looks furtively around as if there was someone listening, but the street is empty. "Just a minute sir, I'll see what I can do." He scuttles back into Betty's cottage.

I continue loading up my van, and after a few minutes, Brown re-emerges. "He says he'll call you on Sergeant McDonald's phone, but if you head for…" he hands me a piece of paper, "he says he'll meet you sometime tomorrow afternoon."

I look down at the piece of paper. A stately home in Oxfordshire. "What..?" I look up to find Brown has disappeared.

I have packed the van, cleared up my mud patch of a garden, taken the dog for a walk, made five cups of tea and failed to finish any of them, and sent Peggy off to the Red House Hotel with a promise that we'll meet at the pub for supper. I've gone round and round the house, checking for dirt, cobwebs, lost CD covers, broken pencils, and all the detritus that my life here has created.

Just the bins to put out. A few guilty bottles that I haven't the energy to wash go in the bin bag for landfill. One last black bin bag in the kitchen and that will be it. I lift it up to take out, and something white catches my eye sticking out from the side of the dishwasher. I curse – surely there's not more dirt and rubbish to clear up. I bend down to see what job I have missed, and find it's just a piece of A4 paper that somehow got stuck down between the dishwasher and the wall. I pull it out intending to add it to my final bin bag. It's covered in dirty cobwebs on one side, making me think that I ought to pull the dishwasher out and clean behind it.

Turning it over I realise it's a page of a police report.

The report that I lost.

The page must have blown off the table when they came in and stole the report after poisoning my dog.

My heart beating, I put the dirty piece of paper on the table to try and read it.

It's just a load of gobbledygook which, I suspect is to do with stuff found on a computer. It makes no sense to me at all, but at the bottom of the page I read:

'Put together with the information on page 16, the conclusion is that this is a large-scale operation – the largest we have seen in the UK. Some of the information taken from the computer is in code and points to them having a comprehensive…'

I turn the page, but it is blank. They weren't saving paper that day. Biggest terrorist operation in the UK? No wonder Dick and his goons have been all over this for months. My abortive drugs raid opened a can of worms, the size of which nobody could have suspected.

I make a careful search of the kitchen in case there's any more of the report that got blown into a corner, but just find a couple of old biros and an ancient mint, which I add to the bin bag.

Then, reluctantly, I don my bullet-proof vest, put my shirt on over it, and strap on the gun. I don my jacket and tuck the folded page of the report in the inside pocket. Then stuffing the bin bag into the already overflowing wheelie bin, I check round the house one more time, call the dog and pick up his blanket, pick up my suitcase, pop the blanket in the van, and walk down the road to the pub.

I'm early, so I settle down in a corner with a pint – the dog, and my thoughts for company. Where now? I have said goodbye to my home of twenty years. Peggy wants us to live in the wilds of Wales. I'm being shot at like some kind of fairground toy, for no good reason that I can fathom. Will this go on for ever? Grimwode seemed to imply that there would be no protection once I had left the force. And then there's Betty. Is she alive? Will she return? I'm in a mess, and likely to end up at the bottom of a ditch with a bullet through my head.

"Hullo." Peggy sits down opposite me, a smile on her face. "How's the house? All sorted?"

"Yes... um, how's the hotel?"

"Brilliant. I went to the spa. Got someone to give me a massage – told them what I needed. I'm feeling much better."

"You look great. But then..." she always does, in spite of her injury.

"You look worried, Arne. Is there something up, or is it just about leaving your cottage behind?"

"No." I lower my voice. "I found a page of the report that got stolen. Must have blown off the table – it was stuck down the side of the dishwasher. Most of it is in some sort of computer-speak but it says that they found the biggest operation in the UK."

Peggy's face turns from post-massage relaxed, to that keen policewoman expression that puts me on the spot. "You've got to get to Grimwode as soon as possible."

"I know, I know. I'm seeing him tomorrow." And dreading it. "Shall we order some food?"

I'm awake. I'm in some kind of machine – a plane, a spaceship, a massive vehicle. The noise of its motion goes on and on. As I open my eyes I see walls around me – all grey and inhuman. They seem to be closing in on me. I can't move, I can't make a sound. I will be crushed. With superhuman force I break out of these bonds and push out my hands to repel the invading walls. Something moves beside me, and I let out a scream.

"Arnold, it's me, it's alright." I feel a warm hand on my outstretched arm. There's a cold wet sensation on the skin of my other hand. As I come to, I realise it's Peggy on one side, the dog on the other. We're in a hotel room with noisy air con, and that's all.

"Sorry," I whisper.

12.15pm 19th November

I turn the van round in the road, and head off for Oxfordshire. My suitcase is on the floor beside me, and the dog is lying on the passenger seat on his blanket.

Peggy and I have had a good time in the morning, making the best of our expensive night in a posh, if noisy, hotel, and using the spa and the swimming pool. We have arranged to meet at a tea room called the 'Teddy Bears' Picnic' (not my idea) in a small Oxfordshire village, after my interview with Grimwode. Peggy will get another mobile on her way, and I have hers so that I can contact Grimwode for an exact meeting place. As usual, she thinks ahead – she thinks of everything.

Driving a white van is a new experience. In the past I have pulled a few over for dangerous driving, but now I can see how tempting it is to be aggressive in a white van. I'm high up and can see well ahead, I'm big, and I'm anonymous.

The confusing lane system in Aylesbury causes me no problem in my van. I just signal and barge – everyone gets out of the way. I begin to wonder if I'm changing personality – the aggressive 'fuck-you' part of me coming out. After all, it must be there somewhere in my make-up. You don't survive in the force without some of that in your personality, and for the first time, I begin to wonder whether I made the right decision about leaving the police.

I bowl along the country roads, humming a tune to myself. I realise it's the cheerful theme to 'The Archers', which seems ironic considering that I'm going to confess a major breach of security to Dick Grimwode – erstwhile colleague turned tormentor. My heart sinks, and I feel the weight of my bullet-proof vest and the bulge of the gun under my left armpit.

I decide to remain incognito at the gate to the stately home, and fork out quite a lot of dosh for the privilege of meeting Grimwode in this sanctified setting.

I text him to let him know I'm here, take the dog with me and head for the grand house. There's a shop, of course, but this is quite a big shop with nice, if expensive, stuff in it. And Christmas is coming up.

I start looking at colourful Scottish blankets, until I see the price. Still, Peggy's worth it. I remember it's her phone I've got. I look down to see if Grimwode has contacted me, and I've missed it. Nothing. For some reason I had 2.00pm in my head as our meeting time, but he hasn't confirmed anything.

I begin to feel uncomfortable again. I don't want this to drag on, this feeling of dreadful confession. I get a coffee at the counter in the shop and sit down and drink it too fast, slightly scalding my mouth. The time drags on – I look at my watch, it's only 2.30. Anyway, the coffee has done its trick and I need the loo. The toilets are at the other end of the shop, and as I get near to the entrance I am struck by a roaring sound that seems to be coming from them. The dog won't stay at the entrance, so I take him with me, following the signs which lead me down a winding corridor towards the men's loos, and the ever-increasing cacophony that sounds like a jet engine.

Clean white porcelain greets me as I enter a palatial room with wash basins and mirrors in the middle, and urinals round the edge. The first thing I see is my face reflected back at me, and behind that I catch a glimpse of another face. I turn round – there's no-one there. The roaring noise is coming from a hand dryer – a man is stooped over it. He is perfectly still, his head resting against the wall and his arms stuck down the two holes that activate the dryer. I recognise his bony back and thin shoulders. It's Grimwode, and he's not moving.

"Dick?" He doesn't turn round.

"Dick, it's Rackham." I go up to him. He is unconscious. I pull him sideways and he slides to the floor, one outstretched hand blistered by the heat of the dryer. The dog growls, and that's all the warning I get as I feel something hit me in the back with such a force that it pushes me to the wall. The dog is barking and I wrench my body round to see my face in the mirror. I'm confused for a moment, then I see my attacker running away between the urinals and the basins. I realise that he must have tried to stab me with his knife, but it has wedged in the fabric of my bullet-proof vest and was torn out of his hand as I turned. I try to get my gun out, but it gets caught in the lining of my coat. Anyway it's too late – he's gone, leaving me looking down at Grimwode's body, blood beginning to ooze from a wound in his back.

I kneel down by him. He's still breathing. I reach for Peggy's phone to get help, and then try and pull him into a better position.

"Ah, Rackham," his eyes flicker open. "You wanted to see me?"

"Yes."

"… didn't… know… I was on the… list…" his voice fades out. I put my hand against his back to slow the bleeding as we wait.

95

I'm walking along a wide beach which stretches into the distance ahead of me. The sand slopes down to a gently lapping sea on my right, but it is stopped abruptly on my left by a forest. It's like some huge hand has taken a giant knife and cut into the edge of the forest to make this beach, leaving broken dead trees strewn around, and great vertical walls of sand with roots of the trees above sticking out every now and then. It looks dark, mysterious, and in places, the sandy walls slope down to make an access into the forest.

I feel the sand beneath my feet as I walk slowly – heel-sole-toes, heel-sole-toes, as I pivot my weight forward gently, going I know not where. I am so absorbed with this walking sensation that it takes me by surprise when I look up and see a small crenellated building in the distance, placed in the middle of the beach, as though by a giant child's hand. As I get nearer, I realise it is one of those early twentieth-century follies that I might have seen on a visit to some manor estate – the windows are arched in a churchy style, and the front door has black metal studs set into light green paint.

BOOKSHOP, it says above the door.

I read the sign, and go inside.

An elderly man, with a long grey beard and half-moon glasses, sits at a low counter facing me as I enter. He takes no notice of me, absorbed in putting some numbers into an enormous ledger in front of him. He is surrounded by books. There are books on shelves, stacked up to the ceiling. Rooms of books lead off in both directions. I turn right, guided by some memory, or instinct, and see that all the books are biographies. Tony Blair keeps company with Brunel, Sir Thomas Beecham with David Beckham. There is some kind of order in the alphabetical arrangement, and I pass the Cs and Ds and Fs before I get to a room that has strange subdued lighting. Most of these books are in darkness but every now and then the spine of a book is lit up as if by some spotlight.

Richard Grimwode. His book is large and thick. I lift it off the shelf and turn the pages. An unbelievable amount of events, qualifications, jobs and accolades fills this volume as I look through. This man has lived, and lived big time.

I put it back and look for more, down a corridor and through another room. And there in a corner is Arnold Rackham. In contrast to Grimwode's biography, mine is thin. Not much there – early life sketchy, a nice bit on my art studies, almost nothing about my police work or personal life until recently. The events of the last few months make up most of the book.

Back on the shelf it goes – disappointing compared to Grimwode.

The other spotlighted books are of people I am less familiar with. There's the young politician, mother of four, who was so tragically shot during a peace rally. Other politicians too, mostly women, well known for human rights and peace negotiations. A mathematician. Some writers. A famous sportsman. But many I don't recognise. As I turn to leave, two names catch my eye.

Brian O'Connell, my erstwhile friend and art thief, and Alan Hunt, the art dealer.

It goes dark, and I hastily make my way out of the shop and back onto the beach. The light is fading and the sea has come in. I look back to see the bookshop awash with sea water. I am holding something in my hand – a piece of paper, but I can't see what it is. I begin to panic as I see the waves coming up the shore towards me, and I run towards the forest. The only escape is up the sandy cliff that hangs above me, and I scrabble desperately with my hands, trying to hold on to the piece of paper at the same time. Every time I scramble up, the loose sand gives way and I fall back into the sea waters that are swirling round beneath me.

The light fades. Everything goes black. All I can feel is this piece of paper in my hand.

7.00am 21st November

I wake up with a start. I have let go of the piece of paper. My eyes focus on it, lying there on the hospital floor:

Some of the information taken from the computer is in code and points to them having a comprehensive...

Then I remember about the confession I was going to make to Grimwode. I have been keeping vigil by him since we brought him in. My slept-in clothes feel sticky, and there's a sore patch where the weight of my gun has pressed against the left side of my chest. I have refused all medical attention. The knife didn't get past my bullet-proof vest, and all I want to do is to see Dick Grimwode through, and possibly make my confession. That's if he lives.

I don't need to be there to protect him. Armed officers are outside the door. The security is so tight, you could crack a million nuts with it. But I don't think it's nuts we're dealing with. His attacker, whoever he was, was impossible to identify – medium height, medium width, medium brown hair, medium everything, except his knife – which was long and sharp. It's a miracle Grimwode survived at all.

"Rackham, is that you?" He's awake. "What are you doing here?"

"Dick, I..."

"Grimwode to you. Aargh… what's the bloody matter with me?" He tries to sit up, but can hardly move for bandages.

"You're in hospital. You were attacked, remember? I found you, and I've stayed with you since they brought you in."

He groans again. "Why you, of all bloody people?"

"I've got to tell you something."

"Can it wait? I need…" he gestures at the door.

"Oh yeah, er yes." I stand up and beckon to the officer outside. "He's come round."

There's a clatter outside, and a nurse and a doctor come in.

"Excuse me, can we?" the doctor points to the door, and the nurse sniffs at me as if I am something that she picked up on her shoe.

"Ok, yes." I shuffle out. My foot's gone to sleep, and all I want is a shower, but I must tell him first. This thing has loomed so large in my mind, that has blotted out all other thoughts.

Oh God, Peggy.

I get my mobile out.

The battery is flat, of course.

She knows what's happened, but where is she now?

"Sir." The armed officer at the door speaks. "Sergeant McDonald came to see you half an hour ago, she asked me to pass on that she would be down at the canteen."

"What, here?"

"Yes, sir."

"Thank you, officer. It's on..?"

"The ground floor, sir. Near the entrance."

"Thank you, er…"

"Green, sir."

"Green."

I stumble off, the life gradually coming back into my left foot. We're on the sixth floor of this modern hospital. If Dick had to choose to be stabbed in the back, he couldn't have chosen a better place. The medical care here seems second to none.

I find the lift, and have to hold on to the wall to stay upright, as it makes its way down. This hospital is vast, and it's a long walk till I get to the canteen. I see Peggy, but she doesn't see me – she's in deep conversation with a young black woman, and neither of them notice me until I am right by their table.

"Hi Peggy, he's…"

"Oh, Arne, this is Amanda." Peggy sniffs at me, about to make a comment, but thinks better of it. "She's an old friend from college. Works in rehab for injured police officers now. Gets them back into work."

"Oh, er, thanks." Why did I say that?

"Hello." She smiles. I sit down.

"The bacon butties are great," says Peggy.

I realise I'm starving, and get up again to go over to the counter.

"No, let me." Amanda is up and off to the counter before I can protest. "Tea?"

"Yes, please. Just milk. Thanks."

"Amanda thinks I should have been in one of the rehab centres. Hannah insisted on looking after me, so I was OK. Still, I can see her point."

"So, can she help with a job? Oh, and Grimwode's come round."

"Have you told him?"

"No, they sent me out. So, I've still got to…" I let it go. "So, can Amanda help?"

"Yes, she's got a whole list of jobs I could do."

List. Now why is that setting off bells?

103

Amanda returns with a mug of tea and a beautiful-smelling butty.

"Thanks, what did it cost?"

"No worries. I'll claim it on expenses. Supporting officers in dire need." She laughs, but looks at me with concern in her eyes.

"Not for long," I say.

"So I hear. Peggy tells me you could work from almost anywhere."

"True, but just at the moment, it seems that anywhere is a risky place to be."

"But once this is over…"

I shrug my shoulders. Will it ever be over?

"But you're getting protection," she insists.

I pat my chest just by the armpit, where my gun resides. "Yes, some. Better than Grimwode." I turn in my chair to look behind me – an armed officer passes the canteen and walks slowly down the corridor.

"Arne, you should stop. Have a shower. Go to bed." Peggy sniffs at me.

"I've got to see this through." I wonder if Peggy's told Amanda about the report.

"And there's a whole list of things we've got to do, and the dog needs a proper walk."

The dog. Yes, I'd better get this over. But bells are ringing again. What did she just say that set them off?

"Yes, I…"

Both women look over my shoulder, and I hear someone clear their throat.

"Commander Grimwode would like to see you sir."

I turn round to look up at a diminutive figure. It's Sergeant Brown, and my heart almost fails me. I hope he won't sit in on my confession.

"Brown. Good to see you," I lie, as I stiffly get out of my chair.

"See you later." I look at Peggy, then nod to Amanda. "Thanks for the…" The unfinished butty sits on its plate, begging me to take it along with me. Thoughts of grease dribbling down my chin as I tell Grimwode the truth enter my head, as I walk with unsteady steps to the lift with Brown.

"So, how's it going?" I ask.

Brown remains silent. This is neither the time nor place to discuss the investigation. I should know that – we're on double-red alert.

Ping. The top floor. Time is running out. Ready to confess.

Grimwode sits propped up on pillows. He would look dead if it weren't for his piercing black eyes looking straight through me as I enter.

"Ah Rackham. Something you wanted to tell me."

I turn and nod at Brown.

"It's alright Brown, you may go. I don't think Rackham's going to try and finish me off."

Reluctantly, Brown leaves, and Grimwode and I are alone, the steady beep of his heart monitor to keep us company.

"Dick, I…"

"Sit down Rackham, you're making me nervous." He spits the words out.

I sit in a chair by his bed, feeling oddly like a member of his family.

"I lost the report," I blurt out.

He looks at me, puzzled. "The report? What report?"

"The one you gave me to read, after the raid on the house in The Avenues."

"Ah, that one." His mind grinds back into gear. "And how did you manage to do that?"

"It was stolen. My dog was poisoned. They took it from… my kitchen table."

105

"Your kitchen table? And what were you doing while that came to pass?"

"Drawing…"

"Drawing?"

"Drawing a picture of the gunman who shot Peggy, er Sergeant McDonald. I was going to read the report when I'd finished."

"So, someone came and poisoned your dog, and took the report off your kitchen table, while you were drawing a picture of the suspect? Good picture, by the way." He muses for a moment.

"Yes, sir." No Dick – I can't do Dick.

"And you didn't think to tell me at the time?"

"No, sir."

"And why was that?"

He's lying there in bed, weak from a near fatal stab wound, and he's got me pinned to the ceiling.

"Well I…"

"Yes?"

"I was afraid I'd get sacked."

He looks at me for what seems like hours.

"You know, Rackham, it's just as well you went off and did your own investigation. We were looking in a different direction, and you found out about the paintings. Also, that report was early so there was not much detail in it. But…" he pauses for effect, "we didn't know that they knew that we knew." He chuckles to himself for a moment, then stops abruptly. "The thing is, Rackham, that it would have been useful for us to know that the report had been leaked, and that they'd know that we'd cracked their code. We could have used that to our advantage. But due to your reluctance in relation to telling the truth…" he weakly waves a hand, "we have wasted time. A couple of months at least, in the biggest investigation into terrorism in this country to date."

106

He looks at me. "What have you got to say to that?"

"Sorry, sir."

"Sorry?"

"Yes, sir."

"And you didn't read the report, which means you don't know about the..." he stops. "I think the less you know the better, don't you? Not the most trustworthy officer in the force, are you?"

"No, sir."

"You can go now, and for God's sake keep this to yourself, if you can manage that. I'll decide what to do about you later. Send Brown in. I need to get this revelation of yours into the system. Then I need a rest." He waves me off, and I retreat in silence, head bowed – I shall join my dog, in the dog world.

11.00am 21st November

"So, you didn't tell Amanda?"

"No. What do you think I am? I wouldn't tell a soul. I wouldn't let you down like that." Peggy looks furious with me.

"Sorry, sorry. It's just that Grimwode wants me to keep it under my hat."

"I think you can trust me with that."

Peggy and I are sitting in our hotel bedroom. It's quite a nice room, with en suite shower which I have already used, but it has the usual problem of how to fit a bathroom, a big double bed, a long desk, two wicker armchairs, a side table, and a wardrobe all into one small space. So although its dimensions are reasonable, I feel crammed in with Peggy, as I unload the essence of my interview with Grimwode onto her. Sitting there with just a towelling bathrobe on, I feel particularly vulnerable.

"Look, sorry – it was a hard interview, and I feel like a dog." The dog looks up from the corner of the room – I forgot to mention the dog bed also fitted into this limited space.

"So, was he angry? Did he tear you to pieces?" Peggy looks less offended, and more like the gentle listener I need her to be.

"Not angry as such. He just put me on the spot – made me feel so bloody guilty."

109

"You're not the only one, you know. I'm a part of this. I should have made you tell them instead of covering up for you."

"That's not fair, and you know it. You were seriously injured. You can't hold yourself responsible."

"Grimwode's seriously injured and he seems to manage." She shrugs.

"Yes, well, Grimwode's made of some undiscovered tough substance…but he started to say something and then stopped."

"Stopped?"

"Yes, mid-sentence. He said he couldn't trust me, he said the less I knew, the better."

"Can you remember the sentence?"

"Something like my not knowing about something that I would have known about if I'd read the report."

"So, there's something going on that we don't know about, and we are just being treated like decoy ducks for someone to take pot-shots at, and we don't even know why." She's getting cross again.

"Looks like this is what being involved with Arnold Rackham means. Sorry love. If I could have avoided this…"

"Let's take a walk."

The dog likes this idea – he is naturally fine-tuned to the word 'walk', so he gets up, wagging his tail. I cram on some clothes and the inevitable protection, and insist Peggy does the same, and we exit the hotel and head for Christ Church meadow.

Oxford is crowded with tourists and students. Cold buskers play half-good music with stiff hands. Peggy finds this environment a doddle after negotiating cliff paths with her crutches.

Down St Aldates and into the Meadow. The grimy regulation notice at the entrance doesn't say specifically that dogs must be on the lead, just simply that dogs must not be allowed to 'harry' cattle. So, as cattle are conspicuous by their absence on the footpath, I let the dog off, and he wanders off happily to sniff the trees that are set out in a convenient avenue leading towards the river. I am ready with my poo bag. He is such a good soul. He offers no risk to other dogs, so they ignore him, mainly. I thought I was the same, but now I know I have dumped my brethren in it. Royally.

Peggy stops, takes my arm. "That's her."

"Who?"

"The woman in the ice cream shop."

"Who, where?"

Peggy holds onto me with one hand, and points at a woman twenty yards away, who is talking to a group of teenagers. The woman turns as I look, so I only just catch a glimpse of her face. I'm not sure – she looks more like some sort of tour guide.

"Got your phone?" I still haven't got one of my own. "Contact Brown or Dawson. I'll follow."

"Careful." She looks at me, full of love. I pat my body armour, and walk off, pretending to take an interest in the activities on the river.

She walks away from the teenage group and down towards the end of the avenue of trees. Her walk is brisk and I have to stride out to keep up. My body welcomes this flow of activity after being stuck in a hospital room for two days.

She turns at the river, and heads away from town. An Oxford rowing team speeds by on the cold water, eight bodies sweating at the oars – their cox swearing at them in some strange, obscene language. I am distracted by them for a moment, and look back to find the woman has disappeared. I run along the side of the Thames until I reach a tributary that joins it from the left, and look up the towpath to see her twenty feet away, and she's looking straight at me. It's definitely her, she recognises me too.

I walk towards her as if nothing has happened. The dog, having finished with whatever he was doing, has caught up with me. I feel him touch my leg with his nose.

A punt passes by me. Three students with scarves and jackets on, sit in its shallow depths, drinking beer from cans. The fourth, wields the long pole with expertise, while quoting Shakespeare:

'Blow, blow thou winter wind,
thou art not so unkind
as man's ingratitude...'

My quarry, who has been watching this merry gaggle, turns and jumps onto the punt, knocking the poet into the river and seizing the pole. She plunges it into the water, sending the punt straight towards the opposite bank. The three beer-swillers, are momently caught off guard, simply staring with disbelief at their hijacker. Then the nearest makes a grab at her leg, but she expertly kicks his arm away and jumps off the punt and onto the bank. The lad in the water shouts to his friends as he waddles waist deep in the shallows.

Another punt coming in the opposite direction, and propelled from one side of the river to the other by a Japanese girl, nearly collides with them, and veers towards the bank on my side, ramming into the mud with such a force that it almost sends the girl into the water.

"Police!" I take my chance. "I need your boat."

I put one foot onto the end that is stuck into the bank, and push off with all my strength, nearly falling in, and sending the punt across the river. The dog, left on the towpath, starts to bark as I scramble over the recumbent occupants, seize the pole from the bewildered girl, and

112

make a final thrust towards the opposite bank. The pole sticks in the mud at the bottom of the river, and I find myself holding on as the punt slides away from beneath me. With a desperate twist, I try to heave myself to the bank, but end up in the mud, leaving the pole stuck up in the air. A testament to my first attempt at punting.

My quarry has disappeared into a jungle of short trees. I stagger out of the water and run in the general direction I think she went, my feet sticking in tree roots and puddles, until I find myself looking up at a tall wooden wall painted a cream colour. It's some kind of building, and I'm guessing it's one of those University boathouses that open onto the River Thames. I walk round to the right of it, squelching in mud and leaves, until I turn a corner and see the river peeping through the trees. I go faster along the side of the building, keeping myself supported by touching the wooden wall, and look cautiously round the corner.

The river is right in front of me, and I can see that I am correct in thinking it is a boathouse. It has a concrete slipway going into the river, and the front of the building is open. It looks like a boat has just gone out, as there are bits and pieces of gear and clothes strewn around.

I gaze at the river wondering what to do next, when I hear a sound coming from behind me. I look round into the dark cavern of the boathouse. Four boats are laid out on special supports, like funeral pyres ready for a river burial. There is a solemnity about the place that makes me want to be quiet. I hear the sound again – a shuffle, then a click. The click takes me straight back to the memory of a young man sitting on a sofa, and the gun he was concealing.

I pull my gun out from its holster as noiselessly as possible, then creep into the boathouse, keeping to the wall and the darkness that it provides. There is no protection in this place. A bullet could go straight through one of the

113

boats, through me, and through the thin wooden wall of the building. I'm glad of my body armour which will at least stop one of those things happening.

There's total silence. If I'm right, and there's another person in here, then we're the only people within earshot. I move round the wall, trying not to trip over anything. A cold hand catches hold of me and I jump, whirling round to meet my attacker, but it just turns out to be the arm of a wetsuit hanging from the wall. I curse silently. That made a noise, and now the other person certainly knows that I'm here. I hear another click and a shuffle. It sounds like it's coming from behind one of the boats towards the back of the boathouse.

Silence.

I'm still, and all I can hear is my heart beating.

Then in the distance, shouting.

The shouting is regular, rhythmic.

Then the sound of oars in the water.

It's the cox shouting the strokes.

The boat is getting nearer.

It's coming here, to this boathouse, and there are two armed people stalking each other.

I hear my quarry then, not running away, but moving in my direction. I shrink back into the darkness of the wall, coming into contact with the cold wetsuit again, and wait. Gun poised. Ready.

I can hear the clatter of the oars being pulled in, as the innocent rowers clamber out of their boat. There's friendly chatter, and the odd groan of a tired student.

The shadow that comes towards me is tall. Not the size of the woman I was chasing. I stay completely still. The figure comes closer. I can see it has something in its hand. It draws level with me, and I lunge forward with my gun and hear the clatter of my opponent's gun on the concrete. Then my life is filled with unbelievable pain. I can't tell

114

where it's coming from, then I realize it's my shoulder and my crotch as I fall to the floor in agony, dropping my gun.

My assailant doesn't run away but is on top of me, knees trapping both my arms as a dazzling light shines in my eyes.

"Rackham! What the fuck?" I hear a hoarse whisper. I recognise that voice.

"Dawson?"

"Yes, I thought you were... oh bugger! Can you get up?"

I can hardly move, but we have to get out of here before the jolly rowing team discover two policemen who've been stalking each other round their boathouse.

"What did you do to me?" My body has gone numb.

"Got your nervous system. Sorry. Quick, pick up your gun. They can't be allowed to see us."

I roll onto my side, and can just see my gun lying there in the light of Dawson's mobile. I manage to reach out and grab it. Dawson helps me to my knees and I ram the gun back into its holster.

We can see the rowing team carrying the boat to the trestle closest to us. They haven't seen us yet, but if we don't get out of the way, they will bump into us.

Dawson heaves me to my feet and half drags me down to the back of the shed. Fortunately, the team are making so much noise, laughing, complaining, and grunting, that it covers up our shuffling as we make our way to the other side.

"We're going to have to get out of here."

The problem is that it's light at the open end of the boathouse, and the students would easily see us if we attempted to get out.

"How come you didn't see it was me when I came in?" I whisper.

"I saw her. Your woman. You must have got in while I was concentrating on her."

"So, is she still here?"

"She disappeared. Then I heard sounds from your direction."

"But she could still be here. Where are the rest of you?"

"All over the place. We came in so fast. The call from McDonald."

"Call them in now. We need to catch this woman."

"We don't want a bloodbath. They're only children for God's sake."

"Do it. Do it now."

Dawson gets his phone out.

There's a sound of rapid footsteps. Too late, we see her receding form, as she dashes out of the boathouse right in front of us and towards the river. Dawson runs after her. I'm still finding it difficult to move. They disappear round the corner.

"Hoy, you there!" One of the team of rowers has seen them. "What you doing?"

They're going to find me any moment now. There's a shuffling noise and I feel a wet nose on my hand. The dog has found me first.

"Hello, hello, what have we 'ere?" A large young gentleman looms out in front of me.

"Er, just finding my dog. Oh, and there's Peggy. Peggy!" I call. "Found the dog."

Peggy turns and sees me. "Thank God, Arne!"

I make a 'go gently' gesture at her.

"Thanks," I say to the rower. "Sorry to come into your boathouse. The dog, you see?"

"Yeah, yeah, but who were those others?"

"No idea, nothing to do with me. Just came to get my dog."

116

I limp slowly and painfully after the dog, and out towards Peggy.

"What happened to you?" she says.

"Don't ask. How did you get here?"

"There's a bridge over the smaller river. The dog found me, and led me straight here."

Good old dog.

1.30pm 21st November

I'm sitting in a bath. I don't know how I got here, or why I ache so much. I look down at my body, searching for some sign. Some bruise. Anything. All I notice, is the large number of warts and moles I have developed. My skin is wrinkled round my belly, and I wonder how I got into such bad shape. My legs look thin and spindly, and the hair has been rubbed off my ankles making an odd bald section after the hairiness of my calves. Is this really my body? Or has somebody put me in it as some kind of joke? Apart from the pain I feel, I'm also beginning to shiver. The bath water is getting cold.

"Arne, are you OK?" A voice I don't recognise.

There's a rattle at the door and a young woman walks in. She looks the age that I thought I was supposed to be. Beautiful, fit, and shapely. Long hair tied in a ponytail. It must be horrific for her to see me like this. So changed, so aged.

She gets down with some difficulty, and I can see she has something wrong with her. Grasping the edge of the bath, she looks into my eyes, searching for something.

"Come back," she says. "Please come back, Arne."

Arnold. I'm Arnold aren't I?

"Arnol'?" I mumble.

"Yes, you're Arnold. Inspector Arnold Rackham." I can see this costs her an effort. I see the pain and worry in her face.

119

"Arnol' Rackham? 'spector?" Yes, that begins to make sense.

She nods. There's something funny about her expression. Then I notice she's weeping.

"How… how did I get here? An… and why does it hurt?" I don't understand. She can tell me. I can trust her – I'm sure I can. Something in her eyes says so.

"Dawson. Inspector Dawson did something to you. I think he used some kind of martial art."

"Art. I do art don't I?"

"Yes, you do." Her voice wobbles. I've caused her pain. "Anyway, he hurt you. It was a mistake. He thought you were someone else…"

"But I'm not someone else, am I?"

"No, you're you. I helped you back to the hotel…"

"I'm in a hotel?" It's beginning to come back. Suddenly I feel worried. "The dog. Where's the dog?" I feel panic setting in.

"The dog's here. It's alright, Arne." On cue a brown muzzle appears next to the woman's elbow. I reach out my hand and he licks it. He's bringing me back. I look at the woman again. A name forms in my head.

"Pe…ggy? You're Peggy."

"Yes, I'm Peggy." She holds out her arms, and I lean forward and hug her. Water streams out of the bath, but I don't care. I've come back. I've found her.

"But how can you love me? I'm so old and wrinkled and…"

"Shut up. I love you, and that's that."

We hug. Peggy gets wet. And the dog barks and wags his tail.

5.30pm 21st November

"So…" Grimwode is propped up in bed, the white of his ghoul-like face almost matching the white cotton pillows. Dawson and I have been summoned to his hospital-room-cum-office. There's no stopping this man.

"So," he looks from Dawson to me and back again. "So you managed to lose the woman?"

"Yes, sir." We both say together.

"And you fought each other in a boathouse, and she got away right under your noses?"

"Yes, sir." It's like a chant.

"I gather, Dawson, that you used one of your methods on Rackham." Grimwode chuckles, and then stops abruptly as the pain of his own stab wound kicks in. "And how did you like that Rackham?"

"Not very much, sir."

"No, I'm sure you didn't. Have you thought of doing a bit more training yourself? Not much good at unarmed, are you?"

"No, sir, but I'm too old, sir, and I'm leaving…"

"Not so fast, Rackham. We may not be able to let you go yet. And as for being too old, you're never too old, are you, Dawson?"

"No, sir," says Dawson, obviously enjoying the prospect of training me up through some painful process.

"So, Dawson," I'm off the hook for the moment, "you managed to lose the woman."

"Yes, sir, we lost her in the grounds of Magdalen College School."

"'Maudlin' Dawson, 'Maudlin'."

"Yes, sir. We thought we had her cornered but then the headmaster…"

"Ah yes, I've heard from the headmaster. Armed officers running round his school. He complained. Naturally."

I wonder if he belongs to the same club as Grimwode.

"Well, to be quite honest, sir, he got in the way and the woman ran out of the school and jumped onto a number 3 bus."

"A number 3 bus. So what did you do then?"

"We commandeered a taxi and tried to overtake the bus, but the traffic…"

"Yes, the traffic is bad. So you didn't catch her."

"No, sir, by the time we caught up with the bus, she had got off. She could be anywhere."

"And the bus driver, what did he say?"

"He said she must have had a ticket to get on, but he didn't notice when she got off."

"So she could be anywhere. Well that's useful." Grimwode's sarcasm knows no bounds. "And have you been able to identify the woman?"

"We are looking into it, sir. We think she may have belonged to the Baader-Meinhof group when she was young. She could be the right age. And…"

"Enough, Dawson." Grimwode looks at me thoughtfully.

"Rackham, you can go for now. You didn't do too badly, and at least you didn't upset the headmaster of Magdalen College School. Keep in touch – someone will give you a new phone, and please try not lose it. And… er… thank you for, er… saving my life."

I see a sign of emotion in his face, and there's a pause while I try and think of something to say.

Then the portcullis comes down. "That's all, Rackham, you may go. Dawson and I have things to discuss."

I leave the room, and walk down the corridor. The pain that Dawson caused me is fading into a memory, but I wonder what Grimwode has in store for me, and what he meant by 'we may not be able to let go of you yet.'

9.15am 22nd November

"We keep the bicycles for a bit and then auction them off."
A friendly policeman is leading me through St Aldates
Police Station to a room at the back where my friend
Dawson and his cohort have been given a temporary
office.

Rank after rank of bikes in various conditions greet me
as I pass through the largest space in the building.

"Don't they ever get reclaimed?"

"Every now and then. We have a celebration when that
happens – it's so rare."

"So you auction them off?"

"And more students come and buy them, and then…
lose them."

"A sort of circular system."

"I couldn't have put it better myself, sir."

I have a sudden urge to buy one of these unwanted
bicycles. Get fit. Cycle off my paunch. But then the image
of bobby-on-a-bike comes to my mind, along with the fact
that I haven't got the faintest what I'm going to be doing
in the next few days, or even where I'm going to end up.

"Here we are, sir." He knocks on a solid-looking red
door set into the wall at the back of the bike room.

The door opens, and I am greeted by a short Indian-
looking woman with streaks of grey in her black hair.

"Do come in, sir." She closes the door gently, but firmly in the face of my friendly policeman, then leads me over to a desk where Dawson is poring over a map.

"Rackham." He straightens up, and gives me a wry smile, extending his hand. I'm reluctant to take it, wondering what pain he could inflict with a twist of his thumb. His handshake turns out to be limp – perhaps he's saving his energy for more aggressive physical contact at some other time.

"Got something for you." He looks down at his desk. To the side of his map, which I'm guessing is of the west coast of Scotland, there is a small, black, cheap-looking mobile phone with charger, and an envelope.

"That's it." He hands them to me without looking up.

I look round the room, wondering if anyone's going to say something, but everyone seems immersed in whatever is on their desk. Nobody makes eye contact. I feel like I've disappeared.

"Well, I…"

"Sir?" The woman who showed me in stands by the door, ready to open it for me.

"Good bye," I say trying to get Dawson's attention.

"Bye," he says looking firmly down at his map.

And that's it – I'm out.

10.00am 22nd November

"That was it. Nobody said anything. Nobody even looked at me." I'm sitting in one of the wicker chairs in our hotel room. Peggy is in the other one, and between us is the unopened envelope.

"Weird. You don't think…?"

"…they know. About my losing the report, and leaving the force. An untrustworthy deserter." My voice tightens as I say this. I see myself in a very unflattering light.

"I didn't mean that. I meant that maybe they were dumping you in it somehow."

"A poisoned chalice, you mean?"

"Well something like that. Come on, open the envelope. It's the only way we're going to find out."

I reach out and pick the envelope up. It's long and a creamy white, and has a textured feel – expensive stationery from Grimwode's office? I slide my thumb under the flap and ease it open. Instead of the quality A4 sheet that I'm expecting, I find a thin blue scrap of paper, hastily torn from a pad. The writing is almost illegible and slopes crazily in both directions:

Good luck in your new job.
Keep the phone charged.

127

There's a knock on the door. A maid enters, pushing a trolley piled high with bedding and plastic bottles. "Can we clean your room now, sir?"

6.30am 5th December

Peggy snores gently, her head resting on my shoulder. I can hear the rain pattering on the roof just above my head.

Two weeks ago we moved into our small and idyllic cottage, nestling in the hills north of the Brecon Beacons. Two bedrooms upstairs in the eaves, and kitchen/dining-cum-living-room downstairs. A freezing cold bathroom is in an extension out the back.

I'm happy like this – her head fits perfectly between my shoulder and shoulder blade, and I could lie like this for a long time. I hold her head in my hands, feeling the softness of her hair. I can smell it too – a gently human smell. Her smell. And in this safe place I can go back over the last couple of weeks in my mind, while looking forward to the day-after-tomorrow when I will finally leave the police and take up my new job.

I took the gun and our bullet-proof vests back to Sergeant Morris at Haverfordwest police station. Nobody said anything, so I think that was what I was meant to do anyway. I was seriously worried about what could happen if I had one of my memory lapses and a gun was at hand. Would I shoot Peggy, or the dog, or even myself? I didn't want to take the risk, so it was a huge relief to get rid of it. I might be a target, but curiously I felt less of one without the gun.

The phone, on the other hand is an enigma. Small, black, inscrutable. There are no names or numbers in its contacts list, and it doesn't seem to have any signal. I assume it's just a tracking device, and maybe they can activate it from their end if they need to contact me. So...I'm still dangling on Grimwode's hook. I suppose it's my fault: if I hadn't been so inquisitive about the wallet that the dog found – just left it, and looked at the sunset – I'd be having a peaceful life now; but instead I'm stuck with this little black phone. It sits on my bedside table, charging away, next to my new smart phone – another enigmatic piece of gear. I'll get the hang of it eventually, with Peggy's help, though by that time it will probably be obsolete in this world of super-fast-moving hyper-technology.

Peggy stirs slightly and snores gently, and I take the opportunity to pull my shoulder from underneath her head – sliding quietly out of bed, so as not to wake her up. Nature calls, so I sneak downstairs to the kitchen – the dog wags his tail at me as I walk past into the freezing bathroom.

Back in the kitchen, shivering from the cold, I let the dog out for his early morning leak, and leaning against the old coal-fired Rayburn, which fortunately I remembered to top up last night, I warm myself up. Restlessly, I move over to the small window to scrape away the ice and peer out into the darkness. The sun will be up in about an hour, but there is already a little light out there, and I can see the frosty trees that mark the boundary at the front of our garden.

A dark shape looms large against the trees. For a moment I think it's two people crouching in the half-light. For a moment I wish I still had the gun. Then I remember the donkey that lives in our garden, owned by our landlord and given free rein outside the cottage. It's up and about early this morning; fortunately it seems to tolerate the dog, a small intruder in its kingdom – but one that causes no problem, and doesn't compete for the tastiest foliage.

I go away from the window and sit down at the kitchen table. I have been working on a picture of water. I am fascinated by the swirling shapes and colours of the sea. The sea that surrounded me as I walked into it a few weeks ago. Not waves so much as motions. I plan to draw the shapes in pen and ink, and then add water-colours to create that precise, yet forever-moving picture that is in my mind. It's the first actual painting that I've done since Peggy was shot in September, and it marks a new departure, away from the strictly representational oils that I used to do. I am much more interested in the feel of nature – visceral, tactile, and in this case, cold.

I shiver as I remember the cold of that water, and the dog touching me, as my brother and my lover called to me from the beach. The cold bath, too, comes to mind. Two memory episodes, both coming after some shock or conflict.

As I work on the pen lines, I begin to see faces appearing in the water. Faces of the dead. Faces of dead girls, denied their right to live by an evil woman who used them for her own ends. A woman who had such a disastrous effect on my family.

I pull myself out of this thinking and back to the picture, but they're still there – the ghosts of children staring up at me from the icy swirling waters.

Tea.

That's what I need – tea.

I go over to the range and put on the battered old kettle. On cue, the dog scratches at the door – I'm obviously better company than the donkey. Or is it just that it's warm? I don't mind, I just want to scratch the dog behind his ears. I know he loves this, like all dogs. But it makes me feel better too. Reassured, comfy, warm.

131

Tea in hand, dog at my feet, I sit down and look at my picture again. The Blake-like terrors have gone, and a peaceful watery image lies there, waiting for me to finish it.

Two days.

Two days, and then I'm free.

I look back at the image I'm creating. What does it mean? Just water swirling round me as I forget. Then the faces start to reappear, and I remember.

Stanley was Paul's twin brother. They were younger than me, my little brothers. Stanley was much frailer than Paul. His beautiful pale face could almost be taken for a girl's. He was so quiet. Kept to himself. Played on his own. I left him to it. Sometimes he would come up with stories. Paul was the musician, I was the artist, but Stanley was the writer. He had such an imagination. He could take you into his world, and make you believe that the things he dreamt up were true. Often his stories were scary. They contained monsters that could eat you from the inside, hidden eyes that watched you to make sure you never told forbidden secrets, and beautiful girls that turned into ghouls with long fingernails and pointed yellow teeth.

I should have known, I should have realised what was going on. Stanley and Paul would go to tea with our school matron, and come back wide-eyed and silent – nightmares would follow. What was going on in the house of our matron Cornelia Witherspoon? I never asked. I didn't want to know. I was only ten, and my father was in and out of hospital. We didn't say mental hospital in our house. We said Dad was ill, we didn't say that he was an alcoholic. Everything was kept buried. And eventually we buried Stanley.

But I got her in the end. I caught Cornelia Witherspoon. After nearly fifty years, the boys she abused came and testified against her. The girl she almost murdered, Lilly, who I'd found living on the streets and who was now in her sixties, came into court and demolished her defence. And I, I put Cornelia Witherspoon into prison, and I dug up the things in my life that had been holding me back. Faced the terrors, and the feelings of failure.

I did it.

I became a true policeman.

And then I discovered the stolen paintings.

I did that too.

And now, only a month later, I'm leaving. I'm leaving the police force, just as I'm finding my feet as a good detective.

I look down again at my swirling sea, and there is Stanley's pale face looking up at me. Vague shapes of girls faces swim before my eyes, and an old face appears. A face that told the truth, suffered, and conquered. Lilly.

Where are you now?

Did you buy your caravan?

Are you on the south coast?

Are you in the warm?

I shiver and drink my tea. My conscience is working overtime. Fat-cat job for art insurance investigators. Is that where I'm going? Anything for an easy life, eh Arnold?

There's a curious bleep from upstairs. I hear a groan from Peggy as she shifts on the bed.

"Arne?" her voice is gruff with sleep. "Arne, your phone…"

That's not my phone. It doesn't make that noise. Anyway I had it on silent.

I go upstairs and find Peggy holding the little black phone that Dawson gave me. She's peering at it with sleepy eyes.

"Look," she hands it to me.

There's a message on the tiny screen: '**Take the job.**'

I press what looks like scroll down buttons, but nothing else appears, and then even that message fades, and the screen goes blank.

"But I was going to do that anyway, I was going to take the job. Why are they telling me?" It's as though they had read my mind – my doubts about leaving the police just as I was getting good at it.

"They must have their reasons…"

"They've got me on a bloody leash." I look at Peggy, and shake my head.

"Arne, you're in the middle of it, you can't just get out now."

"But I'm just being used…"

"We! We're being used."

"And I don't know what's going on."

"Well, let's work it out. We're detectives. Isn't that what detectives do? Come on, you love this stuff. What's got into you?"

"I thought I was leaving. Putting that all behind me."

"You can never put that behind you."

"Tea?" I need to go and do something. I can't quite face what she's saying.

"Tea?" Peggy looks puzzled.

"Yes, tea. Would you like a cup of tea?" My voice is edgier than I intend.

"Arne, what's got into you?"

"Sorry, love. Look I'll go and bring you up a cup of tea. Then we can talk through this."

Peggy sighs as I leave the room, and I kick myself for forgetting what she has to deal with.

Down in the kitchen, I put the kettle on the hob and get the dog his breakfast. He's down to his last tin. I look for the pad where we add things for shopping. It's got to be somewhere. "Where's that list?" I mutter to myself. The older I get, the more I lose. Kettle's boiling, so I make a pot and put everything on a tray to take up.

"I can't find the list," I say to Peggy, as I put the tray down on a wooden crate that does for a bedside table.

"Must be somewhere. I added to it yesterday." Peggy frowns, trying to remember.

I pour the tea, watching the swirling of the milk as it joins the black steaming liquid. Something comes back to me. List. Someone said 'list'. I hand Peggy her mug.

"What's the matter?" she asks.

"That list," I say. "It bothers me."

"Why? It's alright, I'll remember. No-one would come in and nick our shopping list, would they?"

But someone came in and stole my report.

Some of the information taken from the computer is in code and points to them having a comprehensive...

List?

"They've got a list."

"What?"

"Grimwode said he didn't know he was on it. You know, when I was holding him, waiting for the ambulance."

"You didn't tell me that."

"It went out of my head at the time. I was so wrapped up in confessing to Grimwode... I forgot what he said. But..."

"So there's a list. The terrorist group have a list... of targets, presumably."

"I wonder if we're on it?"

"We're small fry. They would be targeting politicians, people in high places. People with power."

"Like that politician who was so strong in the peace movement."

Something is falling into place. Something big.

135

11.00am 7th December

Big. That's what this office building is. Big.

More than I can say for my exit from the police force. No letter. No email. No nothing. Just the little black phone saying, '**Take the job**' – so here I am taking it.

The building in front of me has sweeps and curves that climb to the sky – the modern artist in me is awestruck by its magnificent design. On the other hand, the conservative representational painter part of me loathes the cold inhuman hardness of this building, preferring the old red-brick, church-like office block in front of the Millennium Centre that I walked past on the way to meet my new employer.

But here is where the art insurance company resides, and the dog and I clatter across the shiny marble floor to the reception desk in the distance.

"Arnold Rackham to see Geoffrey Goodchild," I say to the young lady behind the desk. She could be an air hostess; this could be an airport – except there're no queues, only me and the dog.

She looks down at her computer; she looks down at the dog. I look down at my scuffed shoes, creased trousers and tatty old tweed jacket, and I begin to wonder whether we'll be thrown out.

"BGE Insurance," I add in case she can't find a Geoffrey Goodchild. I thought he was the boss. I thought he would be famous in this building.

She turns away and picks up a phone. I can't hear what she says, but she turns round with a bright smile that has been painted onto her face in an instant. A smile that should reassure me that I am welcome, but it doesn't – I used to read faces for a living, and this smile has nothing behind it.

She walks round the end of her curving counter and beckons me. "Please come this way, sir… and your dog?"

"He comes too."

She bends down and scratches him behind his ear. He wags his tail – maybe he can see something in her that I have missed.

We walk towards lifts that go up in transparent tubes. For a moment I worry about my tendency to be affected by vertigo, but then I remember I have my dog, and I feel safe.

"I hope your dog will be alright. It's the seventh floor."

"He'll be fine, thank you."

"Sir Geoffrey is expecting you."

Sir Geoffrey – so that's where I went wrong.

Actually, I enjoy the ride up in the lift. I can see the Bay through the glass front of the building, and more of it comes into view as we rise. There are white crests on the waves out there – looks like a storm is brewing. But in here we are cut off – just the quiet swish of the rising lift.

Ding.

We are there.

Seventh floor.

No-one greets me, but there is an open area in front of me with a desk. Behind the desk is a woman who is looking down at something more important than me. No big smile, or 'welcome, Mr Rackham'.

I walk up to the desk and clear my throat.

The woman has greying hair, I notice, and she is wearing a dark blue jacket. She presses a button in front of her: "Mr Rackham to see you Sir Geoffrey."

She points at a door to her right without looking up. I hesitate, and then muttering 'thank you' under my breath, walk slowly towards it, with the feeling that I'm about to cross a life-changing threshold.

The door is nondescript with no name on it, and fearing it might be a loo or even a broom cupboard, I open it without knocking.

The man who rises to greet me from behind his desk is old. His wrinkled face has yellowing skin and brown patches, and his eyes are red-rimmed with too much looking. His hand as he puts it out to shake mine, is covered in liver-spots. His nails are long, yellow and ridged. His stooping figure, topped by a bit of wispy hair on a shiny bald pate, looks eerie against the backdrop of a stormy Cardiff Bay.

"Well, well, well. Mr Rackham. Do sit down. And your dog. Well, well, well."

I perch on the edge of a posh leather office chair that will swivel if I'm not careful. The dog sits on the floor by my side – so well trained.

"So you've come to join us."

"Yes, sir."

"Well, well, well. And your dog too."

"Yes, sir."

"And you've just retired as a police inspector, with some recent success at finding stolen art."

"Yes, sir. This is my first day as..."

"Well, well, well. Well... we've got a number of things going on at the moment. Not sure what to do with you... mmmh."

There's a pause while he looks at me, and I look back at him, slightly distracted by the storm clouds darkening

139

behind his head. Our moment of mutual appraisal is interrupted by a bleep from Sir Geoffrey's laptop, and he peers down at it.

"Riga," says Sir Geoffrey, reading from his laptop. "Well, well, well, have you been to Riga, Mr Rackham?"

"No, sir."

"Looks like we've got something there for you. Something to look at."

"Look at, sir?"

"It's just come in. Well, well, well."

"What sort of thing, sir?" I'm wondering where Riga is.

"Mmmh…"

I feel a vibration in my pocket.

"Excuse me, sir, I'd better see what this is." I feel irritated and embarrassed that I should be sent a message right in the middle of my first meeting with my new boss.

I get out the little black phone.

'Go to Riga' it says on its little screen. I hastily shove it back in my pocket.

"Mmmh…" Sir Geoffrey takes his time looking up and down at the screen. "Need my reading glasses. Never can find them when I need them. Do you need reading glasses er..?"

"Rackham, sir. No, not yet at any rate."

"Artist, aren't you? Bloody good eyesight I should think."

"Well, I like to think…"

"…aha, that's the ticket." He finds them on his desk – right in front of him. "Now, er… someone trying to sell something. If it's a copy, then our client would like to know, but if it's genuine…" he waves his right hand around, "then he'd like to know where it came from. Just up your street, I'd say."

He suddenly fixes me with such a fierce look that I nearly push my chair back on its castors. The dog pricks up his ears too.

"Alison," he presses his intercom button. "Can you print out the report that's just come in, and send Jake in to collect orders?"

"So, Riga. Where's Riga? Er, sir." The 'sir' thing is wearing thin, I'll be calling him Geoff if I'm not careful.

"Latvia. Used to be behind the Iron Curtain. Free now. Lovely little country. Worth a visit, I'd say. Mmmh... well, well, well."

I feel a lurch in my stomach. Not much good at going abroad. Don't like flying. And the dog. What shall I do with the...

There's a knock on the door.

"Come," says Sir Geoffrey.

The door opens and a young man with very slicked-back hair comes in. "Orders, Sir Geoffrey?"

"Yes, thank you, Jake. Tea or coffee, Mr Rackham?"

"Tea please, sir," I'm not making the coffee mistake – office coffee is like faintly flavoured dishwater in my experience.

"Tea for Mr Rackham, espresso for me. Thank you, Jake." Maybe the coffee would have been fine. "And er... bickies?"

"Yes, Sir Geoffrey." Jake bows and backs out of the room, so royal is my new master. At that moment, as I see Sir Geoffrey in front of the increasingly stormy background of Cardiff Bay, I realise he makes me think of King Lear. I wonder if he has daughters.

The door opens, and the grey-haired lady comes in, holding a shiny, dark blue file. She dumps it unceremoniously on the desk in front of me, and walks out of the room without a word.

"Ah, Alison," Sir Geoffrey confides to me. "Where would I be without her? Where would we all be? Super-efficient but…" he waves his right hand in the air.

"Does she er… speak… sir?"

He looks at me as if I'm a complete fool. "Yes, she speaks… but er… don't get her onto the subject of Pollock. You'll never hear the end of it."

There's a knock on the door.

"Come."

In comes Jake with a tray. There's a mug of slightly milky hot water with a teabag floating in it, and a very respectable-looking espresso. I got it wrong – I should have known the coffee would be fine. The tea, on the other hand, looks distinctly peaky. Whether a bit of stirring will make it give forth more flavour…? The bickies are thick and chocolatey – I doubt Alison would approve.

"So, down to work." Sir Geoffrey takes the plate of bickies, and puts them on his side of the desk next to his espresso. Out of my reach.

I open the file. There is a report, which I glance at. It has names and places, but what catches my attention is the photo underneath. I know that painting. I know it very well.

12.45pm 7th December

"He's an idiot. That painting is so well known, how did he think he'd get away with it?"

We're sitting in a café that is dramatically situated on the edge of Cardiff Bay. It's made even more dramatic by the storm that is raging outside. The windows rattle. Everything rattles, and I glance nervously at a portrait of Nelson hanging on the wall. I could swear I saw it move.

"Have you read the report?" Peggy asks.

"Well, no. But it must be Brian. I saw it just before he knocked me out…"

"Then you don't know the details of how this came to light."

"Well, I…"

"We'll have a proper look through it all when we get back. Have you got it safe?"

"Yes. But Manet's…"

"Shhh." Peggy looks around. There's nobody sitting near us. The storm has put people off coming here for lunch, and we're the only ones mad enough to sit by the windows.

"But that painting," I whisper. "It's all over the internet."

A waiter brings over our coffees and my almond slice. The cakes looked so lovely I couldn't resist, after the torture of watching Sir Geoffrey demolish a plate of chocolate bickies.

"And they want you to go now?"

"Yes." I feel that lurch in my stomach again.

"I'll look after the dog."

"I want you to come with me."

"I can't, I'd miss my physio…"

"…and how are you going to get to physio? I've been driving you so that you get the full benefit. You need me. I can't go. The whole thing's a farce. I don't know what I've got myself into." I put my head in my hands, and then look down at my plate. The almond slice is suddenly less attractive.

"There are such things as taxis, and you shouldn't be driving anyway. Come on, don't give up. You wanted this job. You need to do something."

"But what if I have… one of my episodes?"

"You managed before. You got through it. We'll think of something to help you back. Now come on, eat that bloody cake before I lose control and eat it myself." She gives me a huge grin, and reaches for my hand.

"Ok, but are you sure about the dog?"

She looks down.

"You're not sure, are you?"

I look across the table at her. I read frustration in her face.

"You're right," she says. "I haven't thought this through."

"What about Hannah?"

"She's probably busy. It's the Christmas season, and you know what it's like for musicians. Even Hannah needs to get whatever work she can."

I take a bite out of my almond slice. The sugar hits my system like a blunderbuss.

"More mluddy messah," I mumble, my mouth full of moist ground almond.

"What?"

"Messiahs, she'll be doing Messiahs. She told me that every Christmas she swears she'll never do another one."

Peggy's phone goes. "Oh God, that's witchy," she says, looking at it. "It's Hannah." She puts it to her ear. "Er… er… yes, I'd love you to… but what about work..?"

She covers her phone with her hand and looks at me. "Hannah says she's just got a text from me, asking her to come and stay while you are away."

She picks the phone up again. There's a rattle of words coming from Hannah's end. "Ok, tomorrow… are you sure it's..? yes, but… lovely."

I get out the little black phone and stare at its blank window. It's not telling me anything, but whoever is sending messages is steering us both.

"So is she coming?"

"Yes, tomorrow. She hasn't got any work on offer, except the usual Christmas Messiahs, and she's sick of them. She says she could do with a break, and would love to come out to Wales to get away from London, and all the noise."

"But what did she think about the text?"

"I didn't tell her it wasn't from me. It's them, listening in, just like in your interview. A bit creepy really, but I guess they're looking after us. Anyway, she's coming, and that's that."

"And you're going to be alright with this? Look, I'm worried it's not them. Supposing our terrorist friends have cracked into the system, and are just wanting to get me out of the way?"

"No, you're being over-dramatic. It all fits. Grimwode wants you to go to Riga. They'll look after us. I'll be fine. Don't you worry."

7.30am 8th December

But I'm not fine.

We rushed back to our cottage, driving through the storm. I got things ready for Hannah. Packed my bag. Checked my passport, which was still just valid. Tickets for the plane were emailed to me from Cardiff. Got up very early, even for me. Said my goodbyes to a sleepy Peggy and a dozy dog. And drove through the storm to Gatwick.

I still haven't read the report. I'm sitting in this mausoleum called Gatwick Airport entrance hall, with a cold cup of coffee in front of me and a half-eaten bacon butty, trying to muster up the strength to read it.

People bustle past me with their trolleys, going to their various destinations, and I am aware of the wind whistling round the building. I feel a cold breeze round my legs, and I can see the results of the storm on the departures board – flights delayed or cancelled. My flight to Riga hasn't been cancelled, unfortunately. Still on time. It leaves in an hour, and I haven't even gone through security yet. My legs are like lead, my stomach feels like it's already left on another flight, and my brain won't work.

I hate flying. I knew I hated flying when I took on this job. I took on this job to get away from the police force, but I haven't got away. I'm simply a pawn. It crosses my mind that Sir Geoffrey might be a pawn, and then I imagine him in a leather armchair talking to Grimwode at their club.

147

"'Rackham,'" I hear Grimwode say, in his sarcastic voice. "Yes, he could be useful. A bit like a roll of the dice with him – could come up with a six, but probably not. Send him out to Riga, he won't do any harm there."

Sir Geoffrey nods. "Well, well, well…'"

My brain jerks back into gear. Read the report. Read the fucking report. It's sitting on the café table in front of me in its blue folder. I open the folder and take out a single sheet. Just one sheet. That's all. No detail – can't be at that length.

I try to focus, but my eyes look into the middle distance. The figures of travellers moving to and fro in front of my table.

I look down at the report again. Apart from the preliminary blurb, there's the name and address of the character who's been offered the painting. That's all. I could be wandering aimlessly round Riga for months.

How big is Riga? I wonder.

I reach into my inside pocket to find the little map of Riga that I picked up on the way, and pull out my old notebook which has got caught up with it.

I look at the map.

I look at my notebook.

I open my notebook.

Leafing through various sketches and tiny doodles, I find my latest entry. I must have made a note around the time of the attack on Paul's cottage.

Alan Hunt – Art Dealer
Hay-on-Wye
Herefordshire

Rigby Rogers – Gunsmith
Bright Street
Camden

I put the map of Riga in the folder with the report. Zip it into the top of my small suitcase. With a sigh, I get up to go through security. Get on with the job. I look up at the departures board:

Riga – Delayed.

I sit down again, and take out the little black phone that has followed me about, telling me what to do.

Bloody thing.

Decision time.

I scan the area around me, to make sure nobody's looking, clock the CCTV cameras, and surreptitiously put the phone on the ground under the heel of my shoe. Standing up as though to look at one of the departure boards, I grind the phone under my heel with all my weight on it. I can feel it resisting my attempts to destroy it, so I sit down again and carefully extract it from under my shoe. It's virtually unmarked. I should have known this was no ordinary phone. It's probably bullet-proof. It's my tracker, bug, and instructor all in one, and it's going in the bin.

I pick up my half-eaten bacon butty, stick the phone into the middle of it, and ditch the inedible result into the bin beside the café. Picking up my suitcase, I walk back out of the airport, and into the storm.

I'm not going on an aeroplane.

I'm not going to Riga.

I'm going to Camden.

Midday 8th December

My journey to Underhill car park, Camden, took far longer than I expected. I used the satnav gizmo on my phone, and maybe because of that and me having no detailed map, I seemed to be caught in endless slow moving traffic as I ground my way into London through the rain.

I opted for the direct route, forgetting that I would go straight through the congestion-charge area, and I got caught up in a miasma of one-way streets, pedestrian streets, flyovers, underpasses, and wrong lanes. I was wondering how many times I'd been caught on CCTV doing something illegal, when my phone croaked. Caught in an endless queue waiting at traffic lights, I went to the text page expecting to find a message from Grimwode and co. asking me what the bloody hell I was doing, but it was from Peggy, telling me Hannah had arrived, and brought her cello, and 'it's all fine.'

As I walk through the rain from the car park to Camden High Street, I wonder whether to text Peggy back and let her know that I haven't landed in Riga, but have spent about the same time landing in London. Perhaps no knowledge is the best option at the moment. I don't know what's being intercepted and by whom, so I keep radio silence, and even go to the lengths of blocking Grimwode and Sir Geoffrey on my phone.

Rigby Rogers Gunsmiths lies to the north of Camden Lock. It's a long walk and I'm getting wetter and wetter. I am tempted into the shelter of the market, having no idea just how large it is. It's like I've entered another world. Lurid signs offering body piercing, tattooing and massage keep company with Fairtrade shops selling colourful clothes. There is a hippy-festival feeling about the place, and I become absorbed in the sights and sounds. At one point I feel like I've entered Harry Potter's Diagon Alley. I'm sure I just passed a wand shop – and there right in front of me is a large joke shop. I half expect to see two orange-haired lads pulling me in to buy their wares.

I stop at a street café and get a Turkish coffee and a baclava. The sugar and caffeine hit me with a special kind of chemical explosion as I sit there, dripping. With a shiver I get up, and using the map on my mobile, find my way out of this alternative world and back onto the main road.

Bright Street is quite short and Rigby Rogers takes up most of one side, looking more like a posh gentleman's outfitters than a supplier of deathly weapons. I walk in to the smell of old-fashioned wood and gun oil. Rifles are displayed round the walls like high-quality shoes. Shotguns are arranged in circles in the middle of the shop, with their barrels pointing to the ceiling as though they're playing 'Ring a Ring o' Roses'. Pistols are displayed in glass cabinets – 'Buy me' says a label on a sleek black Walther. Under the counter, instead of men's socks and underpants, colourful boxes of ammunition are piled up neatly – behind bullet-proof glass no doubt.

This is a shop for boys – very dangerous.

I browse, dripping water on the fine oak floor, looking at various attractive articles, and trying to think of a way to find out about Mr Hunt. What kind of gun would he have bought, if he did buy one at all?

"Can I help you sir? Looking for a gun? Haw, haw, haw." A large red-faced man with short black hair and twinkling eyes, appears in front of me. I immediately feel cowed by his racing green gun-sport clothing, displaying the logo 'Rigby Rogers' embroidered in gold. He looks like an up-to-date version of one of Robin Hood's Merry Men.

"Yes... er... um..." Think fast, or you will be out of here before you can say 'Nottingham'.

"Er... a friend of mine bought a gun from you. He... recommended the make, but I lost the piece of paper." I smile at him foolishly, hoping I look like a man who regularly loses pieces of paper with valuable information on them.

"If you can give me his name, I might be able to help you." I pass as a dotty, forgetful friend.

"Alan... Alan Hunt."

He goes over to the counter – I half expect him to vault over it, but he just lifts a flap. "One minute, sir." Instead of the great leather-bound ledger that I expected to see, he has a black laptop, and his fingers dance over the keys like a trained typist.

"When did he buy the gun?"

"Er... I'm not exactly sure. A few weeks ago?"

"Alan Hunt, Alan Hunt, not one of our regulars." He looks at his screen, and scrolls down.

"Could be a rifle. Winchester, or Mauser?" I say, racking my brains for gun information that I had so tried to forget in the past.

"No, no, I can't find anything of that sort." He scrolls down the computer screen some more, while I scroll through my brain trying to think of a clue.

"Couldn't be a pistol. They were banned from being sold, er... years ago," I say, trying not to sound like someone who should know about such things.

153

"Pistol? Now when you say that it reminds me of something… ahh…. Here we are. Air pistols."

"Air pistols?" I am surprised. What good would that do him?

"Yes. This is it. Sold him one a couple of months ago. A Beretta M84. Now I remember he talked about licences."

"Licences?"

"Yes. I remember distinctly. He wanted to buy a pistol, but he knew he needed to get a licence first; but what he didn't know was that he couldn't buy a handgun anyway. So I showed him the Beretta, and he thought that it looked good, so he bought it – it didn't need a licence being an airgun." He looks at me shrewdly. "So you'd be happy with an airgun if that's what your friend bought?"

"Yes… well… I am interested… in buying one. Yes," I say, wondering what it will cost.

"The Beretta M84 is a lovely gun made by Umarex. Small. A real classic. I'll see if we've got one in stock."

Really just a toy, I'm thinking – but why did he want one? Was it to fool the people he was afraid of?

"I've got one in stock." He looks up at me with his twinkly eyes. "I'll get it out for you." He goes out through a door in the back of the shop, and I glance around to see if anyone's looking. I turn his laptop round to see the screen, and there, displayed, are the contact details for Alan Hunt.

Mobile number.

Email.

Address in Hay-on-Wye.

I visualise it, and turn the laptop back round, hoping my photographic memory will serve well. The email and address are easy, the mobile though…

"Here it is sir." He puts a small handgun on the counter, and I can see why Mr Hunt wanted it. It looks just like the real thing.

"Try it. It's got a CO2 capsule in it. Should feel the right weight." He gestures for me to pick it up.

It feels heavy for its size. Fits nicely in my hand. I shiver involuntarily.

"I can see you know your guns, sir. Not like your friend. Haw, haw, haw."

Does it really show that obviously? But then, he sees people pick up guns every day.

"I er…"

"I can do it for… let me see… £130. You've got to have it. It's a snip at that price."

I don't want an airgun, and I don't want to spend £130 pounds on it.

"I'll even chuck in a packet of CO2 capsules, and a couple of boxes of ammunition. What do you say?"

"Well, I er…"

The shop seems to get darker, and I find the walls hard to focus on…

"Don't worry sir. Just need some identification. Haw, haw, haw."

His infectious laugh is beginning to get to me. Can guns really be that funny?

I give him my passport before I realise what I'm doing. I don't want a gun. I don't want anyone to know where I am. Bloody idiot.

Things are really beginning to spin round. I need to sit down.

He taps away at his computer.

Stops. His eyebrows go up. "Just a minute sir." His printer starts printing something out.

"Well, you've definitely got a licence. Haw, haw, haw. Just got a bit of paperwork for you..." The printer grinds away.

"I didn't know I needed a licence." I nervously look behind me.

"Just like your friend. Haw, haw, haw. Now then Inspector Rackham..." he hands me over a sheet with the heading 'Gun Passport', then another sheet with plane flight tickets from Heathrow to Riga. "If you could just sign this, sir."

He reaches under the counter and takes out another gun, finds a spare magazine and a couple of packets of ammunition. "There you are, sir."

It looks just the same as the airgun, except...

"But... this is a real gun."

"We were expecting you – it's on the house, sir. Don't worry, sir, it's all taken care of. Haw, haw, haw..."

The taxi from Riga airport to the city takes half an hour. I sit there in my drying-out coat, wondering where on earth Dick's mob are sending me, and why. Armed and dangerous. They don't know how dangerous. So far I haven't had any kind of memory episode while carrying a gun, though I wonder if this is all a memory episode, ever since I entered Rigby Rogers.

I could have walked out of the shop at any time.

I could have gone to Hay-on-Wye and not Heathrow.

But I gave in and went where they wanted me to. No dog to keep me safe. Just a gun to keep me dangerous...

The taxi stops. The driver gets out, hands me my travel bag, and points down a long cobbled street with old stone buildings. There are signs on most of the buildings saying they are hotels or restaurants. On the sheet that came with my air tickets it says 'The Red Bull', which I can see halfway down the street. Red Bull is the last thing I need. I just hope the beer in Riga is up to scratch.

The taxi driver waves away my offer of payment, and I walk a little unsteadily towards The Red Bull. The street is beautifully lit with old-fashioned lanterns. There is an early evening bustle of tourists, eager for a beer – or, as I see in quite a few places, a cocktail.

I mount the side steps to the small lobby and hand my sheet to the young receptionist behind the counter. She hands me my key without even looking at me, and tells me in perfect English that my room is up the winding staircase that leads out of the entrance hall. I'm right at the top of the building with a view over old tiled rooftops. The room is plain and comfortable. Everything works, and after a shower, I take myself down to the basement which is a bar-cum-restaurant – the tables scattered around the stone archways that support the rest of the building.

I order a beer. The choice being large or small, dark or light. I opt for a large light, which turns out to have a delicious flavour. Slightly nutty, with a deep richness you'd never find in an English lager. The large is, I guess, half a litre, and it goes down very well indeed. The bar is quiet. I think I'm the only one there – I guess people eat later in Riga.

Still, I'm beginning to enjoy this enforced holiday in Latvia. I try a dark beer next, and begin to contemplate ordering a meal, when I notice another customer walk in and look around in a distracted sort of way. His hair is grey and he has a noticeable stoop. His dress is expensive and formal – black suit, grey tie with paisley pattern, and very shiny shoes. Definitely out to impress. A lady perhaps. His eyes light on me and he walks over to my table and sits down opposite me.

"Mr Rackham?"

I really am beginning to wonder if I'm in some sort of demented dream.

"Yes?"

"I'm very glad you've come. Sir Geoffrey said you were his best."

What? I've only just started. Should I be honest? Or just play along? I opt for the latter, and smile in an encouraging way.

"We have painting." The lack of an 'a' is the first indication I have that he is not British born and bred.

"You want come and see?"

"I was just ordering dinner…"

"No problem. I have good cook. You eat with my house. After."

My God, his English is deteriorating as he gets more earnest. I remember this is my job…

"Excuse me, sir, but who am I speaking to?"

"You don't need to know. You come?"

I don't need to know. So now I know, and with a longing look at my half-finished beer, I follow him out of the hotel restaurant.

"Is not far. You see…" He leads me across the cobbled street. There are fewer tourists out now, and more of what I take to be locals. Riga, far from being a downtrodden remnant of the old USSR, looks like a bright, free-feeling city full of young people. I wonder what happened to the old people.

In a couple of minutes we are outside an old building. "Is mine," he says. After the light of the street it's dark inside. I get the feeling I'm walking along by a velvet curtain, but it's so dark I can't be sure. We seem to walk for a long time. Then I feel a hand on my shoulder. I'm being propelled towards the light, which is so bright I can't make out anything. I am encouraged to sit down. The chair feels hard.

"Sir? Sir? Are you alright?" There's a big man standing in front of me. I don't know where I am.

"We'd better call an ambulance. He seems to be having some sort of fit." The man is talking to someone behind me.

"I'll do it, Malcolm. You stay here and keep an eye on him." The man behind me moves away.

I open my eyes properly in the light. It's not so bright and painful now. "Where am I? What are you doing?"

"Hello. Hello sir. Hang on Graham, he's coming to." He puts his large ruddy face close to mine. Merry Men. That's it, he's one of the Merry Men.

"But, where am I?" I look full into his twinkly eyes.

"Rigby Rogers, sir. You came to buy a gun like your friend's."

"But I don't want a gun."

"Well, you seemed very keen, until I asked you for identification. Then you stopped talking, and just stared. We waited for a bit, and then thought we'd better sit you down and call for an ambulance."

"How long have I been like this?" I say imagining that it must have been hours.

"About ten minutes, sir. Look, do you need an ambulance? Do you think you'll be OK?"

"A glass of water, please." It's all coming back to me. And I can visually see the details of a man I was trying to track down, for some reason. I need to write it down, but I don't want 'Mr Merry' to see me do it.

He goes off, calling to Graham to hold on the ambulance, and I quickly whip out my notebook and write down the details of this mystery man.

"Here you are." He comes back and hands me a glass of water. I drink, and as the cool water goes down, the reality of the world I am in comes back to me – a bit like

159

the colour coming into a black-and-white picture. I've had a close shave. They don't know who I am, and I didn't get forced into buying a gun. The last thing I need!

"Thank you. You've been very kind… look, I'm sorry, I'd better go." I try getting out of the chair, and find my whole body is very stiff. I feel like an old man as I grimace, and manage to get myself into a standing position.

"Are you sure you're OK?" He reaches forward to help me.

"Yes I'm sorry, I must be very tired. It happens like this when I get too tired. I'd better get home and have a rest." Play the old man, Arnold.

"Well, if you're sure?" He looks over at his companion, who shrugs, and opens the door for me.

3.30pm 8th December

Depression settles like a thick cloud on my brain. The traffic reflects my mood as I try to get out of London. Every route is blocked by some sort of incident, and I grind along, wondering if the Beamers and Mercs that turn off the main dual carriageway know something I don't.

The slow-moving traffic gives me time to ruminate, which is the last thing I need. I've had a hallucinatory memory episode that completely fooled me while I was in it. My brain is playing horrendous tricks on me, and there seems nothing I can do about it. There's a paranoia there that I recognise: I truly believed that Dick's mob had put stuff on the internet that would enable a man in a gun shop to give me everything I needed to go with their plans – just like that. Do I think I'm James Bond? Am I that central to their cunning plans?

Ridiculous.

My head is playing tricks with me.

I need to get back to Peggy, and my dog. They both make me feel safe, or at least safer than I am now.

I want to get home, but my mind takes a different route. There is a part of me that is still working on that painting in Riga, on the art dealer in Hay, and on Brian. The traffic is pulling me a different way too. The M4 seems to be totally blocked, so I find myself heading for the M40, and thoughts of Hay-on-Wye. I could get there in time to find a B&B and do a bit of my own research. My thoughts are that Brian could not have been stupid enough to risk such a well-known theft being on the open market. The one in Riga has got to be a fake, and having seen how good they can be, it could take a top expert to confirm that – but surely Sir Geoffrey could have found someone closer to hand? Why send me out? He's obviously in cahoots with Dick's lot. Then the penny drops: I'm a decoy. They think that I'm being tracked by someone, and they want to lead them away from wherever their investigations are taking place. Come to think about it, Dick's mob might have put the fake Manet up themselves, just to make it all look real.

This ruminating may be just as bad as my worrying about my brain and whether I have some terrible developing form of dementia, but it has cleared the fog of depression, and as if on cue, the traffic starts to speed up, and I'm heading out of London on the M40 route.

Peggy doesn't know where I am – neither does anyone else. The tracker phone is in a bin at Gatwick, though it may have been discovered by now. I don't know – I've blocked calls from that direction. The one question is, am I being followed by someone else? Someone who would like to do me harm? I look in my mirror at a black Beamer that has been driving too close behind me for some time, and I shiver involuntarily. I can't see anything inside the car, but it's getting closer. I feel my hands clenching the steering wheel ready for some kind of impact, then without indicating, it pulls out to overtake me and disappears rapidly in the faster-moving outside lane.

I breathe again, and try to relax back into some kind of normal state of mind, but I feel shaky, and realise I need some food and a cup of tea. I pull into the services at Beaconsfield, and cautiously get out of my car, looking round to see if I'm being followed. A silver Golf stops a few spaces away, and I risk a glance in its direction: a woman gets out. Opens the rear door and... lets out two lively children. Not my pursuers.

I never like service stations at the best of times, but this one is very crowded. I head for the loos, and hear the sound of the hand dryers, which sets off memories of finding Grimwode.

The cake is good, if expensive, and the tea is... a tea bag in a metal pot. I look around the large cafeteria. They could be here. They could be anybody.

I am feeling hemmed in, oppressed by this crowded place, and I wolf down the cake and narrowly avoid scalding my mouth on the tea, which I leave unfinished. I'm out of there, and back to the car, back on the road, and heading for Hay.

Paul's latest CD is in the car, and I put it on. I haven't really got to grips with it – since he got together with Andy, his life has changed. Things have got calmer and more routine, and I can hear it in the music. Some of the intensity of his earlier songs has gone. There's a space in them now – a hole, where nothing is said. Not the pithy Paul I knew before. I'm happy for him: he has a good relationship now, and he's stronger in the face of life and adversity. But...

Now I wonder what he'll do since he has been vindicated, since he proved that his nightmares and so-called fantasies were founded on truth – that he had been horribly abused when he was young. He didn't make it up; but will his music lack the bittersweetness that was so much a hallmark of his style, or will there be a new feeling – one of release? Acceptance? We're not getting any younger, and perhaps a more accepting way of looking at things would be better for both of us.

'Forgive us our sins, as we forgive those...'

Not original words of his, of course, and the song may be about our own father. But Paul doesn't go into this in any great detail, he chooses to play an instrumental – very simple, spacious – and so avoids it becoming a straightforward Christian song.

I listen on through, checking in my mirror every now and then to see if I have a follower. It's so dark, it's impossible to tell – one set of headlights looks much like another – but I feel pursued. I feel the hairs on the back of my neck in that animal way.

I finally get off motorways and head up towards Hay. It's at this point that I wish I'd left the tea altogether. I need to stop somewhere and find a bush, but it's so dark I keep missing good pulling-over spaces. Finally I find a rutted entrance to a field, and the car bumps and slithers to a halt. I get out, and stagger over to the gate. It's locked and there's barbed wire on the top of it, so even if I could climb over without wetting myself...

There's no-one on the road – though in my haste I have left my lights on – but I relieve myself with my back to the road, keeping an ear open for any cars that might see me. Sure enough, I hear the sound of an approaching car, and it's slowing down. It stops, and I quickly do up my flies, looking round to see what's happening. The car has pulled into the side of the road just beyond me, and I hear the sound of a door opening. A dark figure walks towards me, and I run round and get into my car, slamming the door and revving the engine, skidding out onto the road and round the other car, narrowly avoiding a lorry coming the other way. I look in my mirror, but all I can see is the car's stationary headlights. Was he a pursuer, or just a friendly bloke stopping to see if I'd broken down?

8.30pm 8th December

It's feeling a bit late to find a B&B in Hay as I park in a street leading up into the town centre. I try the first place that says 'Vacancies'. The door is opened by a lady in her sixties with platinum blonde hair, and a lot of lipstick.

"Yers, I got a place dearie." She flutters her eyelids at me, and I wonder what I'm getting into. "Forty-five pounds a night. Full English. Will that do?"

I mutter a reply, and shuffle through the front door, grateful for somewhere to rest my weary head.

"Nice room for you, dearie." She leads me upstairs and opens the door to my room with a flourish. It is pink. The walls are pink. The carpet is pink. The curtains are pink. The bedspread is pink. Pink cushions are scattered on it, supporting the only un-pink thing: a large stuffed toy duck in natural duck colours.

"Keep you company in the night," she says as she sees my eyebrows go up. "Here's the ensuite," she says with a flourish. It's pink.

"All sorts stay here in the Festival. Writers, poets, criticals." She goes on with an endless lists of the good and great who have stayed here. Some presumably in this pink bedroom. Honestly, all it needs is a couple of fluffy handcuffs, and a mirror on the ceiling. I shudder.

"Don't see much of them though. Always got to go out and do things – speeches and the like."

I'm not surprised. I want to get out too, but I seem to have got myself in this predicament where it would be rude to just say 'no thank you' and walk out, so I plonk my suitcase down and turn to her.

"Thank you. It's er… lovely. I've just got to go out to get something to eat. I'll be back later." Much later, I think.

"I usually ask for payment in advance, dearie. Had a bad time with some poets once. Scruffy lot they were. Now you…"

"Thanks." I get out my wallet. "Forty pounds you said?"

"Forty-five please, dearie. People say it's such a nice room."

"I'm sure they do." My sarcasm is lost on her, as I hand over the cash. One last look at my pink prison, and I'm off down the stairs.

"Oh, and I lock up at ten."

"Ah. Can I have a key?"

"For the front door? That'll be ten pound deposit. I've had such trouble with them criticals. Always walking off with the keys."

I fork out another tenner. She hands me a key from a row of hooks, and I'm off into the free air of Hay.

I walk down the street, past the scene of our mobile theft, past the ice cream parlour – now shut up and dark – down through some hilly streets to a sign I recognise. The tapas bar. I just hope they're still serving food. I'm starving.

It's quite full for a cold night in the off season. Spanish music and shadowy corners make it feel foreign. The waitress who approaches me is dressed in gypsy skirt and top – loopy earrings, and bangles on her wrists. Her dark eyes flash at me from a mop of curly black hair, and I half expect her to speak in a torrent of Spanish.

166

"Are you still serving?"

"We serve till ten o'clock." Her accent is local, I guess. She waves me to a small table. "The specials are on the board." She indicates a blackboard just behind me. "Would you like a drink?"

Would I like a drink? After my day, I could do with more than one. I settle for a carafe of house Tempranillo, which she brings over almost immediately. I must look like an ex-policeman in desperate need. I certainly feel like one. I am meant to be in Riga. I thought I was in Riga. I nearly bought a gun. I thought I was being pursued. Then the pink room. This place feels like a sanctuary. I look round the bar – it's full of elderly eccentrics and I think of my landlady's 'poets' and 'criticals.' There are a couple of younger men out with their young ladies, but no-one who looks like they are going to kill me.

I choose potatoes, olives, meats, prawns, and some amazing-sounding stew from the board, and then settle down to enjoy my wine. I get out my mobile, hoping no-one will be offended. There are three missed calls from Peggy, and I realise I've had it on silent.

Guiltily, I press her number.

"Hello. Arne?" Her voice sounds breathless.

"Hello, love. It's me." I speak quietly to avoid disturbing my neighbours.

"Where are you? What's that music? I didn't know they had Spanish cafés in Riga."

"I'm not in Riga."

"What?" Her voice sounds loud like she's shouting to make up for my quiet tones.

"I'm not in Riga. Flight got delayed, and I..."

"You're breaking up..."

"I'm not in Riga, I'm in Hay." I say it louder this time, with my mouth close to where I think it should be.

"You're in Hay?"

"Yes."

"You're in that tapas bar we went to, aren't you?"

A warm feeling invades my body. Shared experience with the one I love.

"Yes. I love you." I mutter the last bit.

"You what?"

"I'm following something up." I go for the less personal approach.

"But you're meant to be in Riga."

"I couldn't do it. It just seemed such a waste of time."

"Arne?" her voice is softer. "Are you afraid of flying?"

"Yes. No. Yes."

"But this job was always going to involve flying. You knew that when you took it on."

"I thought I could take the train."

"The train to Riga? Are you kidding?"

"No, well I didn't think…"

"You'd better go. You'll get the sack… hang on, there's someone trying to get me… fuck, it's Grimwode."

"Don't take it." Grimwode. I thought he was still in hospital.

"I'll let it go to answerphone. They've obviously rumbled you. Have you got their phone?"

"I left it in a bin at Gatwick."

"You what?"

"I was fed up with being tracked and manipulated…"

"You're breaking up again…"

"There's stuff I can't tell you here. Don't tell Grimwode you know where I am."

"But Arne, you're in danger. The reason for their phone is so they can track you and protect you, and now you've bloody screwed it up and nobody's got your back. You've nearly been killed three times in the past couple of months. I care. I bloody care. I'm going to let them know where you are."

168

"No. Please don't. Give me till tomorrow," I say this a bit loudly, and I'm sure people are looking round at me.

"But..."

"Look. I'll text you. Please wait until you've read it before you do anything." I ring off, and text:

I'll be alright. I've got a gun, ammo, and vest.

I lie. Is that a white lie? She'll find out in the end.

A text comes back:

Alright. I'll hold off, but be blooooody careful. And keep in touch.

Then another one:

What shall I tell him?

Tell him you think I'm in London, but don't know where.

I'll get the sack for this...

No you won't. I will. Xxx

"Your food, sir." A young waiter spreads the dishes round the table. It looks a veritable feast. Where to start?

Love you x

Peggy's text distracts me from the prawns.

Love you too x

I'm hungry, and I tuck in to the various delicious dishes, but I find them hard to taste. In my mind, I'm with her now, explaining why I lied.

7.00am 9th December

I awake in a sea of pink. For a moment I wonder if I'm in heaven, floating on one of those pink clouds. But I'm no cherub, and there's no harp. As I focus on this pink world, I see my watch on the bedside table. I've slept longer than I meant to. Perhaps my mind and body knew that I wouldn't be able to stand lying here in this room waiting for my breakfast, and mercifully kept me asleep.

I get out of bed and nearly stumble over the big fluffy duck which has found its way onto the floor. The shower is a dribble of lukewarm water, and I shiver as I dry myself.

Down in the breakfast room I am the only visitor. I hear Elvis doing his worst wobbly crooning from the kitchen, where my landlady is preparing my full English.

On the table there's a pink tablecloth and doilies everywhere. On the wall are the three flying ducks, displayed in the regulation diagonal against a pink background.

"Tea or coffee, dearie?" She's made up to the nines and it's only half past seven.

"Tea please." I don't risk the coffee.

"Hear the news? More immigrants coming in today. I ask you. Taking up all our services, filling up the schools with their foreign languages, sponging off the state, using our health service. I ask you."

She doesn't actually ask me, and disappears into the kitchen. I don't know what I'd have said anyway. I wonder if her pink world only has room for nice white English people, who for some reason don't use up our services and fill the beds in our hospitals.

"Here you are dearie." She puts down a plate of overcooked bacon, plastic looking sausages, whole tinned tomatoes, watery scrambled egg, and toast with the crusts cut off, which looks singed rather than toasted.

I wonder how I'm going to get through this, and wait for her to leave so that I can make a concentrated effort. But she doesn't leave.

"I think we should send them all back. Send them packing."

I wonder how many immigrants are taking up the space in Hay-on-Wye.

"We've had the blacks for years, and look what happens: they're all criminals. And then the Pakis. Keeping to themselves. Never mixing."

Never having the chance, I reflect.

"And now. Syria? Is that our fault? Do we want their brats coming over here? Cheating little Arabs. The Jews are just as bad. Taking all our money."

I feel like I'm back in *'The Remains of the Day'*, at a time when people didn't know Auschwitz would happen.

"Sometimes I think Hitler… 'ere what are you doing?"

I get up. I can't eat her wretched breakfast, and I can't listen to this racist rubbish any more. I go up to my room, pick up my case, which I'd had the foresight to pack, and go downstairs and out of the front door, and into the blessed fresh air. Now I know why she wanted paying in advance. I feel in my pocket – I've still got her front door key. I'm just like one of her 'criticals', but I don't want to reclaim my tenner. I will sneak back later on and put it through her letterbox.

There's a grey dawn light in the streets and nobody's about. I won't be able to get anything to eat or drink for a while. I suspect nothing opens particularly early in Hay, so I carry my case down to the car and sit in the driver's seat wondering what to do next. I feel inside my coat to check where my wallet is, and my hand comes into contact with my notebook.

Alan Hunt. I scribbled his details down yesterday.

His address is in Chancery Lane, so I walk up out of the car park and make my way through the winding streets and into the depths of the bookiest small town in the world.

I turn into Chancery Lane, and a little way down on the left I find 'Alan Hunt - Art Dealer' engraved on a small brass plate displayed on the wall to the right of a pair of high, green gates that fills an archway. The right-hand gate has a handle, and I pull it open. The scraping sound of wood on grit that it makes seems loud in the quiet of the morning. I go through the arch and into an alleyway, with a blank brick wall on my left, and a mews cottage on my right. I presume that the brick wall forms the side of the neighbouring property – there is no door in it. But on the right, the black door to the mews cottage is ajar. I peer cautiously through a low window, and by shining the light from my phone I can see what look like piles of paper heaped on the floor.

I go through the black door and into the darkness, the torch on my phone picking out chairs, a table, and making huge shadows of them. As I get used to the gloom, I can see the place is a mess. It's been ransacked. This is not Grimwode's team – someone else has come in and hasn't cared about leaving signs of their search behind them. Cupboards are open, drawers are turned on their side, their contents spilled out onto the floor.

This was once a tasteful little pad for Mr Hunt. The furniture is antique. I can see the corner of a Persian rug under the piles of paper. I move carefully into the next room, which looks like an office. The mess is even worse here. Overturned cupboards, folders ripped open, paper everywhere. A cold winter sun begins to peep through the windows, picking out dark patches where paintings must have hung. My foot crunches on something, and I point my light down to see glass. Picture frames are stacked against the walls – the paintings have been roughly torn out of them, leaving frayed edges and broken glass.

I walk on through to the bathroom which has been left largely unscathed. A couple of pictures taken from the walls and smashed, the pile of magazines by the loo rumpled and torn. My mind goes back to the drugs raids we did in the Met. We always checked the lavatory cistern – so often there would be something incriminating stuck in the lid, or weighed down in the water. I take the lid off. There's nothing stuck inside it, but peering down into the water I see a brick. Nothing so odd about that: Alan Hunt was saving water. It's a common trick, but something makes me reach in to get it. It looks larger than usual, but as I lift it out it feels lighter than I'd expect. I put it down on the floor and examine its surface. There is a crack going all the way round the sides. Taking the top and bottom in my hands I pull, and after exerting a lot of force, the brick comes apart revealing a plastic bag inside its hollow interior. It's a clever concealing device, and one I've never seen before. But I recognise the contents of the plastic bag straight away – I saw one yesterday – a Beretta. I carefully open the bag with my gloved hands and remove the gun. It feels different – heavier.

'Oh Mr Hunt, you didn't buy this one over the counter.' I check the magazine – no CO_2 capsule, there are real bullets in this one. What happened to his airgun, I wonder?

I look at the other contents – airline tickets, and I'm just opening up the wallet, when I hear the sound of footsteps. I quickly turn off my light and pick up the gun, stuffing the tickets into my coat pocket.

There is no window in the bathroom, I am in complete darkness. I can smell the oil from the gun. I takes me back to the time when…

There's a gurgling sound, and I suddenly realise the oily smell isn't coming from the gun.

It's petrol.

Someone's going to torch the place, and I'm right in the middle of it with paper everywhere.

I scramble to my feet, holding the gun in front of me, and run out of the bathroom, and though the office. A shadowy figure is standing by the front door. I see a flame in its hand.

"Stop, or I'll fire!" I shout, my voice sounding ridiculously loud in the quiet house.

The figure drops the flame and runs out, slamming the door. I hear the turn of a key in the lock, but I snap off the safety catch on the gun, hoping to God that it's loaded, and fire straight at the lock. The door bursts open as the floor in front of me ignites, and I run straight through the fire and out into the alleyway. Small flames come from the soles of my shoes where I trod on the petrol. I catch sight of a figure half turned and caught in the sudden light of the fire. My eyes haven't adjusted enough to see the face.

"Stop, or I…" I don't fire. The figure turns and disappears through the gates, as the petrol and paper turn into an inferno behind me. I run down the alleyway to the street. There's no-one to be seen.

Then I hear voices from behind me. "There's a fire, John! Call 999 quick. It's going up like…" It's a woman's voice – shrill and panicky in the dawn.

10.10am 9th December

I'm sitting in the window of the ice cream parlour, sipping a delicious cappuccino and wondering whether to go for straightforward chocolate ice cream, or ginger and apple.

I managed to get away from the fire unnoticed, and found a café open by the car park. They did a proper full English, and I needed a bit of stabilising food after my near-death-by-fire experience. I sat there feeling rather proud of myself, until I looked down at my knees to see they were shaking. Worse than that, my feet were stuck to the floor – the half melted soles of my shoes had decided to bond with the tiles. Not wanting to be noticed, I surreptitiously bent down with a knife, and managed to lever the melted rubber away from the floor without leaving too much mess.

I went back to the car to move it to the car park and dig out my only other pair of shoes – a pair of smart black lace-ups to wear with my posh suit.

In spite of being winter, Hay is bustling, with a street market just outside the window, and elderly couples coming into the parlour for their coffee and ice cream.

They all look very erudite, clutching their Guardians and Times Literary Supplements. A couple on the table next to me starts talking about vintage cars.

177

"The auction at Hereford is worth a look if you know what you're doing."

I watch as they sip their coffees. Curious how age brings out the muscles in their faces – their expressions seem poised between ones of disgust, and of ecstasy. So much of that plump youthful skin has gone. A skin that covered up emotion, and secrets. Now their structure is laid bare, showing grief or pleasure from the past, and their present irritation or enthusiasm. I get out my notebook and start to make sketches of them, surreptitiously glancing at an unsuspecting model from time to time, to capture another detail, another shift of muscles. They are so rewarding, these faces. But will they give up their secrets? More than they realise, I suspect.

An elderly lady suddenly turns and catches my eye, as I try to pencil in the lines of her pursed lips. I look down at my notebook as if trying to remember something for my shopping list, and then look away from her and into one of the mirrors that are set into the side of the window.

What I see makes me gasp: my dead brother Stan is slowly walking up the street towards the door of the shop. He looks like he's aged in the grave, but he still has that haunted look that set him apart from his twin brother Paul. His eyes are red-rimmed with tears. Has he come back to say he is sorry that he left us? That he took his own life? The expression on his face is just the same as I remember it being the last time I saw him all those years ago, but it has aged with time – the lines of pain and desperation etched deeply in the skin under his eyes and cheekbones.

He sees me in the mirror in the last moment before he passes the window, and his eyes widen. I look out to see his stooping shoulders turning into the parlour. The hair rises on the back of my neck, and I stand up. He has come back. He never died. He's…

"Arne. Peggy told me you were in Hay." His eyes are sunken, and his voice is gravelly.

I am confused. I just stand and look at him.

"Arne. Arnold. It's me. Paul." He reaches out and takes my arm.

"Paul? Oh, sorry. I thought…" I manage to stutter.

"I need to talk to you." He turns and goes to the counter.

I sit down, and look at his back. His sloping shoulders. His drooping head. Where's the Paul I've been seeing in the last few months? Tall, fit, muscular?

Paul returns with a cup of coffee. He sits down beside me, puts his coffee down, puts his head in his hands, and starts to shake.

It's my turn to put out my hand. I hold his arm. "Paul, what is it? You look so changed. I thought you were…"

"Andy…" Paul's sobs become audible.

"Tell me."

"Andy's left."

"What? Why?" I lean closer to him, and his sobbing slows down. He takes a deep breath, takes his hands away from his face, and looks at me.

"All that police stuff. Ever since you brought back that wallet from the beach. All the stuff that's happened since. Andy was both pissed off and terrified, with the police all over the place. He… we both felt so intruded upon… Then we went and stayed in the safe house in the Yorkshire Dales."

"But I thought it was supposed to be beautiful up there. A chance to recover, and be protected."

"Andy felt imprisoned. He couldn't sleep. He was scared to go out, and he kept blaming you."

"Me?"

"Yes. He said if it hadn't been for your meddling – bringing back that wallet, bringing us into your police world… a world he hates. He's been funny ever since I

179

decided to go to court and support your case against Witherspoon. Said it was none of our business. Then he said... he said I was only gay because of my experience with Witherspoon, and... and he could see signs that I didn't want him any more."

"So..." I look him in the eyes, "do you?"

"Yes I do."

"You love him?" My gaze shifts to the next table. Are they listening? The elderly couple of men seem buried in their newspapers.

"I love him. I want him back. I can't live without him."

"So what happened?" I gesture to Paul to keep his voice down.

"I couldn't persuade him to come out for walks with me, so I went on my own. It's so beautiful up there. I always took longer than I said I would. Then I'd come back to find his face all set in that hard look he has. I couldn't look into his eyes – he kept looking away. I'd calm down on my walks, and then I'd try to talk him round, to persuade him that I still loved him, needed him. But he didn't believe me. He said I had changed since the trial. Become all strong and sure of myself. He said I didn't need him any more, and he kept blaming you. He said you'd taken me away from him. All that stuff about blood being thicker than water. And that I'd become more like you. Ever since he first met you, he'd felt an antagonism from you. Like you would want to turn me away from him. You, the homophobic policeman, want your brother to return to heterosexuality."

"But this is all rubbish. I never thought that. I took to Andy straight away. I knew he could be easily upset. But this?" I feel so hurt. "I've never challenged your... I've never even thought about it. I've just accepted it because... you're my brother."

"I know, I know. It was all in his head. I told him that, but every time he attacked you it was like a knife going into me."

Paul leans towards me, and, after glancing round behind him, he continues in a low, shaky voice.

"One morning, we had a particularly bad argument, and I went out, saying I wasn't sure when I'd be back. It was a beautiful windy day, and I walked up on to a long escarpment that overlooked the valley where the safe house was. The wind dried my eyes, and I felt I could see clearly. I believed then that I would be able to pull him round, sit him down, hold his hands, and make him look into my eyes and see the love there.

"I looked down at our valley, and saw someone in the distance, walking up the path towards me. To start with, I thought it was Andy. That he'd had a change of heart, and come out to catch me up. I imagined a beautiful reconciliation on top of the hills. A truly romantic moment. Ha!

"But as I looked, I could see it wasn't Andy. It was a man that I didn't recognise, and he'd stopped on the path and was looking at me. For some reason, I felt very uncomfortable. It didn't feel safe being out there with this man following me.

"If he was following me.

"I decided to carry on and see if he followed and stopped to keep pace with me. I walked up over the top of the escarpment, and then turned off the path and into the long grass and heather. If he was just taking the path he would go in the other direction. I walked for a bit, and then stopped and waited to see if he would appear. He did, and he turned to follow me, then stopped and looked at me. I was beginning to panic now. I had my phone with a special number to contact if I was worried about my safety. I pressed it, and someone replied immediately. They would come out and pick me up as soon as they could. I was to keep my phone turned on so they could find me. The man had started walking towards me, so I headed in a curve, hoping I could get back down off the escarpment and back to the house. The heather got longer, and there were small rocks which slowed me down. I looked back, and the man was still coming after me. He stopped again, and stared at me. He was closer now. I imagined he had a gun, and once he'd got close enough..."

"Was he... did he look like the man who shot up your kitchen?"

"No, he was thinner and taller. No beard. Anyway, I scrambled down a slope only to find that I was heading for a cliff, and there was no way down. So I climbed up again and onto the top of the ridge. He was there behind me. He had caught up even more, because he hadn't made that mistake I'd made. I realised he must know these hills better than I did. I stopped. He stopped. Then my phone made a beep, and I took it out and saw a text:

'He's not one of ours. Keep well away and keep on the top of the ridge. We're sending a helicopter.'

"I really started to panic then, and scrambled up as high as I could get. It was shorter heather on the top, so I began to run. I looked round to see him running after me. When I looked ahead, in the distance, I could see another figure coming towards me. There was nowhere to hide. I couldn't get off the ridge. I just had to pray that the helicopter would get to me before they did."

"Shit Paul, that's horrible!" I feel a mixture of outrage and guilt. If I hadn't meddled, as Andy said... "What did you do?"

"I stopped, got my phone out again, and called the number. There was no reply. The guy behind me was walking deliberately towards me, so I started to run towards the figure in the distance. 'Just give yourself time', I said to myself. Maybe I could suddenly dodge down off the ridge, and then get up again round the back of the man in front."

"It was definitely a man?"

"I wasn't sure. To be honest, I didn't think like that. If they were carrying guns…"

"Yes, sorry. Go on."

"The helicopter came in so fast. It came out of nowhere. I stopped and waved. I heard the crack of a gun and fell flat on my face. The wind from the helicopter blades would have knocked me over anyway. All I could hear was the noise of the engine. I felt a hand on my shoulder. 'Are you alright sir?' I said I was, and was about to get up. 'No, stay where you are, sir.' I could hear more gunfire, and shouts from the men close to me. All I could see was the grass in front of my face. I had no idea what was going on. There was more shouting, more gunfire, then I was told to get up but keep low, and I ran with my helper over to the helicopter. I clambered in, leaving two armed men in flak jackets on the ground. We were up and away, and I heard my helper on the radio calling for more people to come and get my pursuers.

"It didn't take long to get to the small helipad down in the valley. I was taken in a car back to the safe house, and it was then that I discovered Andy had left."

"But how could they let him?"

"Oh, he went almost immediately after I'd gone for my walk. Insisted, apparently. They had no power to keep him, and I hadn't been threatened at that point."

"So where is he now?"

"I went back to Wales, with a minder in tow. And we found that he had taken all his things from the cottage. His clothes, his books, and his pots and pans. He must have acted so fast."

"But it doesn't make sense. How could he have moved so fast? Surely the guys protecting you would have caught up with him…"

"They had no power to force him to co-operate – so they said. I just think they saw a couple of gays and didn't care." Paul's eyes were glistening with anger.

"But why did they care about you?"

"I'm your brother. Someone wants to get at you so badly."

"Everyone thought I was going to Riga, and now Peggy has told Grimwode's lot that I'm in London." I suddenly have a thought. "Where's your minder now, Paul?"

"Oh, he didn't stay with me after we got back to my cottage. They're pretty stretched. They gave me a…"

"Bullet-proof vest…"

"…and a…"

"Tracking device…"

"… so they…"

"Know you're here." I look in the mirror and see a man in khaki gear coming up the street. I brace myself. Nothing happens. No-one comes through the door.

"So Peggy told you I was here. Have you seen her?"

"Yes, I just came from there."

"Has she still got Hannah with her?"

"Yes, but they have no protection."

"So they're vulnerable as well. How's she taking it?"

"They seemed alright. Though I think Peggy's getting restless. She wants you to tell people where you are, and what you're doing. I think she wants you there, with her. That's why I'm here."

"We'd better go. They might get at her next. Dick's lot really don't care, do they?"

"They're going after the people who tried to get me. They don't have enough…"

184

I hold Paul's arm and look him steadily in the face. "You just said it. It's not that they don't care about Andy because he's gay. They're just too thinly stretched. They're not protecting Peggy either, and she's police." I get up and walk out of the parlour, Paul following.

"Are you armed?" he asks.

"Yes, but no bullet-proof vest – long story. Where's your car?"

"I'm down in the car park."

"So am I."

We make our way through the narrow streets to find our cars. Sleet is beginning to fall, and the skies are darkening. Snow on the way.

2.30pm 9th December

By rights, we should have been there two hours ago, but the snow has put paid to that. A lorry jack-knifed on the main road, causing a massive tailback. Then, when we did finally get moving, the smaller road we had to take became increasingly slippery and dangerous – the snow piling up rapidly, visibility almost nil. We crawled through winding lanes, hoping that nothing was already stuck ahead of us, and that nothing would come the other way causing us to have to reverse.

I phoned ahead to Peggy, with various less and less optimistic ETAs. She was happily holed up in our rented cottage. Hannah was playing her cello – I could hear the strains of Bach in the background. The only one not comfortable with the situation was the dog. I heard him bark, and then whine in an unusual way that reminded me of something that made me feel very uncomfortable. Apparently, he'd been getting up from his bed in the corner of the kitchen, barking, and then whining to be let out, but when Peggy opened the back door to let him out, he'd gone back to his bed with his tail between his legs.

"He probably knows you're coming. He's missed you, and he thinks he hears you outside, but it's just the wind," Peggy said.

But I am not happy with that behaviour; it triggers off something in my mind – something recent. But at the

187

moment my brain's all taken up with getting the car to carry on through the snow. I have led all the way, Paul's car has been behind me – just his headlights telling me he's still there. We're not far now, only a couple of miles to go, but I know there's a steep hill between us and the cottage, and the chances are we'll get stuck. The lane goes down, and I feel the car wheels go sideways as I try to control the speed. Gears Arnold, not brakes. I get out of the skid as the lane bottoms out, and start to climb the hill, my mind forcing me to believe we can make it – but the camber of the road slopes sideways, and I can't see where the tarmac ends and the muddy verge starts. The car slides into the side, and gets stuck. Paul stops behind me. He might have made it, but he can't get past. He gets out and tries to push me out, but all that happens is that I go a couple of feet and get stuck even further into the bank.

"It's hopeless. We'll have to walk," I say.

Fortunately for him, Paul has walking boots and waterproof in his car. I am not so lucky. The shoes that got burnt in the fire might have been some use, but my smart black shoes have completely smooth soles, made for dinning rooms, not snowy Welsh hills. There's nothing we can do about the cars except get Paul's into the side as well. We've succeeded in blocking the lane, and I curse myself for my foolishness. Now not even a tractor will be able to get up there – I just hope some poor farmer isn't out in the fields hoping to come back this way.

Paul holds my arm as I slither and slide up the steep lane. When we get to the top, I phone Peggy. The signal is getting poor, and will probably disappear altogether as we get closer.

"We got stuck. We're walking up now. Should take half an hour."

"Can't wait to see you. Neither can the dog, he's going mental." She starts to break up, but I can just hear the dog barking urgently before the phone goes dead.

"How is she?" Paul asks.

"Seems OK. I'm worried about the dog. She thinks he's wound up because he senses I coming home, but I'm not... Oh my God!" I've remembered what's bugging me.

"What?"

"Last time he was barking and behaving oddly was when he was poisoned by the people who stole my report."

"What report?"

"The one Grimwode gave me. The dog nearly died. Oh shit, there's someone out there! He knows it. We'd better get there fast."

"But they'll be armed. We should call for help."

I look at my phone. "No signal. Have you got yours? You've got that special number."

Paul looks down at his phone. "I haven't got anything either. I could go back until I get one, and call them."

"I think we'd better stick together. There's no guarantee you'll get through, and you could be a target as well. Anyway, I need your support. Literally. I'll never get there in these shoes."

"So you've got a gun? I remember you were really good. Then something happened..."

Not now, Paul. Not now.

"I'd better check I've got some bullets in it." I pull the Beretta out of my pocket, and with freezing fingers take out the magazine. I manage to flick the bullets out into my hand. "Only five rounds, I was hoping for nine." Alan Hunt must have tried the gun out before he hid it.

Then as I shakily put the bullets back into the magazine I drop one.

"Shit! Have you got a light on your phone?"

189

Paul shines his light on the ground in front of me. We scour the area around my feet. The snow is deep. It's fruitless in this light. I think of my past in the Met, when we would search a crime scene for spent bullets. We had hours, if not days. Now we have minutes, and there's no chance of me finding the lost bullet.

"We'd better go. Just have to hope I'll only need four shots." We both straighten up, and I shove the gun into an inside pocket to warm it up. It doesn't warm me up though. Cold metal under armpit.

I don't know how many times I slip and fall on our rapid journey to the cottage. It's a nightmare of cold and slipperiness. My knees and elbows are bruised, my progress isn't helped by the fact that I have only got thin gloves meant for city life, and I'm keeping my hands in my pockets in an attempt to warm them up. Cold hands mean bad aim.

Paul helps as best he can, but although he has proper boots, it's a tall order for anyone to keep a six-foot man upright when he's wearing shoes meant for the dance floor. Also, I detect a weakness in him, as though something has caved in inside his fit, strong frame.

We come to a wood, mainly oak, which screens the cottage from the road. It's stopped snowing, and there's that magical silence that follows a heavy snowfall. I decide not to go up the track, but get close to the cottage in the cover of the wood. We clamber over a bit of fence that has seen better days, but as I check I haven't caught myself on the barbed wire, I see a bit of material hanging where the fence is highest. It's denim. So they are here. But somebody's getting cold in their jeans, especially now there's a hole in them.

The ground between the trees has a little snow on it, but it's much easier for me to move now. I motion Paul to get behind me, and I get the gun out, taking the safety catch off.

The quiet is broken by a dog barking.

My dog.

We make our way through the wood as fast and as quietly as we can.

"Can you check your mobile?" I whisper to Paul. There could be signal here.

We come to a halt at the edge of the wood. There's a small field in front of the cottage. Suddenly a dark shape looms out of the gloom to my left. I point my gun at it, but it's just the donkey. I'm surprised it's out in the field and not in its shelter. I look round at Paul, who is nodding to me. He has signal and is texting the emergency number.

"Text Peggy," I whisper. "Warn her."

Then I look back at the cottage. To start with I can see no sign of anyone. The dog has stopped barking, and is whining in a worried kind of way. I can hear Peggy's voice, now scolding, now consoling. I see a movement from the donkey's shelter – that's why it's out in the snow, someone's using it as cover.

"They're coming, but it may take a bit of time," Paul whispers to me.

"Have you texted Peggy yet?"

"No, just doing it…"

The cottage door opens, and I see Peggy framed in the light from the kitchen. The dog runs out between her legs barking furiously. There's someone against the wall to the right of the door. I see the glint of metal reflecting the light from the kitchen window.

It's a long shot, but I take aim and fire at where I think the intruder's legs are. The dog leaps. A shot rings out. And the dog falls.

I can see the gunman clearly now as he moves in on Peggy, intending to use her as a human shield. I won't

191

miss this time. My whole life's at stake. My shot hits him in the body and he slumps against the wall. Peggy looks down at the dog, and hesitates. Her mobile beeps, and she sees the text. A bullet hits the side of the doorframe as she steps back and shuts the door. The next bullet comes in our direction, splintering a tree close by.

"Lie down," I whisper to Paul.

I wait to see what the person in the shelter will do next. They know I've got the entrance to the cottage covered, but they don't know I've only got two shots left.

The next shot grazes the shoulder of my coat. I return fire in the direction of the flash, but it's a forlorn hope that I will hit them. And all the time, the dog is lying there, bleeding to death.

Or dead.

A sudden fury takes hold of me, and I run out of the cover of the trees shouting, "Bastards, I'll get you!"

A shot rings out, but I dodge towards the house. I slip over and fall flat on my face, as a whole volley of shots passes over my head.

One bullet. That's all I have.

I begin to slide my aching body across the snow towards the house. The man I hit has a gun, and assuming he remains unconscious, I will be able to use that. Then I see it glinting in the light from the kitchen window – a green petrol can just inside the donkey shelter. My last shot – but if that ignites it may be enough distraction for me to get the other gun.

I fire. The can goes up in a flash of flame, and I see the face of my assailant. It's the woman we saw in the ice cream parlour. She looks angry. Startled. She's momentarily blinded by the spreading fire in front of her, so I stumble and run to the house. The man is still lying slumped against the wall, and I pick up his gun – a semi-automatic pistol – and take aim. She sees me then, and turns and runs out of the back of the flaming shelter and into the woods.

All I can hear is the crackle of flames, and I wonder whether to go after her. Then I hear the sound of a car starting. Perhaps she'll get stuck. I stand up and cautiously make my way along the front of the house towards the sound. There is the noise of a car skidding. And then it stops, and all I can hear is the drone of the engine getting softer as she drives away.

I turn back to the carnage in front of the cottage, luridly illuminated by the burning shelter. The dog lies on the snow in a pool of blood. I go over, and miraculously, he's still breathing. The gunman lies still, by the wall.

"Peggy!" I call. "Can you let me in? The dog..."

I look down at his gentle face, with its greying muzzle. His eyes are open. They say 'save me, love me' – but even as I look the light fades in them, and he shudders and is still. My dog. My oldest friend.

Through blurred eyes I see the door open. Peggy comes out, and with difficulty, kneels down to look at the dog. Hannah is behind her, the shock in her face telling me how much she cares.

"Is the man dead?" Peggy asks.

"I don't know. I don't care."

"But he might..."

"I've got his gun. Paul!" I shout. "It's safe!"

"I'm here." He's just behind me. "The dog?"

"He's gone."

We all look down at him in the dying fire. The best dog in the world.

193

5.30pm 9th December

"Arne?" I feel a gentle hand on my knee. I look up to see two eyes looking at me. I see love in them – new love, human love. "They're here."

Where have I been? I've been staring into blankness, into darkness.

A man is lying on the floor in the corner of the kitchen. He's covered in a blanket. My blanket. There's a smear of blood on the floor where they dragged him in. I recognise the face, though it has no beard now. Two paramedics are kneeling on the floor next to him, and by the look of it, he's still alive.

There's a tall figure by the open door, looking out. A couple of AFOs are talking to him.

"We've searched the area, sir. No sign of anyone. We found one car down the lane, and Sergeant Gordon's checking the ground where the other car left the scene."

The figure turns round. "Rackham."

"Dawson, you took your time." I spit it out.

"We had to make a detour. There were two cars blocking the lane."

"That was us, we got stuck…" If only we hadn't, would I have got there in time?

"I didn't know you were carrying arms," Dawson continues. He sounds accusatory.

"Just as well I was. Is he..?" I nod at the figure on the floor.

"We're trying to get a helicopter in as close as we can. We might save him."

One of the paramedics looks up and nods. "We've stopped the bleeding, but the bullet's still in there, and we think it's close to his heart."

Oh dear, I think. What a shame.

"Shit!" says Dawson. "Did you have to go for the heart? Couldn't you have just got him in the legs?"

"No, I'd tried that and missed. He'd shot my dog and was moving in on Peggy."

"But..." A thought crosses Dawson's face. "Shit, you're not even in the force now! This is a real fuckup. Shit!"

"You're right there. If you'd been doing your job..."

But he's taking no notice of me. He's on his phone. There's a pause as he gets through. He walks away from me but I can still hear him. "...yes, sir. Still with us, sir... we're there now... doing everything we can... yes I will, sir..." He goes out of the door.

I hear Peggy and Paul talking in whispers behind me.

"I guess that fucker was hanging around, keeping an eye on us, and waiting for the woman to turn up. That's why the dog was behaving so oddly. Poor thing, if only..."

"If Arne hadn't been armed... Do you think I should ask about Andy? The way they're going..."

"No, leave it for now..."

Dawson comes back in. "Helicopter's here." The paramedics have already got my victim on a stretcher, and they quickly get up and leave at a run.

"Is that your gun?"

I realise that a semi-automatic pistol is lying on the table in front of me. I must have put it there, ready, in case we were attacked again.

"No, that's his."

"We'll need that." Dawson stoops down and picks it up, his gloved finger inserted into the trigger guard, and I reflect that he'd hardly need to worry about fingerprints. We know who fired the gun. One of the bullets will be in my dog.

"You're not police now. Better safe than sorry." He drops it into a plastic bag.

It then dawns on me: Dawson thinks I'm in real trouble.

"And is this your gun?" Dawson picks up another plastic bag with a Beretta in it. I nod.

"Look, if it's all the same to you, I'd like to bury my dog." I look him in the eyes then. I *think* I can see a human being in there.

"Sorry, no can do. Forensics."

"I'm coming too. I'm not leaving your lot to hack him to pieces, and then chuck him in the incinerator."

"Don't worry, you're coming with us," says Dawson. "And we'll need Sergeant McDonald as well."

Primary witness, I think.

"You can stay here." He looks at Paul. "It's alright, we'll give you protection. And your friend…" He turns to Peggy. "She'd better stay."

"She's outside with the dog."

I suddenly feel a burning resentment towards Hannah. Why should she be watching over my dead dog? That's my job, not hers. Everywhere I look there's Hannah, looking after my loved ones. She'll be looking after Paul next.

"What's with this bloody dog?"

"As if you'd know," I say quietly as I get up, ready to go with Dawson. I walk out into the snow, stoop down and pick up the cold bloody bundle that was my dog, without looking at or acknowledging Hannah. "I'll carry him, if you don't mind."

197

Dawson looks as if he's going to say something, but thinks better of it as we walk out to the waiting Land Rovers.

10am 10th December

"If you'd…"

"Where did you get the gun?"

"In a toilet."

"Don't be…"

"Listen. If I'd gone to Riga like you lot wanted me to, you'd have three dead people on your hands – or at best, three hostages."

"What makes you think we wanted you to go to Riga?"

"It was bloody obvious. That little phone that kept sending me little messages."

For the first time ever, I see Grimwode looking totally puzzled. "That was Dawson's idea, keeping track of you, but…"

"I dumped it in a bin at Gatwick Airport."

"You did what?"

"Dumped it in a bin, concealed in a bacon butty. I tried to destroy it, but it was unbreakable."

A smile flashes across Grimwode's face. A rare sight. He eases himself off his chair, evidently still suffering from his stab wound, and starts to pace around the room. "So, let me see, you thought we wanted you to go to Riga, you hid the tracker in a bacon butty, and you found a gun in a toilet. Anything else?"

"Nearly got burnt alive when I visited Alan Hunt's office."

"What? Yesterday?"

"The place was a complete tip. Someone had turned it over, papers everywhere, and all the pictures taken out of their frames."

"So you were there when they torched it. Did you see anyone?"

"Just a figure. Could have been a man or a woman."

"Did you find anything else?"

"That's when I found the gun. I looked in the toilet cistern just like we used to in the Met, and found a brick. Fished it out – it was hollow, and there was a Beretta inside. I wasn't surprised to find it until I realised it was a real one. I knew he'd got the airgun version from Rigby Rogers in London a few weeks ago, but where he got the real thing from is anyone's guess."

"You have been busy, and you no longer a policeman." He looks at me thoughtfully. "You do realise we will have to charge you with something? You can't just go round the countryside shooting people."

"But I was protecting my home."

"But how did you know the man wasn't one of ours?"

"He shot my dog. He was going for Peggy. I had to protect them while your lot were off looking after the great and good."

"But you said you took a shot at his legs before he shot your dog."

I look down, feeling furious and frustrated. "I knew it was wrong. The dog kept whingeing and barking. If it had been one of yours, they have let Peggy know. I do your fucking job for you, and now you…"

"Yes, but there are procedures we have to go through…" He puts his fingers to his thin lips, and stops.

"So when Sir Geoffrey asked me to go to Riga, you didn't send me a message supporting that? I thought he was one of your chums, that you were working together…"

"Oh I know Geoffrey. Funny old cove, but no – you were in that one on you own…"

"So someone has infiltrated your system."

Grimwode suddenly looks dangerous. "What? What are you telling me?"

He's slow today. Must be the injury – he'd have been onto this like a wasp onto a jam tart in the past. "I kept getting messages on the little phone thing telling me to go to Riga. And they weren't coming from you."

He turns away from me, and looks out of the window. London's traffic drones by, and looking over his shoulder I can see the Post Office Tower.

I let the silence between us continue. He's obviously calculating something. I don't want to go into custody. I want to protect Peggy and Paul. I want to get to the bottom of what's going on.

"Listen Rackham," he turns. "You know that report you lost?"

"So you did hear my apology."

"I did. The thing you have never known, because you lost it, is that we discovered a list when we searched, er, Hazelbank. You were obsessed with the paintings, but we had something bigger on our hands."

"So that's why you didn't search the basement thoroughly enough…"

"I'm not pleased about that, but I had my mind on other things. This list is of a number of well-known or powerful people involved in peace negotiations, amongst other things. It is long and is evidently getting longer. We know it is a hit list because two of the people on it have been murdered. The organisation we are dealing with is very dangerous."

"You're telling me!"

"We are stretched to the limit trying to protect people, but the list keeps growing. I'm on it, you're on it, your

201

brother and McDonald are on it. We can't keep track of everyone who is potentially going to be eliminated or abducted. It's a fucking mess. And now it seems they've got into our computers." He says all this in a low voice.

"So they're after me because…"

"They don't want you to find the other paintings. Millions of pounds worth are still missing."

"Well they obviously don't know where they are, from the way they searched Alan Hunt's office."

"Obviously. But we need to stop their operation. And that means stopping their money supply. You've done a good job already, though…"

"I know. I should have told you about losing the report at the time…"

"So…" He turns away again, and puts his long fingers on the windowsill.

I feel myself being pulled into working with this man.

"I didn't trust you," I say, as if that's an excuse.

"I didn't trust you either. Still don't, in a way… Look, they obviously think you're a big player in this. It would be a terrible waste of time and resources putting you into custody…"

"So?"

"We can't let you go. You'll have to stay in the force…"

"But I've already left."

"Ah, but there are special measures to recall officers who have left the force, in times when national security is threatened."

"You're kidding!"

He looks at me with that twisted smile of his. "I have the power to bring you in on this operation, Rackham. You have all the qualifications: you know your 'Art', you go it alone, you never give up, and you're a good shot." I shiver involuntarily. "Anyway, you brought yourself back into all this by finding the wallet."

"The dog found it."

"Mmmh…sorry about your dog. You put that man into a coma, you know."

"A coma?" Something inside me is curling up like a spring. Winding, tightening. Am I going to cry? Am I going to shout? My mind goes back to my desperate charge in the snow, and the way I yelled. I'm in this. Deep. And he knows it.

"I haven't got a choice, have I?"

"Yes, but not a good one. Come on Rackham, I know you want to get your teeth into this."

I let out a big sigh. "OK, but no gun."

"Why no gun? That business with the kid was a long time ago."

"There's something I haven't told you…"

"What?" Why does he have to say 'what' like a headmaster about to administer the cane?

"I have these… episodes."

"Episodes?" He looks at me with derision written all over his face.

"I don't know where I am, or who I am."

"Well, I knew that – dithery, arty Rackham all over."

"No, I mean this Dick." He always flinches when I call him by his first name. "I don't know what I'm fucking doing. You remember the time when I ended up on Oxford Street, and was picked up by Peggy? I'd been out of it for the whole night."

"So you think it would be dangerous for you to carry a gun? You could shoot anyone?"

"Yes, even myself. In that state I wouldn't even know what a gun was. I could have shot the dog… but I can't do that now…"

"How long has this been going on?"

203

"It started after the shooting at Hazelbank."

"And you didn't think to tell us?" His eyes pin me to the back of my chair.

"I... I thought I'd be suspended. Lose my job. Lose my pension."

"You're a dickhead Rackham. We look after our own. If you'd thought to have told us, we could have found you treatment. We wouldn't just sack you, in spite of your being one of the most incompetent cops I've ever known." He looks amused. "Funny thing is, you actually became useful after these 'episodes' started. Funny that."

"But if I'd told you, you'd have taken me off the case..."

"I did anyway. You were so bloody disobedient, you just went on on your own." His face changes to serious mode. "Have you seen anyone?"

"I talked to my counsellor."

"Bloody counsellors. Waste of..."

"No, she wasn't a waste of time." I hit the desk with the palm of my hand. "She put me onto a memory clinic in London."

"So that's why you went..."

"They did tests. They are inconclusive..."

"Inconclusive?"

"... but it seems it may be due to depression, rather than anything neurological."

"Depression, Rackham? Everyone suffers from depression in this job. The people we deal with, and what they do, make you depressed."

"But this is different." I look him full in the face. "Are you actually interested? You can see why I never told you."

He laughs. "So, Rackham. You didn't tell me because you were afraid you'd lose your police pension. You then decided to leave the force, and now, after a couple of days, you need to be back in with us to avoid going to prison. Can you see the bloody irony in that?"

"I can. But I don't want a gun."

"You're having a gun and a vest, whether you like it or not. These people are after you, though whether they want to capture you or kill you, I'm not sure. We can't protect you. You're on your own. I want you to go on with your search for those bloody paintings. They will tie up some of their resources going after you, which will help us do our job of protecting the important people they want to assassinate, and weaken their operation at the same time."

"So I'm a decoy."

"You're more than that. You're going to find those paintings. You're going to stay alive, and you're going to fuck up their system."

"Are you going to protect Peggy and Paul?"

"Definitely. We can't let them be taken. It would give our terrorists a lever on you."

"How will you keep them safe?" I really want to know.

Grimwode gets something out of the drawer of his desk, and looks at it thoughtfully. "I am not going to tell you. Which leads me onto something else. We have discovered, you and I, that they have got into our system. There must be a mole. This office is screened, but elsewhere... The thing is, Rackham, I can't trust anyone, so I'm giving this mobile to you so you can communicate with me, but only when you've got somewhere. This is just between the two of us. Understand?"

I nod, smiling at another irony, that we are the only ones in all this that can trust each other. "No tracker on it then?"

"No tracker. You can pick up your gun and vest downstairs. I want everyone to know you're definitely armed. It will force them to put more people onto you."

I get up to go. I wonder if we will shake hands – if this is that sort of occasion. As I put my coat on, I feel something bulky in my inner pocket. "Hang on…" I reach in, pull out a cardboard airline wallet, and put it on the desk. "I found this with the gun in Hunt's toilet."

We both look down at it.

I open the wallet.

It contains open return flight tickets to Riga.

"I think you need to go to Riga after all," says Grimwode, with his sardonic smile.

9.00am 11th December

Back in my home town, the estate agent looks on in astonishment and disgust as I dig a hole in my garden. It's just by the gate onto the common, and it's for the dog.

"Are you really going to bury that here?" she says nodding at the black plastic bag that contains the dog's remains.

"Yep." I don't risk saying any more.

"I'll have to let the tenants know."

"Yep."

"Couldn't you have had it cremated? Or buried it somewhere else?"

"Nope." The dog and I have lived here for so many years. Now, this is where he will rest. Just by the gate that marked his freedom to run out onto the common.

I have dug the hole deep enough, but I can't face just leaving the dog in a plastic bag. He needs to be near to the earth. I slit the bag open, releasing an unpleasant odour, and the dog slithers out, stiff and dead. There's a great gash in his chest, and his fur is all matted. Strangely, it reminds me of when I first found him – starving, and hardly able to stand. The difference is his eyes. They're cloudy with death. No longer asking for love, and wanting to trust. Just gone.

I turn to the woman. "You don't have to stay. I can put things away." But she can't tear herself away from the lurid sight of my dog, and the pit he's going in to. I just

207

want to say 'fucking piss off', but I restrain myself. The dog wouldn't have approved.

I place his body in the hole, put on a spade full of earth, and stand, looking out over the common. I see the bushes that he would make for, because they would be full of exciting smells. The gorse, the browning grass, the trees in the distance. All the walks we had, all the times together. I must say goodbye to them and move on.

I spade the soil back into the hole, covering him up. It leaves a little mound, just like the mounds you see in graveyards after a burial. I want to mark this as something not to be disturbed, so I search around for some large stones to cover it. As I lean forward, I feel the weight of the gun I am carrying push against my side. For one mad moment I think of firing off a couple of rounds out of respect for this dog who died in the course of duty, but I simply place stones on his grave and stand up, brushing the soil off my hands like Father McKenzie. The words 'All the lonely people' come back to me. I was lonely once – the dog was my company for so many years. Now I have human company – someone who cares for me. But I won't forget you, dog.

Walking past my unwelcome mourner, I put the spade back in the shed, close the door, and click the padlock closed.

"Don't let anyone disturb that," I say to her, pointing to the grave.

She looks as if she's about to reply, but thinks better of it.

The spring inside me is tightening, coiling up.

I have a train to catch.

Midday 11th December
London St Pancras

I'm not flying.

No Heathrow.

No Gatwick.

St Pancras is my first place of departure. I knew it so well as a kid when I used to go up to London with my mum. I remember the great steam engines – it was such a huge adventure for a little boy.

Now I am taking my big adventure on the Eurostar – the natural successor to the steam engines of the past.

The little boy part of me is keen to go on this adventure with his little gun and his mission to save the world. The grown-up part of me is tired, sad, and extremely doubtful of the outcome – one shot to the head or one swift blow from behind, and I'll end up dead like the people before me who have tangled with this organisation. I'm like a cat with nine lives, and they're running out. But one thing connects the little boy to the cynical adult: it's this spring coiled up inside me. I realise it's a deep anger, and it goes well with the dogged determination that I have developed over the past few months.

At the ticket counter in St Pancras I decide to go Premier Business Class, trusting that Grimwode was as good as his word and has injected a bit of cash into my bank account. I'm glad I have half an hour to board my train. I'm carrying a gun, and all I have is the document that Grimwode's department gave me that will allow me through EU border controls. But there is no pause in the official's pace as he scans the document and my passport. I just hope it's more difficult for those carrying arms when they shouldn't be. I am hoping that by taking the train to Riga, it will confuse anyone who wants to follow me. It takes a few hours to fly there, but a couple of days to go by train and bus. Who would be stupid enough to take all that time, and put up with lack of sleep, when they could be dining in Riga on the same day?

I find my seat, and slump down in it. It's large, comfortable, and on its own on the right of the gangway. Will there be champagne? As the train silently eases out of St Pancras, I feel my eyes begin to close...

There's a nudge at my knee. I put my hand down and stroke his furry head, reaching behind his ears to give them a scratch. Good old dog...

"Sir?"

I jolt awake. There's a woman in uniform standing above me.

"Would you like the beef, or our vegetarian option?"

"Oh, sorry, er beef please."

"Would you like our red with that sir, or a soft drink? We can offer..."

"Oh, red please." I want to go back to sleep after my Raymond Blanc meal. A bit of plonk should help.

"We can offer a Bordeaux or a Côtes du Rhône."

Not plonk. "Oh, the Côtes du Rhône, please."

A tray of food is put before me, smelling delicious. A long way from the plastic airline food I have experienced in the past. And a nice little bottle of wine with a pretty label. Just the job. Then I can get back to dreaming about my dog.

The countryside whizzes past. The food slips down well, the wine even better, and I relax into a semi-dozing state.

A heavily bearded man wearing dark glasses is walking down the gangway towards me. His coat looks bulky as though he has a gun in each pocket, and I get the impression he's staring at me from behind those dark glasses. I notice he has tattoos on his broad muscular hands. There's something relaxed and deadly about him as he gets nearer to me. I want to reach inside my jacket and get my gun out, but he's already walked past me by the time I've pulled myself together. Looking round, I see him disappear through the doors at the other end of the carriage, without a backward glance.

My heart beats loudly in my ears. I take long slow breaths to try and calm down. Honestly, if I'm going to react to every well-built male I meet on this journey, I'll be a complete nervous wreck by the time I reach Riga.

I ease myself out of my seat and follow in the direction the man went, ostensibly to go to the loo. But I take a peek into the next carriage, and there he is, head down in a copy of OK magazine. His dark glasses are off, and his face looks placid and kindly. Not your murdering type.

Back in my seat, refreshed, I compose myself for sleep. Thoughts and memories about the dog keep coming up, and I hope I will dream about him.

I'm in a corridor that runs along the front of a block of nineteen-sixties flats. To my right is a row of variously coloured front doors, and to my left is a four-foot wall with graffiti on it that looks out onto a car-park five stories below. In front of me at the other end of the corridor is a teenager with a gun.

"Pigs, fuckin' pigs!" he shouts. "Eat lead!"

211

There's a report from his gun, and a bullet ricochets off the wall by me. I press myself into a doorway. There's someone inside my head saying 'Shoot. Get on with it before he kills someone... shoot... shoot...'

I wake up, sweating. My head feels heavy. The wine has just made me feel slightly hungover. So much for dreaming about my dog. The French countryside flies past. What makes it so French? The colours, the shapes of the buildings. The tiled roofs. It seems sun-kissed, lighter somehow, even in winter.

"Tea or coffee, sir?" A waitress has come up behind me. So much for super-alert Rackham.

"Tea, please," I say, realising too late that this is France where the tea will be gnat's piss, and the coffee could be good.

3.55pm 11th December
Paris

'The Gare du Nord' is impressive. Daunting even, still possessing its nineteenth-century feel with its spindly ironwork. In my mind I confuse it with Monet's 'The Gare St Lazare', but it's on a much bigger scale, and there is no steam filling the great roof and changing the colour to yellow ochre.

I need to get a ticket for the next leg of my journey. Typically, I have failed to book my trip online, preferring to follow my nose. But this means standing in queues, and being very visible to anyone following me. I comfort myself with the thought that they probably won't choose to have a shootout in a crowded station.

It doesn't take long, and I'm soon on board the train for Cologne. The super-modern express is super-comfortable as well. Standard class is good enough for me – makes British First Class look a bit shoddy – and I settle down to read a magazine about Cologne. In the photos the cathedral looks spectral – a place to fill you with awe. I remember Andy Warhol's images of the front; I remember how the cathedral stood proud amidst the bombed-out city, at the end of the Second World War. Somehow, this is sparking off an uncomfortable thought process. We did that. Our country bombed and killed people in their thousands. Where are the families of those dead people now? How do they feel about us? The British.

213

I feel a familiar weight on my knee, and absent-mindedly stroke a furry head, scratching the dog behind the ears. The train begins to move gently out of the station. So gently, in fact, that I get the feeling that we are standing still and the platform is going backwards. Takes a moment for my brain to accept that it's the train that's moving. I look down at my knee.

There's no dog there.

I look round to see if someone else's dog had come to keep me company. Up and down the central aisle. Nothing.

No dog.

Is my dog like a limb? When people lose their limbs, they often continue to feel them as if they are still there. Perhaps it's just that. Not one of my episodes, just a natural phenomenon. Comforting in a way. The dog has come back to haunt me, and I can live with that.

Outside, it's getting dark. Lights flash by, and if I look at them in a certain way, they turn into lines of colour streaking past. Then darkness, and a quiet swish of the train moving in air.

I find myself slowing down – switching into a state of suspended animation. Part of me is saying, 'careful Arnold, don't get into one of your memory episodes'. I force myself to look around. There are people reading, listening on their iPods, all in their own worlds – strangely silent. Are they ghosts? Are they real? I suppress an urge to lean across the aisle and prod the woman on the other side who is reading a very thick novel. A child cries somewhere down the carriage and shatters the illusion. I pat my inside pocket and feel the hard bulk of my gun, and it all rushes back to me – this sense of pursuit and being pursued.

The train speeds on, and I settle back into my seat and try to slow my breathing down. I can feel my chest and stomach push against the heaviness of the bullet-proof vest I'm wearing under my jacket. Gradually, though, I feel myself slow down into a state of concentrated relaxation. I tell myself that I'm probably safe here – they will be watching the airports. They won't expect me to take the train, but they will know that I'm going to Riga. Sir Geoffrey knows I'm going. I've had a phone conversation with him explaining that I was unavoidably delayed – sorry sir, sorry sir. He seemed alright about it, especially when I said I would pay for it out of my own money. All this over the phone. So many potential leaks – but I never said I was going by train.

7.15pm 11th December
Cologne

I get off the train at Cologne station, looking round for the information board to see when the next train to Berlin goes.

19:21 the board says. Shit, that's only six minutes, and I'll have to buy my tickets. I doubt I'm going to make it, but I run down the platform towards the main station concourse. As I do so, I become aware of someone else running behind me. I look back and see a figure stop and turn to look at something. I run on again, and this time I look in the reflection of the windows of the booking office as I approach it. I see the figure running towards me. I turn. The figure stops and looks at a poster.

I'm being followed, and there's only three minutes till my train goes. I don't stop at the booking office, but dash for the platform where the train to Berlin is about to leave. A small coffee stall stands near the entrance to the platform, and I dodge behind it, hoping that my pursuer has lost sight of me. It works. A woman runs straight past my hiding place, onto the platform, and boards the train. I stay and watch the train move slowly out of the station. She will be searching the carriages now. Too late to get off. I wonder if she'll wait till it gets to Berlin before she realises I'm not on it.

"Kann ich Ihnen helfen?" A man's voice comes from above my head, and I look up to see him looking down at me from his counter.

"Oh, yes. A cappuccino please." I pretend to do up my shoelace.

"Large or small?" he asks in perfect English. I didn't even attempt German.

"Small, please."

"Chocolate?"

"Yes, please."

I take my coffee and wander slowly back to the ticket office. I might as well book my ticket for the next train. It doesn't go for another four hours. I buy my ticket, and decide to explore the area.

I walk out of the station, and there it is.

Gothic spires. Finest stonework. An icon of survival.

I get into the cathedral through a small side door. I'm in a huge, vaulted space. A place to be quiet, but every step echoes round a thousand corners. There are no visitors here at this time of night. I feel as though I shouldn't be here – a post-Protestant atheist in such an edifice to Catholicism. I sense a movement behind me. My dog is there, padding silently at my side. Are dogs allowed in cathedrals? I look down to pat him, but there's nothing there. It comes back to me, painfully, as though for the first time, I haven't got a dog any more.

I sit down beneath the high vaulted ceiling, cowed and tiny, and bury my head in my hands.

What am I doing here?

I was so angry, I just wanted to be in the middle of this mess of terror. To make a difference. But I'm not even trained for this. I'm just being used as a decoy, a target that our enemies think is worth getting – but on our side we all know I'm nothing.

I look up again and see the pillars and arches receding into the distance. This building is impossibly long. If I walk to the other end it will feel like walking to another world. I grip the back of the pew in front of me and stand up, as though on new infant legs. Stepping out into the central aisle, I walk slowly and uncertainly towards the altar. At my side I feel the presence of my ghost-dog. I don't try to pat him, or look at him. I just accept that he's there. We make our way to the heart of the cathedral, where the transepts meet the main body. Everything around me widens out – more and more stone, and pillars, and faces carved, and cold hands clasped in supplication.

I walk round the side of the altar, and to the back of the building. The sanctuary. Perhaps I could stay here. Seek sanctuary like knights of old. But it doesn't feel safe to me. Not any more. No holy place can be safe any more. All have been desecrated – by what? Anger. The very thing that fuels my desire to carry on with this journey.

I absent-mindedly pat the dog.

I feel his head – his fur.

I turn.

He's gone.

I walk on.

He's there again.

I'm mad. Obviously. But it's a comforting madness. It hurts no-one. Not even me, really. As long as he's the only ghost that follows me round like this. I shiver at the thought of some of the people I have known who could follow me round, constantly at my elbow. I look up. Did I see a ghostly form flying up into the vortex of the ceiling? I imagined it, but as I search the high arches, I can picture Chagall's married couple floating up there. Massive and distorted like some beautiful cartoon.

There's a man looking at me. He has a heavy beard. Didn't I shoot him down a couple of days ago? He doesn't

219

look like a ghost, but oddly I feel that he's looking right through me as if I'm the ghost. He walks towards me. Is this it? The final confrontation? In a cathedral?

"Entschuldigen Sie bitte."

I look at him, baffled. I don't speak a word of German. I slide my hand under my jacket towards the holster. I'm ready.

"Sorry…"

"Excuse me, sir. The cathedral is closed," he says in perfect English.

"Oh, sorry, I thought…"

He leads me to the back of the building, and out of the door I came in through.

I look back at the door as it closes on me.

There's a notice: 'Geschlossen Mitarbeiter nur' in large letters, and smaller translations in various languages underneath.

'Closed. Staff only.'

I am hungry. I find a steak house near the station and order fillet. I never order fillet, but there's money in my account, and my life expectancy is… not very expectant.

God, they know how to cook meat in Cologne. It is succulent, smooth, tasty. The chips are crisp, and the beer… Why do we never get German beer like this in Britain? They keep it to themselves. The bastards!

I take time over this meal. I have still quite a long wait till my train leaves, so I pause to decide on a sweet. Quite a choice.

Then coffee.

Then I wander back to the station to see if my train's in.

Not yet, so I walk up and down the concourse to keep awake and warm. Sometimes the dog is at my side, sometimes he's gone. But he'll always come back… won't he?

Looking at this from another point of view, I begin to worry that I'm having one of my memory episodes. Is the ghost-dog a warning that I'm about to lose my bearings? I concentrate on looking at the books in a news agent. Reality check. They're mostly in German, but quite a few in English as well. I wonder how many books in German I would find at WHSmith's back in Blighty. None. The thing is, the German people can speak and read English. But we, the great British public cannot speak German. Ha!

I hope that these politico-philosophical observations show me that I'm still in the land of reality. The dog comes and goes of his own free will.

I walk back along the concourse, and there, aha, is my train for Berlin.

I get on board and sit down thankfully in my seat. It's 11.00pm, the train leaves in thirteen minutes, and feel myself drifting off to sleep in my comfortable seat…

"It's probably a replica," my boss says, as we look up at the block of sixties' flats. The worst type – unliveable in.

I ease my Browning out of its holster and check the magazine. "With any luck, I won't be needing this. I'll talk him down."

"He's got his nan, Mrs Gamblin, in there. We don't know what he's done to her. WPC Grace tried to get in, and that's when he produced the gun. She's at one end of the balcony, PC Roberts is at the other. If he does have a real gun and is prepared to use it, they won't be able to stop him."

I look up at the brick and concrete building. Five floors up, there're two unarmed officers sheltering in doorways, waiting for backup. I'm all there is, till an ARV makes it from the next borough.

"Take the right-hand stairs. You'll find Grace. She'll fill you in," he says. "But gently does it. We don't want another 'police kill youth with toy gun' incident."

I run up the stairs, my heart in my mouth. This is the first time I've dealt with an armed incident on my own. True, I got exceptional marks for my accuracy at the range, and I have been with other officers who have had to use arms – all too frequently – but now I'm the only one. We've been caught on the hop with this one – our experienced firearms officers are out on two other calls locally. This area is rapidly becoming like Chicago. Drugs. Bloody drugs.

I get to the fifth floor. The stairs stink of urine, and there's graffiti everywhere. I go out on the balcony. Round a right-hand corner are a row of front doors, and Mrs Gamblin's flat is two thirds of the way down.

Urine.

Sweat.

I go to the corner and ease my way round to see what's happening. I can just see the huddled shape of WPC Grace sheltering in a doorway twenty feet away from me. No sign of the lad. I go cautiously along the balcony, my back pressed against the wall of the flats.

I get to the first doorway.

Pull in.

Peer out.

Second doorway.

Pull in.

Peer out.

Still no sign of the lad.

I make it to WPC Grace's doorway.

"I'm really worried about Mrs Gamblin," she whispers to me. "I heard shouting, and then just silence."

222

We listen.

It's very quiet.

I'm straining to hear the sound of a siren. Backup.

Nothing except the drone of London.

Then:

"Shut the fuck up you bitch!"

There's a scream. Then silence.

My heart rate goes up.

"We should do something," says WPC Grace.

"Mr Gamblin!" I shout. I'm finding it hard to breathe. "We know you're upset... Come out and talk to us... We can sort this out..."

WPC Grace is looking at me. "Shall I do it, sir?"

The door of the Gamblins' flat opens, and a thin, flaxen-haired lad in his late teens comes out brandishing what looks like a Walther pistol. If it's a replica, it's a bloody good one.

"Mr Gamblin!" calls WPC Grace. "Gary, put the gun down. We can talk." She stands up and walks towards him.

BANG!

It's not a replica.

WPC Grace collapses in front of me, her head hitting the floor with a sickening crunch.

My radio crackles. "Rackham, what's going on?"

"Grace is down sir, he's shot Grace!" I have my gun trained on Gamblin. I can see PC Roberts peering round the corner behind him.

"Drop the gun," I shout.

"Fuckin' pigs! Eat lead," Gamblin yells, and a bullet ricochets off the wall just by me.

"Shoot," my radio crackles. "Get on with it before he kills someone..."

I aim at his legs.

He ducks and stumbles forward as I press the trigger.

I hit him in the head.

223

Blood spurts out in a fountain as he slowly crumples onto the concrete.
I hit him in the head.
The head.
The head...

I wake up, covered in sweat, the words 'in the head' still echoing round my brain. There's a lump under my left armpit. It doesn't make me feel safe. I have an impulse to take the gun out of its holster and throw it out of the window, but no windows open on this train, so I slump back in my seat.

My mind runs on with the events that followed the shooting of Gary Gamblin. My shooting.

The police hushed it up as best they could. No faces got into the papers. There was an inquiry. Ballistics reported that I would have to have been suspended from a roof twenty feet above Gamblin to have shot him any way but the way I described. A horrible accident. I didn't mean to kill him. If he hadn't ducked right down... bad timing. But lives were at stake.

WPC Grace recovered from a bullet in her thigh, and concussion.

Granny Gamblin was found tied up and beaten round the face, but lived to complain about police brutality.

Gary Gamblin was full of crack cocaine. Hyped up. He'd been chucked out of his gang for being too violent, too unpredictable, but he'd kept his gun. His only answer to a life of abuse. He thought it would protect him, that he could shoot his way out...

'Those who live by the sword die by the sword' - Jesus's famous words from Matthew's Gospel come to me.

Anyway, I was exonerated by the inquiry. Saved lives. Unlucky accident. But I asked to be relieved of any gun-carrying duties.

Then the jokes started. My police colleagues called me Destry, from the James Stewart movie about a sharp shooter who refuses to carry a gun. The other jokes were worse, and crueller. There was an implication that I was a coward, that I didn't have the toughness needed to be in the Met. I saw the meanness, the corruption then. My police partner Dick Grimwode supported me. We had been a good team until the whole gun thing got in the way. He said, 'Don't leave.'

I left.

The train rumbles on into the night, and after churning all this round in my mind, sleep rescues me.

6.30am 12th December
Berlin

I board the train for Warsaw and find that my First Class seat is in an empty compartment. I want to stretch out my legs, and the increase in price was so small it seemed worth it. Hunger drives me to the restaurant car, but it's not open for food yet, so I walk back along the corridors as the train begins to glide out of Berlin Ostbahnhof. I'm going east, and should reach Warsaw by midday.

As I get back to my compartment, I see that someone has put a large amount of luggage on the rack above my seat. It looks like a bundle of old clothes, and I suppress a feeling of annoyance that I haven't got the compartment to myself any more, and that my companion for the next five hours is likely to be eccentric and untidy. Whoever it is must have got on the train at the last minute, and gone to the toilet, or made a fruitless journey to the restaurant car, though I didn't meet anyone on my way back.

I settle myself down in my seat by the window, aware of the weight of someone else's luggage just above my head. Stop grumbling Arnold, you're hardly the cleanest, smartest person on this train – I become aware of the smell of my sweaty armpits, exacerbated by my heavy bullet-proof vest, which is getting increasingly uncomfortable as my journey goes on.

227

"Entschuldigen Sie bitte." A very smart young ticket collector, with perfectly brushed hair, politely looks into my compartment. I get my ticket out.

"Here you are." Again I don't even try speaking German.

"Thank you, sir." Again the perfect English.

"Er, when will the restaurant car be open?" I ask, as my tummy rumbles.

"In half an hour, sir," he replies, making for the door.

"Er…" I am about to tell him that there must be another passenger in my compartment, but he's gone. Not my business, really, anyway.

I settle down to half an hour's hunger, as the lights of the city turn to dark countryside speeding by outside my window.

I jerk awake. Someone's in my compartment. No, I must have been dreaming, I could have sworn I heard someone breathing. Whoever left the luggage has not returned – perhaps I will get the compartment to myself after all.

The train glides on. Then I hear it again – someone's breathing. Close to me. I'm having an episode. My ghost-dog will nudge my leg at any moment.

Relax.

Breathe.

Listen to your breath.

But… there's another person breathing out of time with my breath.

There's a sound from above my head.

Something moves.

Someone grunts.

A shoe appears in front of my eyes, dangling down from the luggage rack above me. It has a hole in the sole.

More grunting.

I look up. The luggage is moving.

My hand moves to my holster.

Another shoe joins the first, and I move rapidly across the compartment, twisting round as I get my gun out.

A small thin man is climbing down out of the luggage rack. He drops nimbly to the floor. His clothes are shabby, and the old overcoat which concealed him, dangles off the rack.

He looks at me, startled. He looks Slavic, with a smooth, slightly pointed face. He is young, maybe about thirty. His hair is very short, and from the neck up he looks neater than I feel.

He smiles. "Don't shoot," he says with an Eastern European accent, as he puts his hands above his head.

"What are you doing – spying on me?" I whisper in a tense hiss.

"Not spying. Can't afford train to Warszawa. Hide here." He smiles and shrugs. He doesn't look like one of my pursuers.

"Right," I say, lowering my gun, and beginning to feel foolish, "so you are dodging the ticket collector."

"Yes. Can I put my hand down?"

"Er, yes." I fumble my gun back into its holster. "Um, sorry…"

"You police?"

"Er, yes, no, not really." What can I say?

"I sit?"

"Fine."

He takes his overcoat off the rack, and sits down in my seat. That smile – it looks genuine.

"Pavel Stasko." He holds out his hand.

"Er…"

"Call me Stash."

"Stash." I shake his hand. I was about to tell him my name. Not yet. "Why do you need to get to Warsaw?"

"No Warszawa. I go to Riga. Is my sister's name day."

229

"Name day?"

"Yes, very important I am there. Have no money…" he shrugs, and gestures to the compartment.

"Sorry about the gun," I say.

"No problem, but why gun?"

My turn to shrug. "I need to protect myself – that's all." My stomach gurgles. "Hungry?"

"No, but you eat."

He looks hungry to me. "I'll get something."

"I come too. If ticket collector comes…" he waves his hands in the air.

We sit down to bread, meat, and good coffee. The restaurant car is nearly empty, we talk in hushed tones.

"Excuse me, you look sad." Stash smiles at me.

"Er, do I? I suppose I am."

"Someone in your family die?"

"Sort of." I feel a nudge as the dog lays his jaw on my lap. I feel his damp nose against my hand. "I lost my dog."

"Your dog?" he seems interested. "How?"

"He was shot."

"But you carry gun." The way he says it makes me feel that by having a gun I am inevitably in a world where dogs get shot.

"I was protecting… oh never mind. What are you doing in Germany?" I say to change the subject.

"I work here and there – all over Europe. Picking fruit, that sort of thing. Sometimes I work in UK. Zero contract I think you call it."

"But where do you live?"

"In hostel, or on street."

I shiver, remembering my night on Oxford Street. "Don't you have any family to stay with?"

"All family in Latvia."

2.00pm 12th December
Warsaw

"Is just wall."

We are standing in front of a brick wall. Grey buildings behind it, and odd concrete flower boxes on the cobbles in front.

"It must have been terrible." I am looking at one of the few remnants of the Jewish ghetto in Warsaw.

"You think is terrible. I show you more in Riga." Stash looks unbearably sad for a moment, and then his youthful optimistic expression returns.

"Riga? I didn't know…"

"Many, many people die…"

"But why?"

"Russians. Germans. Latvia caught in middle."

I shiver as I think of those two murderous leaders, Hitler and Stalin. The power invested in them by people who looked the other way. As I look at the wall, I hear the sounds of the starving people inside the ghetto, the crying, the anger, and then the gunfire.

"Duck." Stash pulls me down hard by the shoulder. There's the crack of a gun and brick splinters out of the wall in front of where my head would have been. I feel adrenaline surge through my body as I reach in for my gun, try to release the safety catch with my thumb. Don't know how to release the safety catch. Can't remember.

"What you doing?" Stash is looking down at me. "Why you on the ground? Police see gun, will arrest you."

I look wildly around me. I'm sitting on the ground with my gun in my hand. I stuff it back quickly into the holster, and ease myself up off the pavement.

"You alright?" Stash brushes down my coat, looking concerned.

"But you pulled me down. We were shot at."

Stash looks at me, and shakes his head. "No. I no pull you down. There is no shot. You just suddenly…"

"Oh shit!" I look at him. Should I tell him? "Lets find some food."

"I have these things. Memory. And sometimes I imagine things." I wave a piece of duck around as I try to explain. We are seated in a very snug restaurant that does Polish food. The ambience is friendly – full of girls in traditional costumes serving plates heaped with duck.

"So is dangerous for you to have gun, no? You could have…"

"No. I have to know how to release the safety catch. When I lose my memory I can't remember how to do it. Quite safe." Bollocks, it's not safe at all. I was just lucky that time. The dog nuzzles my knee, and I stroke him absentmindedly.

"You see my dog?"

Stash peers under the table. "Is no dog. You joke."

"No, I can feel him there sometimes, and then," I look down to where he should be, "he's gone."

"You are so sad for your dog."

"Yes, I miss him. For a while he was the only thing I trusted."

"Now?"

"Now…" I am about to talk about Peggy, and then realise that this man could be anybody. "He's gone."

232

"When we get to Riga, you stay with my family, yes?"

At this moment, it begins to come to me that I shouldn't be on my own. I remember Oxford Street, and being found by Peggy and Hannah. If I got truly lost in mind as well as place, there would be nobody to help me in Riga, except the very people who wanted to find me, and that would be terminal.

I take what seems like the lesser risk. "Are you sure they wouldn't mind?"

"You have given me food, and helped me get back to them. They will want to give you place to stay."

"Thank you, then."

A waitress comes over to see if we want anything, and I ask for the bill.

"We go to coach station now? I know way."

5.00am 13th December
Coach to Riga

I ease myself in my seat, half awake. My body feels cold, stiff and sticky, like I've developed my own permaculture of micro-organisms which is happily getting on with things under my heavy clothes. I shift to the right and try to see out of the coach window, but all is darkness out there as we speed on towards Latvia.

I know where I am, I know what I'm doing, and next to me my new companion snores gently. I look at him in the gloomy half-light of the coach, and there is a smile on his face. And I wonder if he is an angel sent to look over me, or a member of the organisation that want to kill me, put there to guide me towards my death. He seems very assured for someone who has scraped a living round Europe on zero-hours contracts. My nose says he is travelling on the wrong side of the law – not just hitching illegal rides on trains, but working in some unseen way for someone, or something.

I sit back in my seat and close my eyes.

11.45am 13th December
Riga

I am so stiff, I can hardly stand up to get off the coach. I stagger down the aisle after Stash, who turns to help me down the steps and onto the tarmac that is Riga.

"Welcome to Riga. You come to my house. Have shower. Then I show you city."

I need a shower. God, I need a shower.

"I don't want to intrude…"

"No problem. My family will love to meet you. I tell them you helped me. Then…"

"Well, thank you."

We cross the tarmac, and a road, to a park which leads down to the river. On the other side I see old buildings. The Riga I imagined in my dream. We pass grand stucco-fronted houses, ornate and colourful. It feels like a mixture of Amsterdam and Moscow. Tiny minarets top facades coloured in orange and blue. Every now and then an old stone wall or tower is visible down a cobbled alley.

"Is not far." Stash leads me down a side alley, up some steps, and out into a courtyard with windows looking down on every side. Opposite me, are double glass doors – modernity set into an old building.

"We go here." He opens the door and we clatter up stone steps, stopping at a landing on the second floor, and he presses a buzzer by the side of a panelled wooden door.

The door is opened to reveal a girl in her twenties who looks strangely familiar.

"Stash!" she cries, as she runs forward and throws her arms round him.

"Katrina, this is my friend Arnol," Stash says in English.

"Moma!" she shouts back through the doorway. "It's Stash. He has English friend with him."

"Pavel." I hear a voice from inside the flat. There is a spatter of incomprehensible Latvian and a broad-built, grey-haired lady comes bustling down the corridor. Behind her is another girl of similar age to Katrina, and I am struck again by a familiarity. They all crowd round Stash, hugging him in a sort of circle dance.

"Come in, come in." A broad, squat, coarse version of Stash appears behind the hugging throng. "Come on girls, let the poor man in."

"Papa, it's Stash," says Katrina.

"I know, I know... but this man," he gestures towards me. "He is tired from journey, he need rest." He leads us all down a narrow corridor to a small sitting-room with photos displayed in every crevice, and on every ledge. Old, new, black-and-white, faded colour, a big family remembered in film. One faded colour photograph grabs my attention – she's younger, and she's smiling, but it's definitely her. I saw her first in the mirror of the ice cream parlour.

"Who is that?" I turn to Stash.

"My aunt Anna," he says with a smile. "You want tea? Then shower? Then we go out?"

"I think I know her."

"Maybe. She is not here. We have not seen her for long time. Maybe she's in UK." He shrugs.

"What does she do?"

"Courier. I think. Yes, for international. But we haven't seen her for so long. Tea?" He hands me a cup, and we sit down with the family to hear Stash relate his adventures, and how he met me. They clearly don't know what Auntie Anna is up to – or if they do, then I'm in a den of vipers.

I wonder even more about Stash.

5.30pm 13th December

Tea turns into lunch. After lunch we rest. Then a blessed shower, and a change of clothes. I haven't got much in my luggage so I hope I won't be too long in Riga.

Putting the bullet-proof vest back on, after my shower, is not a pleasant experience. It smells strangely metallic and sweaty. I spray some deodorant on it, hoping it won't react in some way, making the vest less effective.

"And now," says Stash, with a grin and a flourish, "now we go to Folk Bar."

I follow him down steps and out into the cobbled streets. Darkness has fallen on this magical little city. Squares and narrow streets are lit in a gentle old-fashioned way. The lights twinkle, and there is no glare from tall concrete lampposts. Stash takes me into the heart of the city, and I lose track of where I am as we walk down the winding old streets. Every now and then I feel the nudge of my ghostly dog, as he follows me faithfully.

Down some steps, into what looks like an old labyrinth of cellars. It is still quite early for drinking, but there is the odd young couple sitting on old pews that line the route to the main bars.

We enter a larger area where ancient brick pillars and archways support the city above. Old battered tables are placed in alcoves and low rooms, created by the forest of pillars, and a few battered upright pianos stand against the

241

walls, waiting for the brave or unwary musician to attempt to get music out of them.

We walk up to the long bar counter that disappears round a corner and into the distance.

"You like strong? Dark or light?" Stash insists on buying the first round.

"I'll try the dark one," I say, thinking it will be closer to my usual poison.

"Is very good. We have two," Stash says to the girl behind the bar.

We take our beers to a long table just by the entrance to the main bar. One of the pianos, that has seen better days, sits against the wall, waiting, pleading, for someone to come and play it.

"Katrina, she will come with her friends," says Stash, settling down on an old bench. "We meet, we talk, we eat."

I walk round the table, and sit with my back to the piano, thinking of Shane in the cowboy movie, and how he always sat with his back to the wall. The beer is delicious – stronger than I expected, but tasty and rich.

"So what are you going to do next?" I say to Stash.

He shrugs. "Is winter. I stay with family. We celebrate."

"Then?"

"Then I try find work. Is more difficult now. So many immigrants."

But we see you as an immigrant in England, I reflect. "I'm sure you'll find something. You must have so much experience…"

"Yes, true." He smiles in that warm way he has. Live for the moment, his face says.

I look down at my beer. It has miraculously disappeared. Stash's is almost finished too.

"Another?" I get up and take our glasses back to the bar. A bit of a queue has built up, and the person before me has a long order, so by the time I return to the table, Stash has settled at the piano next to a woman who is playing rhythmic groove-type jazz. Stash is joining in with the odd top note, but the main music is coming from the hands of this woman. She makes the slightly out-of-tune honky-tonk piano work beautifully, and I just stand and listen – not wanting her to stop.

The music comes to a natural pause, and Stash turns round.

"Hey Arnol', thank you." He gets off the stool and takes his beer.

"One for the pianist?" I say.

"You want I introduce?" he gestures at her back.

"No. Don't stop her. She's brilliant."

"She like wine. White. Sour. Thank you."

Dry white wine I think, and I'm off to the bar again, but now I'm keeping an ear to the music – listening to the gradual build and change it makes as she adds complexity to her simple riff. Where has someone that accomplished come from, to play on a beaten-up old piano?

I return with a large dry white, and sit opposite Stash while we listen to the music reach its climax, and groove gently to a halt. There's scattered applause from round the cavern, and she turns to smile at her audience.

I know that face.

"Aunt Anna," says Stash. "You were asking about her. Here she is."

Her face gives nothing away, and I wonder if I could be mistaken.

"My friend, Arnol'", says Stash.

She sticks out her hand, and I take it. The hand of a musician – supple, strong, but sensitive. Is this the hand of a terrorist?

"I hear you helped my nephew out. Thanks. And thanks for the wine." She takes her glass and raises it in my direction.

"My pleasure. Thanks for the music. Stash didn't say you were a concert pianist."

"I'm not," she responds with a grimace, looking me straight in the eye – and then I know it's her, and that the last time we met we were trying to kill each other in a field in Wales as I ran to my dying dog.

"Stash!" Katrina's voice cuts through my realisation that I am sitting opposite my nemesis.

Katrina and two girls, all dressed up for partying, squeeze round the table to hug Stash.

"Anna! You here? We didn't know." More hugs.

"Now we have music," says Katrina to me, and Anna turns to the piano and starts to play again.

They are all so excited that their aunt is here, and they talk fast in Latvian, so I have time to reflect on my situation.

Was Stash set up to join me on that train and bring me here?

Are the whole family in on it?

Or are they all completely innocent, and just having a good time?

After all, Anna would have known I was coming to Riga. If Stash wasn't in on it, she might have been surprised to see me in his company, but she wouldn't be surprised to see me.

I wonder who else is in this bar, armed and ready to take me on. I don't think she'll be acting alone, and if her family aren't in on it, then there must be others out there in the shadowy archways.

But she won't want to take me here and now. Not with Katrina celebrating with her friends and family. Surely I'm safe if I just stick with them.

"You like we eat?" Stash's English interrupts my thoughts.

"Yes, thanks Stash." Let me pay, I was about to say, but felt that might be patronising or rude even.

"We get, meat, potato, veg. Big dish. We all share. Or would you like pizza?"

"I'd love to share – thank you." And I'll sit here sipping my beer very, very slowly while I watch what happens next.

What happens next is that Anna stops playing.

"Oh play more Aunt, you see how Arnol' enjoys it!" cries Katrina. "Please, please play for us all!"

"I must go," Anna says gently. "I will be back for pudding. Maybe I will play some more then." She gives Stash a look, and leaves the table, heading into the far reaches of the cavern.

"Where's she gone in such a hurry?" I ask Stash. "That's not the way out."

"Maybe she join some friend for chat. I not know, but..." Stash eases himself off the bench. "I need toilet. Excuse. Food come soon."

He goes off in the same direction as Anna, and I wonder whether I'm safer to stay where I am, or try and follow him. I stay, sitting, undecided, for a moment. Then get up.

"Where are the toilets?" I ask Katrina.

She smiles and gestures into the cavern. "Is not far. You find."

The bar is becoming crowded now. I guess, from the language around me, that many of the young local population come here. I sidle through the crowds trying to work out which way Stash went. The toilets loom suddenly in front of me, and I glimpse Stash coming out, but instead of coming back my way, he heads for another part of this underground maze. There are fewer people in this area, as I follow him, and I lean against a pillar, trying

245

to look nonchalant as I watch him make for Anna, who is sitting at yet another broken-down piano, placed against the end wall of a long low room. There is a table full of locals talking loudly, and I squeeze past them, trying to keep out of Stash's sightline. He goes up to the piano, and joins Anna. They both have their back to me. I so want to hear what they are saying, and I risk being spotted as I get close to them, settling behind the archway that supports the roof right next to them.

There's a spattering of Latvian from Stash, and I wonder if I will be able to make anything of their conversation. But I was right about that look Anna gave Stash: they needed to talk, and they didn't want me to hear.

"Speak in English," Anna hisses at Stash. "They won't understand us if we speak quickly and quietly." She looks round at the merry throng of Latvians at the table.

"So look, Aunt," Stash lowers his voice, and I find it hard to hear the next bit, but I notice my name.

"But he is dangerous, Stash. He is with British secret service. He has a gun, you told me yourself. He tried to kill me." She is facing slightly in my direction, so I can hear her more clearly.

"But he is good man," Stash gesticulates, forgetting to keep his voice down. "He no want to kill anybody. He help me. I no want…"

"Shh…Look, Stash, you brought him to me. Now leave me to get on with this. It is not your business any more. You have done well. Good boy." She passes something to him. I am guessing an envelope with money in it.

He looks down, and I can see his back sag as he accepts the money.

"Now, you go back to Katrina and her friends, and I'll join you later. You've taken long enough as it is. Don't worry, I will deal with your friend. We won't spoil the

246

party." She says this brightly, as though all will be OK for Stash and his family.

I turn and almost collide with a waitress carrying a tray of beer. I am needing a pee now, anyway, so I make my way as fast as possible to the toilets, hoping Stash hasn't caught sight of me. I stand at the urinal, and hear the door open. Stash comes in, sees me, flinches, and then decides to join me at the next urinal.

"I wondered where you'd got to," I say.

"Oh, met old friend. You know how is. We got talking, but I still need..." he glances down.

"We'd better get back to our table. The food will be there, won't it?"

"Oh yes, you go on."

"I'll wait for you." I stand by the basin, washing my hands slowly. There is no way I am going anywhere without Stash and his family.

We return to the table, and Katrina looks up at us. "What have you two been up to? You've taken your time." She giggles, and I wonder what she thinks we could have been up to in the mens' loos.

Stash looks at me.

"I got lost," I say looking him straight in the face. "Stash says he bumped into an old friend."

"Who was it?" asks Katrina eagerly. "Petr, Stan?"

"You don't know him."

"I know all your friends, silly."

"No this is new friend. Mac."

"Mac? Where he from?"

So Stash has been talking to a new old friend. He must guess I don't believe him.

The food arrives at this point, and distracts Katrina from her interrogation of her brother. We all sit down, and curiously, Stash bows his head, and gives what must be a blessing in Latvian.

247

The food is good hearty stuff. Plenty of meat and potatoes, and a tasty gravy. I order more drinks from the waiter for everybody, being careful to go for a small beer for myself.

"So, you come to Riga on business." Katrina comes out with this, as the drinks are brought round.

"Yes. Art."

"Art, that's vey interesting. You come to see painting."

"Yes." A thought suddenly occurs to me – Riga is a small city. "Do you know Michael Dimanta? He's an art collector."

"Ah yes, I know him. He's vey nice man. You want meet? He come here to Folk Bar vey often. Maybe he here. We go look. You come?"

"I don't want to take you away from your friends."

"No problem. We go before pooding." She holds out a hand and takes mine as if we're about to take to the dance floor.

"But…" I look at Stash, who is about to say something. He stares at me open-mouthed, his fork halfway from his plate.

"Come on." She tugs me away from the table and through the throng of drinkers that surround the bar. As we go on, her leading me by the hand, I realise that this place is even bigger than I thought.

"He often eat on other side," Katrina shouts at me. "We go look. Maybe he there."

We pass through lower tunnels and more caverns, and as we go on, the crowds thin, and the clientele looks older and more well-heeled. We round a corner, and there, sitting at a smart table with tablecloth, candles, and elegant wine glasses, is a group of four people. What looks like a mother in her fifties, flanked by her two daughters, is facing a man with his back to us. His hair is short and greying at the temples. His neck is thick, and his shoulders look muscular under a black jacket.

"Is him. I introduce." Katrina drags me round to face him. "Michael."

He looks at us for a moment. He has a smile on his face, which gives me the feeling of covering any emotion that he may actually have.

"Sonja?"

"Katrina."

"Ah, Katrina..." He has obviously forgotten who she is.

"This Arnol' who want to meet you. He come from England to Riga about art."

His eyes widen slightly. "Arnold Rackham?"

"Yes."

"I have been looking forward to meeting you. Will you come to my house later? I have something to show you." He has very little accent.

"I'd be delighted to but..."

"No worry about us. You go later," Katrina says. "We are by entrance on the other side. See you after pooding?"

"Yes." Michael smiles broadly at us, completely ignoring his guests, who have sat there as though in a trance.

Katrina drags me off through the crowds and back to our table. Anna has returned and is talking to Katrina's friends. Stash has been joined by a man who looks the same age – leather jacket and jeans. Looks sporty. And I wonder if this is Anna's reinforcements come along to pick me up.

"Play for us Aunt. Please. One tune before pooding," Katrina pleads.

"Please, Anna, please play," her friends join in, and Anna turns to the piano and starts to play something very slow and rhythmic.

"This Petr," says Stash. "Friend of Anna."

"Hello," I say, but he just looks at me, and turns to Stash to continue a conversation in Latvian.

"I just take Arnol' to meet Michael Dimanta," Katrina says to her friends, with a sideways glance at Stash. The other two girls coo, and giggle. Mr Dimanta is obviously very popular with the women of Riga.

Anna's music gradually increases in speed and volume. It's almost impossible to keep my feet still. Another man joins us at the table. He looks very well built, and there's a bulge in his jacket that suggests he's carrying something similar to me. He enters into conversation with Stash, who is looking more and more uncomfortable.

We four men at one end of the table. The three girls at the other, and in between, Anna playing with increasing tension and vigour. It feels like it is going to explode, and I mentally go through the steps of how quickly I can take my gun out, ready to shoot.

The music stops.

The pudding arrives.

Anna turns round, and I am surrounded.

The pudding is sweet, and there's plenty of it, but all I am aware of is the need to be ready. I feel the adrenaline surging through me – the policeman in me taking over all my muscles. A bit like the Incredible Hulk, but not very incredible, and definitely not a hulk.

Anna turns swiftly to me. "We go." She looks at her acolytes. One is reaching into his jacket.

"I think not," I say, with a steadiness in my voice that amazes me.

She looks down at my gun, which is pointing up at her heart from just below table level, and shakes her head at her artillery.

250

Stash looks pale. Shocked. Not really understanding what's going on. Katrina and her friends at the other end of the table certainly don't understand.

"What you all looking so sad for? We have fun. Yes?" She grabs the attention of a passing waiter, saying something in Latvian. "We have music, yes? We dance."

After a short pause while we all try to smile horribly, and look normal, Katrina and her two friends get up and grab Stash and Anna's acolytes, leaving Anna and myself sitting behind the table.

"Come on you two. Don't be cowards. Dance."

"You first," I say, keeping my gun out till the last moment.

It's a curious collection of dancers. Anna and her henchmen jig about trying to look happy. Stash is dancing close with one of the girls, and Katrina and her other friend dance in circles round Anna's two men.

"So…" I say in Anna's ear.

"So?" she replies.

"Why are you…?"

There's a shout from Katrina. "Michael!"

I look round to see Michael and his three dinner companions walking towards us.

"Can I take Mr Rackham away from you for a while?" Michael says to Katrina.

"Of course. You go," she says to me. "We stay, have party."

I sidestep Anna, who tries to block my way. Her men stop dancing, uncertain what to do.

"Bye, and thank you," I say to Katrina, as I join Michael who grabs hold of my elbow and steers me firmly into the corridor. I glance over my shoulder – Katrina and her friends are trying to keep Anna and co. dancing. It looks chaotic – at any moment one of them will escape and follow me.

251

"I have a car. We take Mrs Cibulskis and her daughters home, and then you come with me to see the painting." It is an order, not a request, and I wonder whether I'm getting into even deeper water.

We go up the steps to a waiting black limo. Michael gets in the front, and we all climb into the cavernous back. Plenty of room – no need to rub knees. I glance out of the window, and there is one of Anna's men, standing at the top of the steps and hailing a taxi. We drive gently through Riga – the old narrow streets limit the speed we can go, and I feel tired, very tired. The ladies in the back talk quietly in Latvian, and I find myself straining to keep alert as the car comes to a halt outside a decorative block of flats.

Michael opens the car door to let the ladies out. They exchange a few words in Latvian, and are gone. Michael gets in the back with me, and as he does so I see a taxi slow down and stop behind us. My weary body jerks awake again, ready for another confrontation, but our car is off before I get a chance to see who is in the taxi behind.

"Did you have a good flight?" Michael asks.

"I came by train and bus," I say stifling a yawn.

Michael laughs. "Why?"

"Don't like flying, and…"

"And?"

"Look Mr Dimanta…"

"Michael, please."

"Michael, there are other people who are interested in your painting, and where you got it from…"

"Yes, I know." Michael leans forward and says something to the driver. We speed up, and take a couple of turns down narrow streets. We head into a cul-de-sac and a big black gate opens up before us. The gate shuts behind us and we are in an underground garage with two men coming out of the shadows to open our doors.

Michael mutters something to them in Latvian, and then gestures to me to follow him up the stairs at the end of the garage.

At the top of the stairs all sense of modernity disappears, and we are in an old house, beautifully kept, with polished wooden floors, and ornate stucco ceilings.

"Come and see my gallery," says Michael.

Down the end of the corridor, we come to double doors, painted in blues and greys. He opens them, and we walk into a high-ceilinged room, lined with paintings that are almost exclusively impressionist. On the right-hand wall is the Manet that has caused such interest. From a distance, it looks completely genuine – but I know, now, how easy it is to be fooled by brilliant forgers and copiers.

"So this is it. Have the other paintings here all been verified as genuine?" I ask.

For a moment, I think he is going to hit me. A look of such anger crosses his face, I suspect he could be a very dangerous man indeed.

"Of course." He manages to smile.

"So why am I here? Couldn't you have got an expert opinion from your usual er... experts?"

"Ah, well, I'm not very keen to let other people see this painting. As you know, the genuine original was part of a heist many years ago. I thought it must be a copy. An exceptional copy, by someone contemporary. But..."

"That is unlikely, so..."

"The people who are selling it want a lot of money..."

"And they think you will pay that if it's genuine. If it's a copy, they will rip you off, if it's genuine then it's stolen goods."

"Correct."

I get out my magnifying eye glass, and go up to the painting. It's old, certainly. The way the paint is cracked when magnified. I sniff it and I smell old paint. But there are two other smells as well. Very faint. Coal, and apples – and I have the feeling that the last time I saw this painting was in the cellar of Hazelbank, in my home town. I look for the tell-tale signs, of a genuine Manet – the signature, the way he used his brush – and I become more and more sure that this is the real thing.

"Who is offering this to you?" I ask, still poring over the painting.

"That is not your concern. Is it genuine?" His voice has taken a harsh, slightly excited edge.

"You invited me here as an expert in art fraud. My company…" I turn round to face him. He is pointing a gun at me.

"Is it genuine?"

"Yes," I say. "Where did you get it from?"

"Move away from the painting," he hisses.

"Why?" I stand stock-still, wondering how bullet proof my bullet-proof vest is at this range.

"Get away from it." He doesn't want to hit the painting.

"Was it Brian O'Connell? Or Alan Hunt?"

His eyes flicker slightly at the mention of Alan Hunt's name. He starts walking towards me, and I make a decision. This time I won't miss the legs. I see his eyes widen in disbelief as I take my gun out and shoot him in the knee. Then with a howl of pain, he falls to the floor, letting go of his gun. I walk over and put my foot on it, still pointing my Glock at him. I hear running footsteps coming towards the double doors, and then the rata-tata-tat of automatic gun fire. There are cries from outside, and it sounds like an entrenched gun battle is going on.

I pick up Michael Dimanta's gun and move to the wall by the doors. Dimanta lies on the floor curled up in agony, and in the distance I hear the sound of sirens. There are shouts from outside and the door bursts open. Another volley of shots, and a man pitches forwards onto the floor, and lies there motionless. More shots just outside the door, then silence.

Anna walks into the room, holding an automatic. She looks down at Dimanta and asks a question in Latvian – I recognise my name. Dimanta looks straight at me, and Anna turns.

"Drop your gun," I say between gritted teeth. I never wanted to be in the middle of this sort of thing.

"Why? Will you shoot me?"

For an answer I point both guns at her legs.

She fires her gun full into my chest, knocking me over. The breath is knocked out of me, and I feel like I've been kicked by a mule. I aim at her legs, but she nimbly jumps aside and runs out of the door. The sirens have stopped, and there are shouts. I try to get up, but the pain in my chest slows me down. I realise that if she dodges the police I will never catch her now. I get out my phone and dial Grimwode's special number.

"Yes?" His voice is sharp as usual.

"I'm in the house of Michael Dimanta. The Manet is here. Dimanta pulled a gun on me. I have immobilised him. The police are here, and our main woman suspect, Anna, has attempted to kill me, and is on the run."

"What?"

"I can't say it again." I look up to find two armed Latvian police with their carbines aimed at my chest.

11.30pm 13th December
Riga

"You soon feel better." A nurse has applied ointment to the great big bruise on my chest. I have been thoroughly checked over at the hospital, and I am lying on a bed in a private room. Number 13 seems like it might be my lucky number. We have found the Manet, exposed an art fence, and Anna is on the run.

"Good work, Rackham," said Grimwode, when the police finally let me contact him. "Shame you missed her legs. Not very good at hitting legs are you?"

"They tend to move, Dick. You know, thin and a bit hard to hit."

"Sounds like you're getting into this gun thing, Rackham."

"I'm not. They're filthy things. They make the world less safe, not more."

"Enough preaching for now. Have a rest," – kind of him I thought – "and then see if you can track down this Anna woman. She seems to be a key player, and she's awfully keen on putting you out of business."

"What about O'Connell, Hunt, and the rest of the paintings?"

"Hmm, we're looking for them, but you do seem a bit of a magnet, so concentrate on her."

"And my wife? Are you looking for her?"

"We found her DNA on the shoe your… er dog picked up."

"Thanks for telling me!"

There was a funny grumbling noise from the other end of the phone. "I thought she was the last person you wanted to see."

I didn't say anything – he was right, but I still wanted to know where she'd ended up, without one of her shoes, and without her solicitor.

It seems the Latvian police had been keeping an eye on Dimanta for some time. They suspected him of dealing with stolen paintings, ideally situated as he was between Europe and all those Russian oligarchs dripping with money. The foolish man had wanted to check the provenance of the Manet, using a distant art fraud company in Wales. Never suspecting that someone like me, with police connections, would turn up. Somebody must have tipped him off while I was in his house. They found a text on his phone, but it couldn't be tracked, and he's still refusing to co-operate.

Nobody expected the attack by Anna's crowd. Two people dead, and two more with serious gun wounds. A veritable battle.

For my part in this, I was interrogated, heavy-handedly at first. Until a certain phone call came through. Then it was like they didn't want their hands burnt. Shuffled me off to hospital.

Still, good news, one more painting back. Three to go, I think.

But where are Brian O'Connell and Alan Hunt? They know that we are after them, and, worse for them, so are the terrorists. I wonder if Hunt is still alive – he's lost his wallet somewhere off the coast of South Wales, his office has been raided, and he is without his gun. Something made him frightened, and then he fled. Maybe he was caught out, and didn't have time to go back to his office and pick up his gun and tickets. Whatever happened, we're pretty sure that Dimanta had dealings with him.

And is Brian holed up somewhere with the last three paintings? Millions of pounds worth of art in his hands, but so difficult to sell. Perhaps Hunt was only one of his outlets, and he's already sold the rest, and is living the life of Riley on some Caribbean island. But I should think he's looking behind him, wherever he is.

But that's a bit like me. I think that I must be the most unpopular person with the terrorist group. I have cost them millions, and could cost millions more if I track down the rest of the paintings before they do. I am on a special list all of my own.

My chest is very tender, and it's hard to sleep in the hospital bed. I am not sure that I have any protection from the Latvian police, so I keep waking at the slightest sound. The police still have my gun, and my body armour is too damaged to be safe. Anyway it would be too painful to put on. So I am lying, defenceless, in this bed wondering whether I'll be alive in the morning.

7.00am 14th December
Riga

I awake to a bustle outside my room. People are talking rapidly in Latvian – there's a shhh, then the voices start to raise again. The door opens, and a nurse comes in.

"You ok? Awake? You have friend," she says.

"Yes. But…" I hope this isn't another group trying to get hold of me, but Katrina walks in, still wearing her party frock, and looking as though she's been up all night.

"Arnol', you ok? What happened? Police have asked us but we don't know."

Stash is just behind her, looking even more dishevelled. "Is bad. Seems Aunt Anna is mixed up in this…"

"… and Michael, Michael Dimanta. I introduce you. I not know what he is. He is with police now. I know this."

"I'm alright. Somebody tried to shoot me in the chest." I look directly at Stash. "But I was wearing protection, so she…"

"She?" Katrina asks.

"She didn't succeed in killing me." This to Stash again. He knew I had body armour, but he said nothing of this to his aunt.

"She tried to kill you?" Katrina looks horror-struck. Stash looks down at the floor.

"Yes, but here I am," I say with a grimace, reflecting that shooting people in the chest is one of the standard ways of killing them.

My phone buzzes – it's Grimwode. "The Latvian police have agreed to let you have your gun back. Get down there as soon as possible, before they change their minds." He clicks off, and I wonder whether someone is listening in.

"Sorry, I've got to get up and go and see the police."

"We wait for you. Get you breakfast after," says Stash.

The hospital is happy to dismiss me. A bit of bruising is no reason to stay in a bed, the cost of which is coming out of somebody's budget. I find Stash and Katrina at the entrance – I am glad of their company, and they know the way to the police station. I am given back my little Glock 26 and its holster, but no bullet-proof vest. They keep that for evidence, along with the shirt I was wearing which now has a neat hole in the front.

Latvian breakfast proves to be great coffee and the most beautiful almond slice I have ever tasted. Stash and Katrina sit opposite me, watching me eat. They both look dog-tired, and conversation is sporadic.

"We think it our fault all this happen to you," says Katrina. "You come to our country to look at painting, and poof!" She makes a gesture of me going up in smoke.

Stash looks down again. "We take you back to collect your things, then I show you something."

They see I have finished and get up with a scrape of chairs. I rise too, but more stiffly and slowly. That pain in my chest really is just bruising, I say to myself.

It's a short walk to their flat. Mr and Mrs are out, but as I go into the sitting room to pick up my bag, I notice that one photo has been turned to the wall. Anna no longer smiles out at me in faded colours. Katrina goes to bed, but Stash waits for me by the front door, and leads the way down the stairs and out onto the street.

262

"You think Riga is very pretty?" Stash says. "Is very poor. I show you."

"Where are we going?" I say, hoping this is not another trap.

"Moscow District."

Old factories keep company with smart shops. The remains of the Jewish ghetto is marked by a stone Star of David. It all has a feeling of poverty and wealth and turmoil.

"Many, many people very poor in Latvia. We have terrible history. Terrible things done to us by Russians and Germans. People like me leave, because... because we can't bear it."

Stash turns to me then. "Look I'm sorry."

"You led me to your Aunt Anna, didn't you."

"She ask."

"Why did you do it?"

"She give me money."

"For money?" I can't believe he's so callous.

"I need money. I don't know she wants to kill you. I think she just wants to talk."

"Talk?"

"But when I see her friends..."

"I thought you knew them."

"One, but the other... I no like look... I see what they are up to."

"I'm sure you did."

"Then I tip off police."

"When they'd gone after me."

He nods and makes a throat-cutting gesture. "They mustn't know. Is dangerous for me."

"I bet it is."

Stash takes me to a modern, glass fronted building that sticks out from the decorative old houses around it. The

263

Holocaust Museum. A strange tourist attraction for someone coming to Riga for the first time, but he insists we go in.

"Is very important you see this. Know about Latvia and how we happen in wars."

So I follow him round the museum from room to room. Huge black-and-white photographs of people starving, people behind barbed wire, mass graves, swastikas, Russian stars, Stars of David. And so much English writing describing the horrors of the last century:

The Ukraine, and how Stalin starved a population without showing any mercy;

The Jews in Latvia, and how they were treated, and mistreated, depending on who was in power;

The massacre of half of the population of Latvia during the Second World War as Germany and Russia played tug-of-war with this tiny, unprotected country.

"If we had proper arms, we could have defended ourselves, but…" Stash looks at me intently. Is his face angry or sad? I can't tell.

I nod slowly, not sure where this is leading.

"A country must have good arms to defend itself, or this happens."

I think I can see where he is coming from. It's all very well for us in the UK. We are an island, for a start, and we have nuclear weapons, and a well-trained army, even if it's shrinking. We are so safe, comparatively. Here in Riga, if Russia decides to annex them, they will have to rely on the rest of the world for protection. It's happened so many times in their history, and nobody came to their aid in the past.

The last part of the museum is dedicated to Hitler's disgusting attempt to eradicate the Jews. Chilling how one man could lead such a mad campaign – treating humans worse, much worse, than animals. And all the time, people were going along with it through fear, ignorance, and hate. It makes me wonder about us in the UK. We see things from a certain, ignorant perspective. Most of us have no idea what cruelty we as a nation are supporting throughout the rest of the world. We turn our backs on it all, and get on with our lives.

I leave the building – my head is reeling. So many images. So much buried past. I buried my past and suffered for it. But the world tried to bury this past – still tries. The cold air wakes me up, and I feel a familiar nudge of a cold nose on my hand. The dog. I look down at him, but he's not there. He's just a ghost.

"What you do now?" Stash asks.

"I don't know." I feel an urge to go back to Peggy. This is all finished. Surely.

Then I hear a piano. I look up. The music is coming from an open window in a decrepit tenement built of brick and rotting stone. I know that piano-playing.

I hear a sharp intake of breath from Stash, and I look at him. Our eyes meet.

"Is her," he says.

"You should go," I say. "I need to deal with this."

"No, I stay. I must talk to her. She kill you."

"Just go," I hiss, and walk away from him to the front of the building. The old double doors, which are slightly ajar, have blue and grey peeling paint, and I get the feeling that this was once an expensive apartment block. I pull the right-hand door towards me, and it creaks as I drag it over mud and dead leaves. I stop and listen, and feel something touch my elbow. It's Stash. He's not going to go away. I shrug, and walk into the lofty hallway. Rubbish and leaves are strewn round the stone floor, and opposite me, an old marble staircase leads up into the gloom. I can hear the piano echoing eerily down, and I guess it's coming from a room on the first floor. I go up the stairs quietly, pulling

265

my gun out. There's someone at the top of the stairs. All I can see is a dark figure. I hide my gun in my pocket, hoping they haven't seen it, but as I get closer I see that it is an old woman dressed in black. I see old lace, and a gnarled hand holding the banister as she starts her descent, and as I get closer, I realise she is blind.

"Kas tur ir?" she says in a clear voice.

"Tas ir kārtībā," Stash replies gently.

She stops, and seems to stare straight at us with her milky white eyes; then continues her descent as we pass her.

The piano-playing continues to lure me on along a corridor at the top of the stairs. The door at the end is slightly open. I pull my gun out again, and walk quietly up to the door, push it open, and there, with her back to me, is Anna, playing an old grand piano. There are dust and leaves on the bare floorboards. The only things in the room are the piano and the stool she sits on.

"Anna!" Stash shouts, before I can stop him.

She turns, and in one swift gesture pulls out a gun. I point my gun straight at her, and I try to find the safety catch with my thumb, but I can't feel it. What's the matter with this gun? I think frantically. It feels completely unfamiliar. Panic sets in as I watch her, and everything seems to go into in slow motion, as she points her gun at me and pulls the trigger. A dark shape appears in front of me.

"No!" Anna shouts.

I am pushed back by Stash's body falling against me and I involuntarily pull the trigger of my gun. I hear the bullet hit the piano – it's a terrible sound, a cacophony of splintering wood and shrieking metal.

'Just pull the trigger – no safety catch, you fool,' a voice says in my head, as I fall to the floor, the weight of

Stash's body on top of me. I pull the trigger again, and a bullet hits the ceiling.

I find myself looking straight into Anna's eyes as she looks down at me.

"Fool, bloody fool!" she cries, and she turns and runs out of the room. I hear her sobbing, as the sound of her running feet on the bare floorboards recedes into the distance.

Where am I? What am I doing? Everything's chaotic. The gun is still in my hand, I am pinned down by a body. I feel something warm and wet on my stomach. The body groans and moves, and I gently push it off me and look down at it.

Pull yourself together, Arnold.

Think.

Remember.

This person is Stash.

He has just saved your life.

His aunt has shot him, and is getting away.

But Stash is still alive. There's a mass of bloody flesh between his shoulder and his neck – I can see the broken fibres of his muscle surrounding the wound. It's disgusting – huge. The dampness on my stomach is his blood.

Reach for phone.

Dial Grimwode.

"Yes," harsh voice.

"Anna's shot her nephew. Need ambulance," I whisper.

I shouldn't have worried. I can hear a siren getting closer.

"Go," gasps Stash. "Find her. Stop her."

Grimwode's voice comes from my phone. "Leave him. You need to follow her. Find out…" The phone goes dead.

I look down at Stash.

"Go." He looks up at me, pleading.

I can hear voices in the building. The clatter of feet on the stairs. I get up and run out of the room. There's a door just down the corridor, half open. I slip in. Listen to the sound of feet running down the corridor. They stop, and I peer out. They're all looking at Stash. One man is kneeling by him. I slip out and run quietly down the stairs, hoping I won't meet anyone.

I'm out the door, clutching my coat round my blood-stained shirt, and hailing a taxi.

"Airport." I have a hunch Anna will not be hanging around in Riga. She'll be getting on a plane as quickly as possible.

After half an hour, we arrive at the airport and I reach down to get my bag, only to realise that I have left it somewhere.

5.00pm 14th December

Pain on a plane. I touch my bruised chest, feeling the crisp fresh shirt I managed to buy at Riga airport. The blood-stained one is in a litter bin outside the loos. Miraculously, I caught sight of Anna queuing for the Dublin flight, so I waited till the last minute to join the plane. It all feels dreamlike. The officials waved me through as if they were expecting me – gun and all.

I sip my G&T, the only way I'm going to cope with being trapped on this noisy winged coffin, and I feel the pleasant sugar-surge pervading my body. Anna is somewhere behind me. I hope she hasn't seen me. I saw her get on the plane, and I'm sure she didn't get off at the last minute. I wonder if she still has her gun concealed somewhere. I doubt it. They were pretty thorough with everyone else going through security. One up to me, I think, on the gun front. But curiously, it doesn't make me any happier. She's a killer. She's tried to kill me three times, but I just want to nab her in the time-honoured policeman way. Set of handcuffs. "You don't need to say anything etc…" Trouble is, I suspect she will be joined by others when she gets to Dublin, and anyway I want to follow her and find out what she's up to.

Second G&T? No, Arnold. You need your wits about you.

They serve some sort of food. Comes in plastic and foil. Not sure what it is, but I eat it. Another policeman habit –

never turn down food, you never know when your next meal will be.

There's a dog on the plane. I can feel him nuzzling my knee from the aisle. The woman on my left has fallen asleep. I look down, but there's no dog. For a moment I wonder if he walked off, before I remember that he's my ghost-dog – the only dog that could wander freely on a plane.

Now my bladder is giving me messages. I would have liked to stay in my seat for the entire flight, so that Anna would have less chance of seeing me, but when you got to go... I peer round the edge of my seat and down the aisle. Anna is walking away from me towards the loo at the back of the plane. Synchronicity of toilet need? The loo is free at the front end, so I quickly make for it, hoping that I can get back to my seat before she comes out and starts walking up the aisle again. As I come out of my loo, I see her walking towards me, head down, looking for her seat. If she looks up she will look straight into my face. A tall man gets out of the seat just behind mine, and I walk quickly towards him. He stands still, making a perfect screen.

"Er, sorry," I say as I barge round him, and into my seat.

He gives me a funny look, and mutters something in German. He probably thinks I'm a typical rude Brit barging his way through Europe.

The plane drone changes pitch, and I feel the same panic I always feel on a flight. We're going to crash. The engine's failed. We're going down in the Irish Sea. All hands lost.

We are going down.

To Dublin Airport.

Now my ears start playing up. Swallow, hold your nose. Everything's become painful and muted. Fortunately, I won't be using my ears to follow Anna.

Bump.

We're down.

I imagine kissing the tarmac like the Pope, which makes me wonder if that particular Pope hated flying as well. But no time for that – I get off the plane in front of Anna as fast as I can, hoping she won't recognise my back. As we make our way to passport control, I pretend to drop something on the side of the walkway, and dodge behind a pillar to bend down and search for it, letting the people behind me pass. I look up and see Anna walking fast down the slope to the passport hall. I follow slowly, letting a few people get between us to provide a screen, and queue behind her to go through control.

I follow her rapidly through customs, trusting that I won't get stopped, and we're out into the main entrance of Dublin Airport.

She walks quickly across the concourse and out of the entrance marked for buses. I keep her in sight, and see her board the coach for Rosslare. Looking up at the timetable I can see it's about to depart, so I run and get to the doors just as they're closing. The driver gives me a grumpy look as I board, but still sells me a ticket as he puts the bus in gear. I see Anna's back as she walks down to the rear of the coach. I manage to find a seat near the front by a plump gentleman who smells of pipe smoke, and quickly sit down, hoping Anna hasn't turned round and seen me.

I feel someone nudging me in the ribs. The nudging gets more irritating and urgent.

"Scuse me. Time to get off. Change…" The smell of pipe smoke is overpowering.

I wake up. We're the only people left on the coach apart from the driver who is looking round at us.

"Oh, sorry. Must have…" I quickly get up, and bump my head on the luggage rack. Stumbling off the bus, I find my pipe-smoking companion pushing past me and walking rapidly down a dark underlit street. I feel the dog by me, urging me on. Got to catch the next bus, the dog says in my mind. You're meant to be following… following… Anna. That's it, follow the pipe-smoker. Find the bus.

I race after him, and we make our way rapidly through the streets of what must be a small Irish town. I am hungry and thirsty, and I am not sure how much longer I can carry on without some sort of sustenance. We round a corner, and there is a queue at a bus stop. The coach hasn't arrived yet, and I can see Anna standing separate from the rest, talking on her mobile phone.

The coach arrives, and people start shuffling on. Some wait by the side with their suitcases, and I overtake them, getting in ahead of Anna who is still deep in conversation on her phone. I find a seat near the back, sitting next to a young lad who is deep in the world of his iPod. From what's coming over on his headphones, there's a lot of frenetic drumming, which has evidently sent him off into a trance, and I wonder if I'll be able stand this for a hour or so. But my position is good – I can see the entire aisle and will know when Anna gets on, and where she is sitting.

But Anna doesn't get on. The coach doors close, the bus starts to move, and I look out of the back window to see Anna getting into a black BMW. Too late, I'm stuck on this bus going to Rosslare, and I have no idea where Anna's headed.

11.00pm 14th December
Rosslare, Ireland

It occurs to me, as I tuck into fish and chips washed down with a pint of Guinness, that Anna might be headed this way as well. I am sitting in a late-night restaurant, which caters for late-night travellers to Rosslare who are wanting to board the ferry to Fishguard in the morning. I have been told that there is accommodation down the street – last check-in by midnight. So no sleeping on the streets for me tonight. No repeat of my demented Oxford Street experience. In fact, apart from my imaginary dog, I seem to be quite lucid and sane at the moment.

But, as I say, Anna could be headed this way as well. Our discoveries on the coast of Pembrokeshire point to something going on in the Irish Sea: the wallet, the dead solicitor, Betty's shoe, all washed up within a few miles of each other. Of course, Dawson and co. will have thought about this too, but they might've missed something – it wouldn't be the first time. Or an incident could have happened on a boat that was passing close to the Welsh coast. Whatever, it all looks a bit nasty, and I feel a sudden tingle of fear for unfaithful Betty. I never wished her that kind of harm – not even in my angriest moments.

Rosslare is a port – the port for this crossing from Ireland over to the south west coast of Wales. Supposing Anna was picked up by the BMW for some kind of

273

conference with her terrorist group, but she was still making for the Irish Sea? Rosslare would be her destination, and whatever is going on somewhere between the coasts of Ireland and Wales. I could do with a map, I realise, detailed enough to show the coastlines and any islands, big or small that might be significant. Or if it's a boat I'm looking for, it might be harboured up at Rosslare. Maybe that's where it all started: a boat crossed the Irish Sea, something went wrong, at least one person was murdered, then the dog found a wallet washed up on a beach in Pembrokeshire, never knowing it would lead to his death.

I'm beginning to get sad, and that's no good to me. I need my sleep. I need to charge up my batteries, and be up early before the ferry departs, get a map, and see if I am right about Anna.

I leave the restaurant, and find the late-night hotel. Get booked in. Order an early breakfast, and just manage to get undressed before sleep takes over.

7.30am 15th December
Rosslare, Ireland

I feel a nudge against my hand. A wet nose. What's the dog doing up in my bedroom? He knows he's meant to stay in the kitchen. I look at him – if he could smile, he would, but he wags his tail instead.

"What are you doing up here?" I say in a fake admonishing voice. I look at my watch.

7.30am.

I need to be up. I look back at him, but he's gone. I'm not in my bedroom, I'm in a hotel room. The dog is dead. How long will I be haunted by him? Part of me hopes I always will be. But that's … mad.

But for now I'm pursuing a terrorist. I need to catch a ferry.

Still, I reflect as I quickly shower, and bung my stale clothes back on, it's an improvement on my demented episodes. Being haunted by a ghost-dog is harmless enough, and who knows, he might lead me to something, like in the old times.

The ferry for Fishguard goes at 9.30am. The breakfast is the usual Great British, even though I'm in Ireland. All the stuff I need for the day ahead: processed meat, salt, sugar, carbs, beans.

I eat a bowl of fruit while I think about Peggy. Is she alright? Has she been protected? Grimwode is the only one I can trust, but has he managed to keep her and Paul safe?

I get up from my table, pay my bill, and walk quickly down to the harbour. A newsagent is open, and I buy a couple of maps that will hopefully show me what happens between Ireland and Wales.

Down at the ferry, the cars are driving on. I look out for a large black Beemer and spot three of them. All have privacy glass. Maybe Anna is in one of them, maybe not.

Up on deck, I look out at the harbour. Not many boats are around on this cold December morning: a couple of container ships, another ferry – going to France I guess.

But close to, there's a large, white motor yacht. Sleek. Beautiful. Millions of quids worth. The place for millionaire parties. I look down at it, half expecting to see some famous actress swanning along in an evening dress. This boat would be more in place in Cannes – Rosslare seems a bit rough and ready for such a beautiful beast.

The hooter goes on our ferry, jerking me out of my reverie, and we start to move. I look back at the yacht and see a small figure hurrying down the gangplank.

I could swear it's Anna. No binoculars, but my most reliable physical attribute – my eyesight, tells me it's her. Too late for me to get off the ferry, I sail away from my quarry, wondering where she's bound for.

The name of the yacht is visible now: The White Crusader – a provocative name, if ever there was one – and I wonder who owns this boat, and how they are connected to Anna, and the wide network of terror to which she belongs.

I ring Grimwode. It goes to answerphone, and I just say, "Call me." I leave no message about anything that someone else could pick up.

We are slowly going out of the harbour, and into quite a choppy sea. It's very cold on deck, and I need to find a nice café so I can sit down and look at my maps. I take a last look at The White Crusader and notice that it's already

276

moving off. It speeds up, and effortlessly passes us as it heads out to sea. I watch it till it's just a dot in the distance. Same direction as us? Maybe?

In a café with all the tables and chairs attached firmly to the floor, I gradually warm up with the help of a large watery latte, and something pretending to be an almond slice. The dog has come back to haunt me. I can feel his presence by my side. So much so, that I'm tempted to drop him a bit of my ambiguous confection.

I spread the maps out on my table, and look for islands in the Irish Sea. Not many. A few as it gets closer to Wales.

Bardsey up north – too far away for my theory.

Skomer, Skockholm, Ramsey. They are all closer to the place where I found the wallet, and where Mrs Braithwaite's body got washed up, and where Betty's shoe... But surely Dawson and his men would have searched all those thoroughly – particularly Skomer, which is so close to the mainland?

But maybe not – Grimwode made it clear how far they were all stretched, chasing the terrorists and protecting the long list of intended victims.

I wonder about Ramsey Island. It's got some big caves. The problem is it would have visitors around it all the time; but maybe not so much in the closed season. Whatever happened out at sea happened in November...

My phone goes.

"Yes?" Grimwode's voice is sharp. Unemotional.

"I'm on the ferry to Fishguard. I saw a yacht in Rosslare: The White Crusader. Anna's on board. They're heading out into the Irish Sea."

"You're sure about the name?" There's something in his voice – an uncertainty.

"Yes."

The phone goes dead. Well, thank you Mr Grimwode, I think. A little more support would be nice. Anyway, he

277

knows now, and hopefully he's the only one. But he did sound surprised – maybe the owner goes to his club.

The ferry lurches, and some of my coffee spills onto one of the maps, creating a new island. It's going to be quite a rough crossing, and I wonder whether my trust in my sea legs will be over-challenged today. I put my maps in my coat pocket, and take the stairs up onto deck.

The spray hits my face, and it would be refreshing if it wasn't so bitterly cold. I probably won't be able to stay out here long, but I stagger along the deck, holding onto the rail as the ship lurches from side to side.

Proud sailor, I.

I look out to sea, and spot a couple of tankers – dark shapes against the heaving sky. I came out on the port side of the ship, and I make my way slowly round to the starboard. To my surprise, there, not far away, is The White Crusader, not making much headway and wallowing in the waves. That yacht must have every gizmo under the sun, but it appears to be in trouble. The ferry sounds its horn, and seems to slow. I imagine the captain in the control room asking if the yacht needs any assistance. There's a pause while our ferry slows; then the yacht starts up its engines and, with a great churning-up of water at its stern, zooms off to the right and is soon a small black shape on the horizon.

I wonder what that was all about. A sailor comes towards me, looking revoltingly assured as he walks down the stairs from the control room.

"What were they doing?" I shout to him.

"Nets caught in their propellers," he yells back in a broad Irish accent. "Didn't thank us for offering assistance. Feckin' fools, drifting into our lane... accident..." I just catch the words as he walks jauntily up the deck as if we were sailing on a millpond.

Another person has come out on deck. They are too far away for me to see, but I'm guessing adult male. He stands, looking out to sea. Doesn't look like he's going to be sick. There's just the two of us – the rest of the landlubbers are in the warm, either heaving in the loos, or taking full advantage of their sickness pills.

Just to see, I walk round to the other side of the ship again. The wind buffets me so hard, I nearly fall, and grab the rail for support. There's no-one there. The swell of the sea seems impossibly large. The ferry is big, but…

I look back along the deck, and there is the figure, too far away to see clearly.

I am getting wet and cold, and I decide to risk the sickness inside and go back down to the café. The sweet smell of vomit greets me as I go inside. I look at my watch – only two hours to go. I'm damned if I am going to be sick. I make my way cautiously to the café, expecting to find it closed in these conditions, but there are two cheery-looking stewards ready to offer refreshments to anyone who would dare. As it happens, I am the only taker.

I plump for tea, a Mars Bar, and a packet of crisps.

"Bit wild today," I say, trying to sound nonchalant.

"Not bad for December. Pretty average…" The steward smiles. "Careful, sir," he continues as I nearly spill my tea due to a sudden lurch to starboard.

I put two sugars in – for some reason, I think sweet tea will work against any feeling of sickness. I grab the nearest table, and concentrate on getting my tea to my mouth while holding on to my unhealthy goodies. I think of Peggy, and what she would say about this kind of food – it reminds me that I had fruit for breakfast. Just now I wish I had stuck simply with the full English – something about the complexity of what's in my stomach increases my feeling of queasiness.

279

It takes a while to negotiate tea, crisps, and Mars Bar into my system. They do have a calming influence. Worth the work, I reflect.

I look up, and I realise I have company. A man has come in and is sitting in the corner of the café. It occurs to me that he might just be another passenger that can sort-of cope with this stormy sailing, or he might even be a figment of my imagination like the dog. But my suspicion is that he is perfectly real and has been asked to keep an eye on me by the occupants of The White Crusader. I wonder now whether the nets-in-propeller thing was just an excuse to get close enough to the ferry to send a signal. Whatever, it's taken my mind off my innards which seem to have settled into some kind of rock-hard state.

Ignore him, says one part of my mind.

Go and talk to him, says the other.

He knows I know he's there, so there's no point in pretending I haven't noticed him. He may be a figment of my imagination, or just another firm-gutted traveller, but I want to find out.

Getting across the morass of tables and chairs is a bit like clambering from one wooden motorbike to another on a merry-go-round. I try to keep my eye on him, but one particularly steep lurch nearly sends me over, and when I look up, he's gone.

So he's either a figment of my paranoid imagination, or he's tailing me. I think a fellow traveller would have waited.

Now follows a curious game of hide-and-seek. My aim is to hide from him and turn the tables on him so that I can be the stalker. When we finally get off this accursed ferry, I need every lead possible to find out where Anna went in her little white boat.

But suppose I'm simply imagining him?

Well, at least this game is keeping my mind off my stomach.

With the ship rocking this much, it's easy to have an excuse to stick close to the walls. I creep round a corner, and there he is, looking down the transverse corridor to the other side of the ferry. I slip back round the corner so that I can pull back if he turns.

He gets his phone out and looks like he's texting. He looks at it and then shakes his head impatiently. I guess the text wouldn't go.

Something nudges the back of my knee, and I look round.

It's the dog. He looks up at me, his tail wagging from side to side. He is apparently unaffected by the lurching motion of the ship.

I look back, and the man has disappeared again.

What is real?

The man, or the dog?

The dog is still by me, licking my hand and wagging his tail.

I follow the dog, and he leads me to a row of seats at the side of the ferry. I sit down. He lays his muzzle in my lap, and I scratch him absent-mindedly behind the ears. The heavy motion of the ship becomes a cradle rocking, and I feel sleep coming.

1.45pm 15th December
Fishguard

"Sir, excuse me, sir, we're disembarking." A friendly hand is on my shoulder, shaking me gently.

I wake from a beautiful dream. A dream I don't want to leave: I am walking down the common in my home town, the dog at my side. It's dawn, and the lights of the town are twinkling in the distance. He talks to me. He says, "I can guide you now. I can help you find what you're looking for. Just follow me…"

I am awake. There is no dog. Just a man in a uniform trying to wake me up and get me off the ferry. We must be at Fishguard.

"Uh, sorry. Must have fallen asleep," I say, stating the obvious.

I get up stiffly. The rocking motion of the ship is still going round my head, and I wobble. The steward holds my elbow, guiding this poor elderly man out of his seat.

"Thanks." I stand still for a moment, gaining my equilibrium, and follow him up the stairs, out of the doors, and onto the gangplank. I am the last passenger. The cold air hits me, and I wake up properly – fully aware of where I am and what I'm meant to be doing.

I walk down the quay and into the town. Find a cashpoint. Find a chippy. Find a taxi. And we're on our way to the south tip of the Pembrokeshire coast. It isn't long before we're going down narrow lanes with glimpses of the sea round every corner. It looks quite calm compared to my rocky crossing, and I'm hoping that it will remain so.

I have a plan.

Down in my brother's village, there is a fisherman that I have talked to on many occasions in the past. He's called Pete. He's told me many stories about his fishing exploits. He's proudly shown me his boat. It's quite small. A coastal vessel, more suited to finding and pulling up crab and lobster pots than going out on the high seas. It's the low season for him now, and he'll be doing repairs. Maybe repainting his boat, though I hope he isn't today. I need him and his boat.

I pay off the taxi, and hope that there is enough left in my wodge of notes to satisfy Pete's financial requirements.

Skomer Island is my destination. It could well have been the first place that Dawson and co. searched, but whoever put a bullet through Mrs B's head might have cleared out as quickly as possible to avoid discovery. My thinking now is that if The White Crusader was going across from Ireland to Wales, they will have a destination, and that might be offshore, and Skomer is the most promising island if they wanted to hide something.

I find Pete repairing a lobster pot. He's quite a short man, with narrow but muscular shoulders and big hands. It's like his hands have grown with his work, leaving the rest of his body behind. He looks up at me – twinkling blue eyes under a thatch of white hair. He must be a few years older than me, but he's much fitter.

"Inspector Rackham, not much for you today. I haven't been out for a while." He looks out to the bay, considering the December seas. "I've got some mackerel in the freezer. Do you like bass? Class fish that. Caught some with Don a couple o' weeks ago…"

"Actually, I was hoping you could take me out in your boat."

Pete stands up slowly from working on his pot. He looks up at the sky, looks out to sea at the waves, and strokes his chin.

"When?"

"Now?"

"Now… hmm…" He looks at his watch. "Give me a minute… er… Inspector." He walks over to a hut on the little quayside. Disappears inside. I guess he's on the radio checking the local forecast. After five minutes he reappears.

"Now's a good a time as any. Where do you want to go?"

"Skomer. I want to look for caves."

"Caves?"

"Yes, I think someone may be hiding something in a cave somewhere off this bit of coast."

"If you think it could be Skomer, then you'll be wanting The Neck."

"The Neck?" It rings a bell, but it was a long time ago that I went out to the islands.

"It's joined to Skomer by a thin bit o' land. Lots of caves and cracks round The Neck."

He goes back into the hut, and comes out with a lifebelt. He helps me into it – I make sure I can reach the pocket that contains my Glock.

Pete notices. "Expecting trouble, Inspector?"

"Er no… just… how much do you charge?"

Pete leads me over to a small dinghy that's bobbing up and down by the quay. I step down into it stiffly, making the boat wobble from side to side. Pete steadies it with his big hand, then climbs in himself without disturbing the balance.

"Let's see how we go. We'll settle up at the end." He starts the outboard motor, and I wonder what the end will be. I feel like I have just taken an irreversible step by getting into his dinghy. We chug round to a small fishing boat moored to a buoy. It has a cabin at the front but is open at the back. He's painted it recently – it looks old but smart. He helps me in, then ties his dinghy up to the stern, starts the engine, goes to the bow and casts off, and we chug our way slowly out of the little bay and into the churning sea.

"Seems quite rough," I shout over the sound of the engine and the wind – the spray comes up over the bow, making everything slightly wet.

"Oh, average for this time of year," he shouts back. "Weather should hold for a bit. There's something coming in a bit later, but we'll be back by then."

He seems very sure we'll be back by then, or maybe he is referring to himself and his vessel.

We keep in the shelter of the coastline, following the rugged outcrops that make the Pembrokeshire coast so beautiful. After a while, I see a string of islands heading out into the sea, their dark sloping backs curled against the weather. Skomer is the largest one at the end of the group. The waves are bigger now, as we make directly for Skomer. Pete's obviously not the slightest bit worried about his small vessel taking on this large rolling swell. Looking back to the mainland, I notice a small beach with a jetty built into the rocks, where the land juts out in the direction of the islands. I look forward again as we get closer to The Neck, and I can see the odd cave and fissure. I wonder how the hell I'm going to search them, or even get to them. Near the landward end of the island is a tunnel created by a natural fissure that goes right through to the other side – I can see light, and something moving at the other end.

"There's a boat out there," Pete shouts.

I look and find it hard to see anything, as I bob up and down with the spray stinging my face. By screwing up my eyes, I can just see the stern of a large white motor yacht moving slowly up the other side of the island.

"Do you want them to see us?" Pete shouts.

"No!" I shout back.

He gets us as close into the island as he can, and the boat stops rocking like some kind of demented fairground ride. I am cursing myself – I don't know what I expected to find, but now we can't even have a look at the other side of the island without being seen by The White Crusader.

"You looking for an accessible cave, Inspector?" Pete asks. We don't have to shout any more as we keep as still as possible out of the wind.

"Yes."

"There is a little beach and a cave on the other side that can be reached at low tide. Used to go there as a kid for larks until the nature reserve people asked me not to. They don't want people disturbing the birds. One o' the best places for Manx Shearwaters, though not so much goes on this time o' year, but best keep out o' sight o' the warden's house." He nods in the direction of the main island. "You want to see the cave, but you don't want the white yacht to see you?"

"Yes, but…" I'm thinking this isn't going to work, and there's a feeling of relief flooding through my veins.

"We're nearly at low tide now. There's a way through from here, over the rocks and through that tunnel. You could do it if you're…" Fit enough – I fill in for him. "They won't see you while you're in the tunnel, so you can wait at the other end until the coast is clear.

"Right. How?" My feeling of relief wilts away.

"You can take my dinghy to that little inlet there. Tie it up to a rock. I'll pick you up in an hour."

287

"But…"

"You can do it, Inspector." He looks at me with such trust – I wonder where he got that from.

I get into the dinghy, and he shows me how to start the outboard. I take the rope from him, and steer my way through the waves to the inlet. I get out too soon and end up with sodden shoes and socks, but manage to pull the dinghy in and fasten the rope to a solid-looking rock. Pete waves at me from his boat and points to the tunnel, and I start to make my way carefully along it. I look back at him, but he's already turned the boat and is starting to chug back along the coast, leaving me alone to search the island.

I scramble along the rocky floor of the tunnel, my wet shoes slipping from time to time, but I still manage to stay more or less upright as I make my way across to the other side of The Neck. The wind gets stronger as I get to the end of the tunnel, and as I pull back to remain concealed, I can just make out the outline of The White Crusader apparently stationary off the coast of the island. As I look, I see an inflatable making its way out towards the yacht. It's difficult to work out how many people are in it. The whine of the engine slows to a putter and I see the inflatable stop at the side of the yacht. After a couple of minutes, two people climb out, and up a ladder. The inflatable is hauled up, and with a burst of churning water The White Crusader heads off out to sea.

Slowly and carefully, I slip and slide across the rocks – sometimes shuffling on my bum, sometimes crawling on my hands and knees. The beach comes as a surprise, and I nearly fall head first onto the sand. Out to sea the yacht has disappeared, but looking to my right I can see a small cave opening at the top of the beach, just big enough for one person to squeeze in on all fours.

I look all around the area for a sign of someone else – the place seems deserted. No guards for the cave – at least not outside.

Very slowly, I crouch down and ease my way into the cave mouth, gun in one hand. I can hear an eerie sound of crying somewhere up ahead, but it's pitch black and I have no idea how this cave works, or how big it is. The ground slopes up sharply, and I think it must be the cave Pete was talking about. I reach up and find nothing but space above my head. The crying gets closer, and something about it makes me gasp. I know that sound – it's Betty. At the same time, I notice a horrible rank smell. Something has died here and is decomposing, filling the air with a sickening odour. My mobile phone battery is probably on its last legs, but I take it out and turn on the torch.

A lurid scene greets my eyes: propped up against the back wall of the cave is a painting, still in its plastic wrapping, and next to it is Betty, hands and feet bound and a large bruise on her face. To the other side of the painting is a figure lying curled up, and it's from that that the ghastly smell is coming.

"No, no, no, no!" Betty shrieks. "I can't…"

"It's me, Arnold," I say, trying not to gag on the smell. I turn the torch on my face.

She lets out a long high-pitched scream, and tries to struggle out of her bonds.

"Calm down, it's me…"

The scream turns to sobs. I get to her and try to hold her hand, but she wrenches it away from me.

"Where have you been?" I whisper it, to myself as much as to her.

"In hell," she gasps.

"What have they done to you?"

"You don't know?"

"Tell me."

289

"They want Brian… think I know… where he is…" she starts wailing again, and rejects any attempt I make to touch her.

"I'll get help," I say, and look down at my phone which has almost run out of battery. There's no signal. I scramble down to the cave mouth to see if there's any signal outside. Betty starts to scream again, but it sounds like some weird seagull outside the cave. The phone is almost dead. I text Grimwode:

'On Skomer. Found Betty in cave on seaward side. Need help.'

It goes.

I go back in, Betty is sobbing, and I use the last of my torch to find her.

It goes dark.

Just us. The smell. The painting.

"Betty. Listen, we've got to get out of here."

"I can't… move…"

"I'll try and cut your bonds."

"They'll be back soon…"

"I've got a gun."

"A gun? You're not Arnold. He hated guns. He killed a boy by mistake…"

"Listen, Grimwode made me have one. I hate it too, but I need it now to protect myself… and you."

I feel her bonds. They are made of some thick tape. I search round to see if I can find a corner to tear them off. All the time Betty is pulling away from me. She has clearly lost her mind. They have evidently tried every psychological trick in the book on her, including leaving her in the dark with a rotting body. I have to bring her back. I can't find the end of the tape so there's no way of levering it off. I haven't got a knife so I search for a sharp stone, but all I can feel are smooth round pebbles and sand.

After an agonising time of trying to find a way to release her, I have got no further.

"We'll just have to wait. I've called for help. I hope it comes before your captors get back."

"Is it really you?" There's a sob, then a gasp. It's like she's just woken up.

"Yes, Betty."

"Prove it." She's sharp now. They could be playing another trick on her, and she can't even see me now.

"Do you remember how we used to meet at my cottage for a glass of Rioja after work?"

"Yes."

"Do you remember you gave me a coffee machine last Christmas, and I kept forgetting how to use it?" Not many intimate details – we didn't have an intimate life.

"Yes. But…" she's still not sure.

"Who's that lying dead in the cave?" I try a different tack.

"Alan…"

"Alan Hunt?"

"Yes…"

"He was meant to help Brian sell the paintings, wasn't he?" I realise I've gone too far, but it's too late.

"Brian? You want to know about Brian? You're one of them aren't you?"

"Sod Brian! The idiot went off with the paintings thinking he could sell them, but just bringing death and torture to anyone who came near him. He's got two left out of the four he took. I'm guessing there's one in this cave, and I found one in Riga."

"Riga?" Betty gasps.

"Yes, Riga. Why?"

"We used to meet there. There was this millionaire, and we'd stay at his house. That was before…"

"Malcolm was murdered."

291

She starts to cry. Part of me is cold to her pain – her unfaithful life with Malcolm Smith-Rogers. But also, I can sense that I'm getting through to her.

"Listen. Listen, there's not much time. They may come back at any moment. Tell me what you know about these bastards who've done this to you."

She stops crying. "If you really are Arnold… what have I got to lose?" this to herself, "but don't hurt me… please…"

"I'm not going to hurt you." It pains me, but I reach out and gently squeeze her arm. She doesn't pull away. For a moment, we're man and wife – but then the illusion goes.

"The boss isn't an Arab or a Muslim or anything like that."

"You've seen him?"

"Yes, he's the owner of the yacht. He's helping them, the terrorists, gives them arms."

"But I thought they were using the paintings to raise money for their cause?"

"Yes, they are, but it's not easy. Stolen art is normally done to order. They found the cache, but can't find anyone who wants to touch it."

"You know a lot about this."

"I heard Malcolm and Brian discussing it before… before…" she starts to cry again. I'm thinking, didn't she have enough? Why did she want to get involved in all this stolen art grief?

"So, this man," I have to get her back on track.

"He hates YOU!" she shouts. Then she laughs. It's an eerie, bitter sound. "They all do."

"Because I spoil their plans?"

"I think they might have used me to get at you, but then they found out about fucking Peggy."

"Peggy?" I shudder involuntarily. Have they got Peggy? Has Grimwode managed to protect her?

"Your girlfriend." She says this with a nasty edge to her voice. I feel angry, but my need to get this back on track overrides my impulse to say 'yes, she actually loves me.'

"The boss. Tell me about him," I continue.

"I don't know anything about him."

"OK, describe him. What does he look like?" I'm gearing up to do a sketch of him if I ever get out of here.

"He's heavily built, brown eyes. Dark brown. They frightened me, his eyes. The way he looked."

"Good, what was his hair colour?"

"Black with grey flecks."

"Receding?"

"Re… what? Oh yes, he was losing some at the front."

"So he'd be about fifty?"

"Older, I'd say. Could be in his sixties. He looked so fit and rugged. His face was a ruddy brown colour. He sounded British. I wondered if he was ex-army."

"This is great, Betty. You never heard his name, I suppose?"

"No. I'd have told you if I had, you idiot."

I swallow that sign of what she really thinks of me. "The shape of his face – oblong? Square? Round? Oval?"

"Oblong, and he had these creases that went from his cheekbones to his jowls. He looked like he was always smiling, but he never really smiled."

"Were they afraid of him? The terrorists?"

"They worshipped him. Treated him with huge respect."

"Eyebrows?"

"Eyebrows? Oh, you're back on his face. Why do you keep jumping about like this?"

"Just trying to get the whole picture."

"Bushy, and quite white."

"Anything unusual about his face? Marks?"

293

"One ear was bigger than the other. It made me laugh to myself…"

"What did his face make you think of?"

"Granite."

"Granite?"

"He was so hard, so impenetrable."

Then she starts to sing:

"Granite is the hardest stone my boys,
Granite is the hardest stone,
Dee dee dum, dee dee dum,
Dee dee dummy dummy dum,
Granite is the hardest stone."

It's the chorus of a song we both heard in Cornwall on one of our rare holidays a few years ago. It was a time when I felt closer to her. A time when I had no idea what was going on.

She starts again, in her quavering but accurate voice, and I join in in a rumbly sort of way:

"Granite is the hardest stone my boys,
Granite is the hardest stone,
Dee dee dum, dee dee dum,
Dee dee dummy dummy dum,
Granite is the hardest…

There's a blinding flash of light in our faces, followed by a volley of gunfire. Betty screams. I hear bullets ricocheting all around the cave. I roll sideways away from Betty, and towards the painting and the decomposing body of Alan Hunt.

"Don't hit painting," I hear a shout. It's Anna's voice.

I struggle to get my gun out from under me, and remembering for once how it works, I shoot straight at the light.

The light goes out. There's a yell, and the sound of something heavy being dropped.

I fire off more rounds in the same direction, no idea who or what I'm hitting. There's a scream.

"Fuck you Rackham!" I hear Anna's voice again. Then a scrabbling sound from the entrance to the cave. Then silence.

I lie still for what seems like an age, listening.

There's no sound except for the sea.

No sobbing, no gasping, no breathing.

I slowly crawl towards where I think Betty must be. I touch her leg, then find her arm, her wrist still bound with tape. I can't feel a pulse through the plastic, so I reach up to her neck. It's warm and wet, but I can feel no pulse. I try and try, but there is no sign of life. My Betty. I put my arms around her, and rock from side to side. I can't help it – I weep. The Betty I loved, protected, supported, is gone.

Then I pull away, and cautiously make my way down to the cave mouth. I come into contact with someone's head. Like Betty's, it's perfectly still. Like Betty's it's warm and wet. I feel its neck. No pulse. Crawling past the body, I find cold metal. A machine pistol. Could be useful, I think. Then I remember the painting.

Crawling back up the cave in what I think, is the right direction, I come into contact with another body – but this one stinks. I recoil away from Alan Hunt's remains, and find the painting still leaning against the back wall. I carefully lift it, and shuffle my way back to the entrance.

It's dark outside, but compared to the cave I can see the shape of things. I have to get back to the dinghy, across rocks and in the dark, and the tide's beginning to come back in.

Machine gun, or painting? I can only carry one.

I can't leave that painting behind. Not after all that's happened. It's almost as if my identity is tied up with finding art.

I shuffle to my feet, holding the painting, and use the gently sloping rock face of the cave to find my way along and off the beach. It's very tricky slipping and sliding over the rocky shore. I hope that I won't miss the tunnel back to the other side of The Neck; then through the rock wall, as though by magic, I see lights. I move cautiously, and I can see the lights of some large ship out to sea on the other side of the island. I can feel the edge of the tunnel entrance, and I grope along the wall, stumbling and slipping on the wet rocks. Every now and then, I feel water coming over my shoes. The tide is coming in.

As I reach the other end of the tunnel, I try to remember where I moored the dinghy, but the sea is higher now, and the boat must be floating off away from the rocky inlet.

The sea is cold as it washes over my feet, then up to my calves. It's almost up to my knees when I find the rope. I feel along it to the prow, and with huge effort I heave myself over the side of the boat, and lie inside it as it rocks. I could die now, just go to sleep and never wake up; but I feel a wet nose in my face, and a gentle growl. The dog has come to help me keep going.

Gathering my thoughts, I wonder whether I should wait for Pete to return, or wait for Grimwode's team to rescue me. I have the horrible certainty that my message to Grimwode was intercepted. Why, otherwise, would Anna and her friend have come into the cave, guns blazing? They might still be searching for me. They might get to me before help arrives.

I come to the conclusion that the best thing to do is to try and make my way back to the mainland in my little dinghy. The sea has calmed – I wonder if it's the calm before the storm – and I remember the bay that we passed on our way to Skomer. Could I make that? I don't remember there being much open sea.

I sit up, and after a few attempts, start the motor. Fumbling with the rope, I manage to release the dinghy and turn out to sea. I chug along as close to the island as I think is safe, then feel a swell pushing me away from the dark shape of another island that I can see ahead of me. I must be between The Neck and the next island that is closer inland. Further ahead I can see some lights, and I hope that they mark the little harbour I'm making for. The swell feels like it will tip my dinghy over, and it's a relief when I get into the lee of the next island.

Carefully steering my way along by the sharp rocks, I make for the last bit of open sea that separates me from the mainland. The swell feels bigger now, and I can feel the wind getting up. This part of water is wider than I remembered. More than once, my little boat nearly capsizes. As I move from side to side, frantically trying to keep it stable, part of me visualises how Pete would calmly be sitting there, not panicking in this swelling sea.

It's then that I hear the sound of a chugging motor, and looking out along the coast, I can make out the silhouette of a small fishing boat heading for The Neck. It's Pete's boat, I am sure of it, and he's come to pick me up. I've lost all track of time – it could have been an hour since he left me.

I wave frantically at the boat.

"Pete, Pete, over here!" I'm floundering in the swell, wondering if I'll capsize before he sees me. The boat continues on its way, and in desperation, I take out my gun and fire a shot into the air. The boat turns then, and a powerful searchlight comes on, its beam slowly sweeping in my direction.

"Pete!" I wave again.

A shot rings out, and a bullet whistles over my head. The full beam of the light is on me. Whoever is behind it can see me clearly now, and is intent on shooting me out

297

of the water. More shots come from the boat. I fire back, trying to take out the searchlight, but a wave hits my dinghy and I nearly fall overboard.

The boat is getting nearer, and a bullet just misses me and ploughs into the bottom of the boat. I am getting into the lee of the peninsular now, as the fishing boat closes in on me. Steadier now, I fire straight at the searchlight, and it goes out. I head my dinghy towards the little harbour. I can see some navigation lights there now. There's a rending, crunching noise, and an angry shout behind me, and I look round to see the dark shape of the fishing boat grounding on the rocks that come out from the coastline. A bullet hits the bottom of my boat for the second time, and water is coming in so fast that I'm not sure it will get me to the beach. I urge my sinking craft on, not looking back. My pursuers are evidently taken up with their own problems now. The wind is getting up, and they'll have the devil's own job getting off those rocks in one piece – and if it's Pete's boat, as I suspect it is, then I've got their dinghy.

The sounds of shouting and cursing fade as I steer my sinking boat towards the beach, and I hit the shingle and nearly fall out, trying to keep the precious painting out of the water. Soaked to my waist, I walk quickly up the beach, looking round for signs of pursuit. The climb up the road is hard, and I'm fast running out of energy. I need to find somewhere safe as soon as possible, and a farm comes to my mind, where the farmer has been friendly and helpful to me and my brother in the past. It's off the beaten track, and I make my way through fields walking as fast as I can, keeping my head down, and looking behind me at regular intervals for signs of pursuit. Every now and then I feel the dog at my side, spurring me on, as my past history unravels through my mind.

Betty. That safe cold life. Regular. Easy. But dead now.

The farmhouse is near a single track road which runs round the coastal peninsular. I knock on the door, and hope.

The farmer opens the door, and light floods out. I look down at the painting. There's a neat bullet hole right through the middle.

3.00am 16th December

The shadows are closing in. I'm captive in a strange house, but they've forgotten to tie me up. Stiffly, I get out of bed. The room is wired, a CCTV camera looks down at me from the corner, its little red light blinking. As I look at it, the red light gets bigger and bigger until it feels like it will take over my brain. I close my eyes and turn away – the light's still there. Blinking.

There's something I need. It's metal and short, and it comforts me. It will get me out of this mess. I am addicted to it. I have to have it. It's precious. I get on my knees and crawl around the room. It feels more like a cave now. There's someone in the corner watching me. His face is in the shadow, but I know it's made of granite.

I crawl on round the room-cave. There's no way out. There are dead bodies in the corners. I don't want to touch them. I must find this thing. This metal thing. My head comes into contact with something soft, and I recoil. I reach out to touch it. It's soft. Not warm, not cold, not human. I push at it, and it gives way. I push and push, and it moves easily – softly.

My hand comes into contact with something cold and hard. A bone? Again I recoil, but then I reach back and feel it. It's not a bone. It's made of metal. It's the thing I've been looking for, the thing that will save me. It's then that I realise that I've had my eyes closed. I look at the thing. A glint of dark metal. It's L-shaped and fits neatly

301

in my hand. If I turn it round so the end of it faces me, will it free me from all this torment? The dead? The man in the corner?

There's a little bit that moves between my finger and thumb, but then it gets stuck. It only moves slightly and then it gets stuck. Gets stuck. Gets stuck. What is it that I don't understand about this thing?

I hold it so that it feels comfortable in my hand. Then I stand up.

I turn my back on the man in the corner, and the dead bodies, and find the door. It isn't locked and opens easily. Light floods in, but I don't look round, I look down at the thing I'm holding. I find it both attractive, and repulsive, like an addiction. Its sleek shape is penis-like, and I am sure it shoots things out of the end I am pointing away from me.

Again I feel the urge to point it towards me. Bring all this death to an end. The ultimate victory.

I ponder on this idea. But I still don't know how to make this thing work. It seems to jam. Maybe if I use more pressure? A firmer grip? I point it at me, but the thing doesn't fit any more. It feels strange. Wrong.

A hand grabs my hand. It has come from nowhere. I look up. There's a man standing in front of me. Do I know him?

"No," he says, gently. He takes the thing away. My thing. I start to cry.

"Come downstairs, I'll get you something." He has a gentle Welsh accent. Welsh? Wales?

He takes my arm. I look at his face through my tears. He has a kind face. It's weathered, but not made of granite. Farmer. He's a farmer.

He leads me gently downstairs and into the kitchen. Kitchen.

It's all coming back to me. I used to have a kitchen, and I kept a gallery of sketches to remind me of people when I forgot... who... they... were.

He goes over to the sink and fills the kettle. There is an old range and I can feel the warmth coming from it.

"There," he says simply. "We'll have a cup of tea."

It's then that I realise that he has just saved my life. My gun lies on the windowsill out of reach.

"Thank you," I say huskily.

"After what you said last night..." He leaves the rest unsaid, and pours hot water into a flowery teapot. Something about the sweetness and gentleness of the crockery makes me want to laugh.

"A text came through on your phone. Woke me up. Just as well." He looks at me with a serious expression. "Are you OK now?"

"Yes, I think so," I look him in the eyes. "I could have killed someone. You or your wife. Shit." I start to shake.

"Well you didn't," he says this in a fatherly way, as though his children were always walking round at night with loaded guns. "Have a cup of tea. Sugar?"

"Please." I wonder if I can trust him. Maybe it doesn't matter anymore. My position is so different from the old secure life I had once.

I grasp the warm mug with both hands, like an anchor. "I have these episodes when I forget things. I didn't know I was holding that gun. I was afraid this might happen, but I couldn't tell my boss. You saved me."

"I know. I wondered if you were suicidal. I wouldn't have been surprised. Your wife dying like that."

"I told you that?"

"You told us you'd tried to rescue your wife. Not much more except you didn't want us to call the police. You were in quite a mess last night. We fed you, gave you a bath, and lent you some of my pyjamas. You went out like

303

a light, but you asked if we could charge up your mobile phone. I found a way to do it, and a message came through. Woke me up." He shrugs, and looks at me, letting his breath out in a slow whistle.

"What was the message?"

"I didn't look."

"Can I see it?"

"Will you be alright if I go up and get it?"

"Yes, I'm fine now," I say shakily.

He gets up from his chair, picks up my gun from the windowsill, and goes upstairs.

I close my eyes, and a face appears. It's granite and I have to draw it. All that's left of Betty's last hour of life. I need to give it meaning.

He brings down the phone.

'Keep your phone on I'm coming to get you' the text says. No time. Just that. So that's why we haven't had a phalanx of armed police turning up at the farm. He's sent them to the cave. He's waiting to see where I am. He doesn't trust anyone.

"Can I have a piece of paper and a pencil?" I ask.

"Got something in this drawer." He goes over to a Welsh dresser. He's still holding my gun, I notice.

I start to draw. The face that looks back at me is formidable. The dark eyes under white eyebrows, the lines that don't really smile. That feeling of granite. I shudder, but I think this will be useful for Grimwode. I remember the way he sounded when I told him about The White Crusader, as if it was the last name he expected to hear.

"That's impressive," says the farmer.

"Part of my work," I say. "Used to be an artist. Comes in useful in the force."

He smiles. "Have another cup of tea. I'll make some toast."

7.15am 16th December

There're voices downstairs. I don't know how I got back to bed, but I must have slept soundly. I wonder how long they've been up. I get up, and find my mobile on the table by my bed. There's no sign of my gun.

There are clean clothes hanging on the back of a chair – not mine. I remember how I arrived, soaking wet and smelling of rotting flesh, with flecks of blood all over my clothes. They put them straight in the washing machine – no questions asked – and now the farmer has lent me his clothes. They are a bit wide for me – he's a well-built man – but the height works. I tuck the plaid shirt into his cord trousers and tighten them up with a belt. In the mirror I look like I've shrunk in the night, and it's true that a part of me has gone missing. The part that had a wife, and never tried to kill anyone. With a sigh, I wash my face and clean my teeth, open the door and quietly walk downstairs. The voices have stopped, but I can hear the clink of spoons on dishes.

"Ah, Rackham," Grimwode looks up at me from his bowl of porridge. "Come and have some breakfast, then we'll leave these good people in peace."

I can see that the 'good people' are slightly scared of Grimwode. He gives out an aura of power and authority. His face is steel rather than granite, but this morning, there is the saving grace of a kindly glint in his eyes that appears every now and then.

"Thanks for last night," I say to the farmer, wondering whether I should ask where my gun has got to.

"No problem. I had to get up for the animals at four. This is my second breakfast." He smiles, looking at me enveloped in his clothes. "You can borrow those, your clothes are nearly dry. Cerys has put them in a bag for you. Oh, and there's this:" He goes over to the Welsh dresser and picks up my drawing of the granite man as described by Betty.

"Thank you," I say.

"He did that last night. Good, isn't he?" The farmer's all smiles.

"Rackham and his drawings," Grimwode says. He glances at it, and nearly chokes on his porridge.

"Are you alright, D... Sir? Is it your injury?" I look at him, and he's using all his formidable skill to regain his composure.

"Yes. Eat up, Rackham," his voice is slightly gravelly. "We'd better get going."

I finish my porridge, then thank Cerys and look at the farmer wondering how to tackle the gun thing. Standing up, I pick up the bag of damp clothes, and go over to the painting – the bullet hole is obscured by the bin liner they have put it in.

"Have I got everything?" I ask.

The farmer walks over to the dresser and unlocks a drawer. Pulling out my gun, he looks from Grimwode to me.

"Thought I'd better look after it last night after... well, er, Mr Rackham seemed to be very upset."

Grimwode puts out his hand and takes the gun, checks the magazine, his face inscrutable as ever.

"Thank you, you've been very kind to er...my friend. Mr..."

"Evans. No problem. I've seen Mr Rackham around this area for many years. Glad to help."

I follow Grimwode as he walks stiffly out to his sleek black car.

"Hop in," he says. "Thought I'd better drive myself today."

"So you're better."

"Getting there. Thing is, Rackham," he laughs in his sardonic way, as I get into the comfortable leather seat beside him, having put the ruined painting on the back seat. "It's thee and me now. I can't trust a soul."

He switches the car on, and we purr out of the farm.

"So," he says as we drive slowly down the lanes towards St David's.

"So?"

"What did you do last night that made Mr Evans take your gun away and lock it in a drawer?"

"He thought I was going to shoot myself."

"And were you?" He sounds vaguely interested.

"I have these…"

"… episodes, I know."

"And I got confused. I was always afraid that would happen. It's why I didn't want to carry a gun in the first place."

"But you'd be dead at least twice by now if you hadn't been able to protect yourself. Listen, Rackham, I want you to carry it for a little longer…"

"I killed a man last night, and I meant to."

"We think you missed, but the bullet ricocheted off the wall of the cave and hit him in the temple."

"So you got there? You saw Betty?" My voice wobbles a bit. "Listen Dick, it was dark. I fired in the general direction. I killed him on purpose."

"You had to, Rackham. No choice."

"That's the problem with guns."

307

"Anyway, there were no bullets left in the magazine. You couldn't have shot yourself," he says, as if that dismisses the whole matter. "Fortunately, I have brought along some more ammunition for you."

I shudder at the thought of more ammunition. "So, what next? Why still the gun?"

"Last night, you turned things round. They're on the run now. That woman…"

"…Anna…"

"Anna, as you say, did not get back to The harrumph…White Crusader. When we got there, there was no sign of it. She took her dinghy round the island. Dawson said he turned up in a borrowed boat and gave chase, and the fool managed to get the boat grounded on the rocks. Shots were exchanged and she shot out their searchlight."

"Dawson?"

"Yes, why?"

My mind goes into overdrive: Dawson should have searched Skomer island after Braithwaite's body was washed up; Dawson stopped me from catching Anna in Oxford, and then managed to lose her; Dawson gave me the treacherous little black phone; Dawson sent my brother to the safe house; Dawson recommended the ice-cream parlour in Hay-on-Wye.

"So it was Dawson taking pot shots at me."

"What are you talking about, Rackham?" Grimwode has that old edge to his voice.

"I was the one in the dinghy escaping from the island. Anna had long gone back to the yacht."

"The fool said it was the Anna woman."

"And you believed him? That was me he was pursuing, and he knew it perfectly well. He must have got a full view of my face. It was me that shot his bloody light out. He, or one of his goons, put a bullet through the middle of the painting."

"What?"

"Well, it could have been worse, it could have gone through me."

"Harrumph!" is all Grimwode can say.

"I ended up with two bullet holes through the bottom of the boat. Was lucky to get to the beach."

"So the dinghy we found on the beach…"

"Was mine. Well, Pete's actually."

"Who's Pete?" Grimwode is beginning to sound very out of sorts.

"A fisherman from Haven, just down the coast. I hired him to take me out to Skomer in his boat. He lent me his dinghy so I could get onto the island, and said he'd return in an hour. When Dawson arrived, I thought it was Pete until they started shooting at me." A nasty thought crosses my mind. "And where's Pete? What's happened to him? If Dawson was in his boat…"

"You're sure about all this?"

"Were there any other boats out looking for Anna?"

"Not at that point. Dawson was first on the scene. He said he'd spotted this Anna woman and tried to cut her off. I did wonder how he got there so quickly." I can hear the cogs turning in Grimwode's mind. "This puts a different complexion on things." He presses something on the car's display screen. There's a short pause. "Jackson? Grimwode. We think One's gone AWOL… grounded a boat trying to eliminate Duck… yes, him… no, it wasn't by mistake… yes, definitely AWOL. Yes… goodbye."

I remember Jackson – a powerful woman, who must be Grimwode's equal in another department. I trusted her. I hope that was well founded.

"My message to you asking for help must have been intercepted. That's why Anna and her friend turned up so soon, and came into the cave with guns blazing. They knew I was there."

"Yes... bloody leaks everywhere. The whole ship is full of holes. No safe communication. Like I said."

"But you can trust Jackson?"

"Sometimes, Rackham, you know nothing, which is probably just as well," he mutters to himself as much as to me. "We'd better go and find this Pete. Haven, didn't you say?"

"Yes. Just hope he's OK."

"Dawson wouldn't be stupid enough to leave a trail of dead bodies behind him."

I find myself hoping he's right about that as we drive down the narrow lanes to Haven.

"So they found the bodies in the cave, and that was all?" I ask.

"Yes, two fresh, and one very dead."

"That was Alan Hunt."

"I thought so. We will check of course."

"Betty told me." It's like she's still alive.

"Ah yes, your wife. Sorry about..."

"I'm surprised they shot her and missed me." Something catches in the back of my throat.

"Maybe they thought she would tell you something."

"We were singing when they opened fire." It suddenly comes back, and I swallow hard.

"But they didn't get you. That is curious."

"I dived in front of the painting. They didn't want to damage it. Millions of pounds' worth."

"Have you looked at it?"

"No. Haven't had a chance. But it does have that bullet hole through the middle."

"Yes. So you said." He breathes in sharply. I don't know if it's the pain of his injury, or his sudden realisation that we've damaged millions of pounds worth of fine art. "Anyway, it won't do them any good."

We go down the steep winding lane and into Haven.

"He works from the quayside," I tell Grimwode. "On the left after the bridge."

"Home ground to you, eh, Rackham? I hope we don't have to search the place for this..."

"Pete."

We park by the quay. Grimwode eases himself out of his seat with the merest of grunts.

"Lead the way, Rackham."

We walk down the quay, past a couple of sheds, and see a small figure with his back to us, crouched over a lobster pot.

"Pete!" Relief floods over me. At least he's not dead.

Pete turns round slowly. He has a scowl on his face. Stands up. Looks Grimwode up and down, standing there in his black suit. "You must be the insurance," he says. "That was quick."

"Pete, this is a police colleague of mine. We've come to find out what happened last night." I look at Grimwode – the expression on his face is difficult to read, but there's a smile somewhere.

"I thought you'd know. They were your friends, waving their bloody police identities in front of my face. Said they needed to get out there fast to rescue you, but it was too dangerous for me to come." Pete spits on the ground. "Phil said he saw my boat in pieces on the rocks, when he went out this morning. Your fuck...ing friends never came back. I was waiting to see what would happen, and here you are. Safe and sound." He looks as though he thinks I should at least be in hospital.

"Listen Mr..."

"Davis."

311

"Mr Davis," Grimwode continues, and I can see he has caught Pete off guard. "We think Inspector Rackham's 'friends' were taking pot-shots at him from your boat. We need to know who they were."

"They what?" Pete looks from me to Grimwode and back again.

"Pete. Did you hear any names?" As I ask this, I am conscious of Grimwode playing with his phone.

"No. No names. It was all so quick. Just thought I should co-operate with the police. Help them rescue you."

"Can you describe any of them?" I ask, gently.

"The leader was very tall, and he had a very prominent, what's that thing... oh, Adam's apple."

"Is this him?" Grimwode suddenly thrusts his mobile phone in front of Pete's face.

"That's the one."

I catch a glimpse of Dawson's image, and Grimwode and I exchange glances.

"About my boat," Pete is back on the attack.

"You're insured, aren't you?"

"But I loved that boat. She was like a wife to me."

"Worse things happen at sea." Grimwode looks at me, and I look down at the stone and grit. "We will make sure the police co-operate with your insurance, but in the meantime, I would advise you to talk to no-one about our discussion here. For your own safety, you understand?"

Poor Pete. He was so willing to help. "Pete, I'm really sorry this happened to you. You helped me out, and now..." I wave my arms in the general direction of the sea.

"If they come back, here's a number to call." Grimwode gives him a card. "Don't let on that we've spoken to you, but keep in sight of other people if you can."

We walk back to the car. I can feel Pete's eyes boring into the back of my head.

"What are you going to do about Dawson?"

"Let him run. See where it leads."

"But he must know I'll say he knew it was me in the searchlight."

"He'll say it was dark, and he couldn't tell."

"But you don't believe him?"

"No I don't Rackham."

So Dawson's One, and I'm Duck. For how much longer? I wonder.

"They're safe," says Grimwode, as we drive smoothly down the dual carriageway from St Clears to Carmarthen.

"And you're sure about that?"

"I keep telling you."

"But how can we trust anyone now?"

"Listen, Rackham, much though it pains me to say so, you are a key player in all this. We can't afford to have them getting to you through your loved ones. They're safe."

"But I can't..."

"No, you can't contact them. Like I said..."

I take a deep breath and try to trust him.

"So what now?"

"The National Botanic Gardens of Wales."

"The what? Why?"

"Meeting Jackson there."

"Oh, right."

We sit in silence like the old couple that we are, as Grimwode negotiates us round Carmarthen and off the A40 towards the Botanic Gardens.

"Didn't I see a sign for the gardens just up there?" I say after we've gone a few miles through smaller lanes winding across unknown countryside.

"Satnav says up here," says Grimwode, but he doesn't sound convinced.

"And you trust it?"

"Mmmh, can you look at the map?" Grimwode is so used to being driven, that he's lost the 'finding places' instinct.

I get the map out. "Looks ambiguous. Can't tell exactly where..."

"Bloody hell! Idiot! Keep on your side of the road!" shouts Grimwode as a small silver car coming from the opposite direction nearly collides with us. I catch a glimpse of the driver. Looks like Anna. Can't be. I am imagining stuff now.

"I think we need to turn round, go back a couple of miles. We must have missed the turning."

It's a while before we can find anywhere to turn. The car skids and complains on the frozen muddy surface of the track we back into. Ignoring the satnav, which is trying to leave us in a field, we find the entrance to the gardens. Not many cars are parked in the various bits of carpark. The little silver car is parked behind some trees, I notice. I make a mental note that it's a VW Polo, and try to remember the registration number. Grimwode pulls his black limo up by a large and equally black Range Rover, creaks his way out of his seat, gesturing me to stay where I am, and gets in the back of the Range Rover.

Ten minutes go past. I can't see inside the Range Rover as it has privacy glass, but I can guess there's a heated discussion going on. The emotions of the past twenty-four hours begin to catch up with me – the image of the body and the painting, the feel of Betty's warm dead weight in my arms. I'm going to start breaking down if I don't do something, and I begin to wonder whether that really was Anna in the silver Polo. Perhaps I should go and check out the gardens.

I get out of the car, just as Grimwode gets out of the Range Rover.

"Where are you off to, Rackham? Get back in. Need a word." He creaks back into his car. I slump back in my seat like a sulky teenager.

"What's going on?" I mutter.

"None of your concern," he says. "Jackson and I need to get back to London. I'm going with her, as we have a lot to discuss. You know how to drive a car?" he carries on in his most sarcastic tone of voice. "You can have this one – but leave here a bit later, and try not to go the same way or catch us up. Here's the key. Ammunition is in the glove compartment, and, oh yes, here is another mobile which won't have been hacked into... yet. Try to be circumspect if you have to contact me. We don't want to set Dawson onto you with another gun-happy troupe, do we?"

"How do I...?"

"The car is traceable. Stick close to it and we'll know where you are."

"I meant..."

"Goodbye, Rackham. Go carefully." He's out of the car surprisingly quickly.

"But..." how do I start it? I meant to say. It looks nothing like my battered old Vauxhall.

The Range Rover beside me glides off, leaving me in this large posh car that's as foreign to me as a spaceship. Instead of a speedometer and a few other instruments, a small blank screen greets my gaze. I wish I'd paid more attention to what Grimwode was doing as we drove along.

There must be a manual in the glove compartment, but all I can find in it is a box of bullets. Do I really want to go this way? Continue on this path of destruction? Am I going to kill someone else?

'Go carefully,' Grimwode said. He's lent me his big fast car, given me ammunition, a phone. He knows how dangerous this is.

317

"Go carefully," I say to myself as I load the magazine and push it into the handle of my gun. It feels so familiar now, this gun. So necessary. Images of the shooting outside our cottage – the dog being gunned down, protecting Peggy – all come back to me. Then, with a jolt, the feeling of Betty's dead body. I don't know where my head is, and I don't feel safe – I shouldn't have this gun – I need this gun…

With a deep sigh, I put it in my pocket. Time to go and explore the gardens – maybe it was Anna I saw in the Polo, in which case I should go and look for her. I lock the car by pressing the little padlock icon on the lump of plastic they call a key, and the car obliges me by tucking its wing mirrors in with a rasping squeak.

Having paid to go in, and picked up the leaflet, I realise this garden is on a big scale – plenty of places to lose Anna if she's here. To my right there's a lake with small white huts by it, and woodland behind. To my left there are a number of old buildings. Signs point to a walled garden, a butterfly house, an apothecary. In front of me is a small circle of water that is the bottom end of a winding stream that comes all the way down from the top of a hill. As I look up I see a large glass dome. Checking in my leaflet, I read that it is the largest single-dome greenhouse in the world, and it has a café.

There are very few people about as I walk up the hill, occasionally hopping over the little stream. They all look retired – not much different from me – taking advantage of their free time to explore this place before the hordes of children descend on it during the Christmas holidays. It is designed to appeal to children – one massive playground of botanical information. I feel a deep pang of sadness at never having had a child with Betty – the ruin of our marriage, and her death.

Large glass doors slide open to let me into the dome. The main part of the building is taken up with a number of concrete paths leading past flowerbeds with plants from all over the world. To my left are a series of rooms set into the side of the dome. The World of Fungi, various art and craft displays, and after following these round I find the Café Med – appropriately named, as the temperature in the dome is comfortably warm, and there are tables set outside the café so that you can have your coffee looking out over the mass of exotic plants that makes up the central part of the dome.

I get a cappuccino from the counter, and a healthy-looking confection made of oats, and sit down to look at the strange shapes of the various plants in front of me. My position doesn't give me full view of the dome, and I am slightly concealed behind something frondy, which could be useful if my quarry should come this way. I sip my coffee and eat the pleasantly sweet oat bar, waiting and wondering. Dark images start to come back into my mind, and I realise that action is the only way I'm going to dispel them. Reluctantly, I get up from my table and start my search of the dome.

I walk back towards the main entrance, intending to make a thorough search down all the pathways that circle inside the dome. I pass the entrance to The World of Fungi – a dark and colourful sign inviting me to explore. I feel the nudge of the dog pushing me to go through the doorway, and who am I to ignore such a good ghost?

"Is not working."

The exhibition is in two rooms. The darkness is lit by cases exhibiting various fungi – from the well-known to the strange and unfamiliar. Low voices drift to me from the next room. One of the voices is Anna's.

"We think it's working very well." A man's voice. Clipped. Public-school.

"But we can see no new order. We're losing ground…" Anna's voice is blotted out by the sound of a trolley rattling on the concrete outside.

"… paintings. You said you wanted help…" The man's voice again.

"… Rackham…" Hearing Anna's voice spit out my name makes me jump, and bang my head against the glass case exhibiting a particularly colourful fungus.

"Shhh. Someone's…" I hear their footsteps getting quieter – they must be leaving The World of Fungi. Cautiously, my hand on my Glock, I ease my way into the next room. It's empty. A display showing how fungi saves the world greets me – Anna and her contact have gone.

Looking out of the doorway into the main dome I can see two figures walking towards the entrance. They pause, and then turn down one of the pathways that run past the flowerbeds showing plants from all over the world. I walk quickly to the entrance, and see them in deep conversation down one of the central aisles. I take another path, which will bring me level with them, but hopefully I'll be concealed by the tall plants that separate each route. The sign says they are South African plants. They're broad and bushy, giving me good cover, but as I get closer to Anna and her friend, I find that my path is going downhill as theirs goes up. They stop. I am looking at their feet through a lacework of greens and browns.

"… O'Connell…" Anna's voice.

"Leave him to us. He's still worth a fortune. We can…"

They start walking off, and I am destined to sink as they rise. My path leads me down, and as I turn a corner I see a shallow lake, and a high wall in front of me. The path seems to be circling round, and I am hoping theirs will do the same above me. Fish of various sizes and colours dart away from the side of the path as I pass, and I turn the corner to see the path rising. Looking up, I can see them on a metal bridge directly above me. They have stopped and are looking down at the lake. I quickly make my way under the bridge, where I can see their feet through the grating. I stay there till they move on, and then start to walk up my path, hoping that they are going in the same direction on the higher path. As I pass a sign telling me I am with plants from California, I can see their feet on the path above me, and I realise that we are heading for the main exit.

"...you'll tell him?" Anna's voice sounds tentative, uncertain.

"Yes, I'll..."

I am almost at the end of my path and they at the end of theirs when Anna turns in my direction and our eyes meet through the green fronds of some exotic plant.

Her eyes widen, "Rackham!"

I round the corner to face them. The man is tall, in his forties, wearing a dark suit and tie. For some reason he makes me think of an accountant. There's an uncertain pause, as I wonder whether to take out my gun and arrest them there and then. But they turn and run back up their path.

I run after them.

I don't shout.

We are all silent.

They run away.

I chase them.

It's like a kids' game in this beautiful playground.

Anna suddenly turns and jumps through the flowerbed labelled Western Australia, and her companion runs on up the path. I pause, uncertain whether I should follow Anna and trample through the precious plants. I can't bring myself do it, so I run back and round onto the lower path.

I can't see Anna, but I run on, thinking she must be making for the lake. She can't have got far enough to be out of my line of vision. But as I round the corner, there's no Anna.

I hear the bang of a door behind me, and a high-pitched alarm starts up. Back up my path there is an alleyway on the left. The sound is coming from there, and I run down the alley and turn a corner to find an emergency exit door open. She must have set the alarm off.

I go outside to see her running down the hill towards the main exit of the gardens.

"Sir. Excuse me…" A young man is coming towards me wearing a green sweatshirt with the National Botanic Gardens emblem embroidered on the front.

"Police!" I shout, as I run down the path after Anna. I have no warrant card to wave at him. I just hope he believes me. He doesn't try to stop me.

Anna is going through the front building which marks the way in. I notice that the way out is to the side, and obediently go that way instead of following her the wrong way. Maybe she won't be able get out that way, I hope. But as I go through the exit gate, I see her running across the car park towards the little Polo. She starts the engine.

I run for my sleek black limo, but as I watch, a little girl runs out onto the road and falls flat on her face right in the path of Anna's car. Anna screeches to a halt and gets out of her car, lifts the crying girl up and puts her by the side of the road, gets back in and drives off.

As I go towards my car, I'm fumbling for my key to open the door, but as I get near, the wing mirrors move out with a little creak, and I find that the door opens without needing me to press any key fob.

Anna's driving towards the entrance of the car park. The crying girl is being comforted by her parents. I try to start my car.

Nowhere to stick the key in.

There's a button labelled 'Start'. I press it. Nothing happens. Then the blank screen where the instruments should be blinks alive with the words 'depress brake to start car.'

I depress the brake.

Nothing happens.

The car is on but there is no engine.

There's no clutch pedal either.

I try the accelerator pedal.

Nothing.

In frustration, I jab randomly at the start button and the brake pedal.

Nothing.

Anna has gone.

'Calm down, Arnold,' I say to myself. 'Take a deep breath.'

The trouble is that I've always driven cheap, old, geared cars. I've been driven by others in more modern expensive ones – I have never paid attention – never asked.

Now I have to work this out.

Do things in order.

Press brake pedal.

Press 'Start'.

No.

Press brake pedal and leave foot on.

Press 'Start'.

The engine hums into life.

I move the lever that has taken the place of gears.

D means drive, I guess.

I don't move.

Ah, foot off brake.

I start moving towards the tree directly in front of me.

Quick! Brake! Nearly bang my head on the windscreen, the brake is so sudden.

R must be reverse.

Foot off brake.

Start moving backwards.

Someone toots their horn from behind me.

Quick! Brake! Bang my head on the headrest behind me.

Struggle to get seatbelt on with foot on brake.

Looking round, there's nothing behind me, and I slowly back out of my space.

Brake, shift lever into D, and we're off.

God knows where Anna is by now.

1.02pm 16th December

I'm on the A40 heading east. I'm guessing Anna drove this way – away from the coast and her latest crime that she has left behind. It's been slow getting the hang of this car. It's basically quite simple to drive, but so full of distracting gizmos that I find myself losing concentration and drifting into the middle of the road. I've managed to work out the air con, where the lights are, how to turn the windscreen wipers on. I've fried my bum on my heated seat, and now am wrestling with the onscreen media buttons trying to find Radio 4. Ah, here we are. Press onscreen button. Try to keep on your side of the road.

"… helicopter came down off the coast of Scotland last week. Government has now confirmed that it was carrying a number of peace negotiators and a senior military figure. No survivors found…"

Putting all those important people in one helicopter? A risky thing to do.

"… eyewitness accounts say they heard a roar and saw a bright yellow flash as the helicopter exploded…"

Doesn't sound like an accident.

"… McNeil said he saw a flash from his fishing boat. Called the coastguard…"

I was out at sea last night, being shot at, but this sounds…

"... minister spoke to us earlier. 'We now suspect that the helicopter was deliberately targeted by terrorists trying to prevent a settlement...'"

My mind wanders onto that list, the list that's been at the centre of all this – Grimwode wouldn't tell me details – he didn't trust me. Who was being targeted? Peace negotiators? Peace-promoting politicians?

"... 'suspect this is part of a long term campaign to destabilise any attempts to end conflicts peacefully. This is the third incident in the last month. Two political figures murdered, and also other members of the security services under threat. We are on high alert...'"

And I'm getting hungry, really really hungry. I feel like I haven't eaten properly for a week. Thoughts of Hay-on-Wye and the tapas bar and the ice cream parlour invade my mind, blocking out anything else.

"... which makes that seven incidents since September, doesn't it minister?"

After Brecon, I'll head up to Hay-on-Wye. After all, I met Anna there in the first place, and Grimwode told me not to go directly to London. Makes sense.

"... dog ownership is at an all-time high, our home correspondent reports. Incidents of canine fights and attacks on people are also up, and there is the problem of dog poo. Councils are reporting that they don't have the funds or manpower to collect the plastic bags from the containers provided fast enough to keep up with demand."

Me and my dog are not a part of this anymore, unless you count ghost-dogs with ghost-poos. But isn't the radio wonderful? From terrorist threat to our nation to the overflowing dog-poo containers. There must be a metaphor there somewhere. There clearly isn't enough money around.

I pass through Sennybridge, a name I connect with training army officers. Wonder if I'll see some. Does this make me feel safe, or threatened?

"... reports that arms sales are up massively since the last election, especially to repressive regimes. The Guardian newspaper reports that nearly five billion pounds worth of..."

I wonder what Anna and her terrorist organisation will make of that? Aren't they fighting 'repressive regimes'? Are we a repressive regime? We certainly seem to be supporting them elsewhere.

"... has found that of the forty-nine countries that are classed as "not free" by Freedom House, the independent organisation that promotes democracy, thirty-six have bought British-made weapons under the current government."

Is this what I'm working for? I feel the gun burning a hole in my pocket. My gun? Or Grimwode's gun? And what are Grimwode and Jackson up to? Is it just about tracking down Dawson and co, or is there something bigger? I am driving his car. Who knows it's his car? Am I a decoy duck again, pulling pursuit away from him? 'Go carefully', he said.

A tremendous bang on the side of the car wakes me from my reverie. And then something hits the windscreen with such a force that a fine crack appears in the bottom right-hand corner. Must have been stones thrown up by a passing car. I look in my mirror and see a Land Rover disappearing rapidly in the opposite direction. Grimwode won't like this. His nice car being scratched and dented by passing Land Rovers.

I drive on towards Brecon, trees and fields on either side, and the massive beauty of the Beacons emerging in front of me. I notice a helicopter flying low, and coming towards me at speed. Mountain rescue? I wonder. The helicopter comes lower, and literally zooms over my head. I duck involuntarily, and the car swerves. It's gone past me and is shooting down the road, flying low. Army? Practising manoeuvres? Seems a bit excessive.

The radio has been on, chuntering away and unheeded by me, but I hear a sudden change of tone:

"... breaking news: Sir Reginald Stone has been arrested in what police describe as a successful naval operation in the Irish Sea..."

Irish Sea? I was there...

"... his yacht, The White Crusader. Navy vessels gave chase after it refused to respond to a request to board. Government sources have refused to comment so far..."

What? Sir Reginald Stone, Sir Reginald Stone... the name is irritatingly familiar. Is he some kind of philanthropist?

"... a blanket of silence. Our Middle East correspondent..."

Middle East?

"... friends in the highest places. Nobody seems willing to comment on what must be the most embarrassing scandal to break out in government. The weather..."

Abrupt change? I wonder if they got a signal to shut up. I personally know how the owner of The White Crusader is connected with terrorism in the most direct way. I guess this is highly embarrassing that this news has broken, for everyone. From government to security services. I bet they didn't want this coming out into the public awareness. So Reggie is our man with the granite face – my drawing that made Grimwode choke on his cornflakes. "You're sure about the name?" I remember Grimwode's uncharacteristically uncertain tone when I told him I'd seen The White Crusader at Rosslare.

I set this up. I started it.

The heated discussion in Jackson's Range Rover must have been about that. God, they acted fast!

I'm driving on the ring road round Brecon. A convoy of military Land Rovers passes by on the opposite carriageway at speed, and it makes me wonder about the Land Rover and helicopter earlier. Things are moving. Forces are gathering, and I am hungry.

At the roundabout I turn up the road to Hay. I might pick up something nice at the ice cream parlour. Certainly ice cream.

It begins to snow, and I wonder how Grimwode's limo will cope with slippery conditions. There's been no sign of snow anywhere since I got back from Riga, but now there's snow, and it makes me think of Peggy. Where is she? Locked up somewhere for her own safety. I can't contact her. I long to contact her, to hear her voice.

I feel cold inside.

Dead dog.

Dead wife.

Injured love.

Nobody's safe. And I used to think I could make people safe!

2.35pm 16th December

The car park is nearly empty when I arrive at Hay. The snow has settled – not deep, but enough to cause the car to send me alarming messages about skidding. The brakes make a grinding noise, and the steering wheel has got a mind of its own. I manage to manoeuvre my prima donna car into what I think must be a parking space by some recycling bins. Looking round, I think I can see a small grey VW at the other corner of the car park. There's no-one around.

I step out into the snow – it's spookily silent, as though waiting for something. I have that feeling of being watched, and I walk away from the car and look up to the town. Was there a glint of binoculars caught by the sun, which has made an appearance to brighten up the white world the snow has left?

Something about Grimwode's car catches my eye. The stone damage is far worse than I expected. Grimwode will not be pleased at what has happened to his precious limo while I was driving it. I take a closer look: the dent on the driver's door, just below the window is deep, as though something pointed has been driven hard into it. The point of it, which I stick my finger into, has penetrated the paint and some of the metal, but has come up against something hard. The windscreen damage is odd too: whatever hit it got so far and then bounced off, leaving a small crack.

Something with that force should have shattered the windscreen.

It dawns on me that this is a bullet-proof car, and these were bullets, not stones, that hit me. The Land Rover, the helicopter, the fast military convoy, all going in the opposite direction – a drama was being played out right in front of my eyes. Now I wonder if those bullets were meant for me, or for Grimwode.

I shiver and pull my coat round me, lock the door with the remote key, and walk up through the car park with my ghost-dog at my side. I cross the road and go into the alleyway that opens out into a small cluster of shops.

"How's your garden?" A voice behind me makes me jump, and reach convulsively for my gun.

I turn, expecting a threatening figure, and see a tall man standing in his shop doorway, with a gentle smile on his face.

"Did you find what you wanted?" He speaks gently, and I remember going into his shop, and Peggy thinking I was having one of my episodes. I pull out a tissue, and make the pretence of blowing my nose.

"No, but it's too late now, isn't it?" I reply.

"There are things you can plant in winter. Come up in the spring."

Spring. Will I ever make the spring?

"Actually, I'm looking for food."

He looks down at his watch, and frowns.

"You could still get a baguette at True Ewe, and there's…"

"…ice cream." I look at him and smile a goodbye, turn, and make my way past the shops and down a narrow alleyway to the town centre.

There're a few people about, mainly elderly – looking for books no doubt. I step off the pavement, and nearly get mown down by a car, driven slowly by an elderly lady intent on running over anything in her way. I see the welcoming front windows of the ice cream parlour, and enter the warm café, hoping that they are still serving baguettes.

The Polish girl behind the counter frowns. "No, we run out. Sorry."

I settle for a double scoop of chocolate ice cream, and a large double-shot cappuccino. I am the only customer, so I settle down in the window, and watch the people as they walk past, reflected in the mirror that faces me.

Nearly everyone is old. This is a place for the old person who has seen the earnest bustle of life, and just wants to reflect, read, browse books, eat good ice cream. I could live here. Settle here for the final stage of my life, however long that might be.

But not very long, the way things are at the moment – and anyway, if I survive, there's Peggy, my rejuvenator. I can't go all old and fusty on her.

I absent-mindedly take my Glock out and put it on the table in front of me. Looking round, I can see that nobody would be able to see it, and I look down at it as if a gun could give me the answers I am looking for. Since September, I have been shot at how many times? I have shot, I have maimed, I have killed. I even tried to shoot myself. This thing in front of me – it's not a good thing. It is made to do harm.

'Go carefully.'

'… arms sales are up massively…'

'White Crusader.'

'Granite is the hardest stone.'

The gun glints at me. It is an attractive shape. Comfortable to hold. Comforting to have. Pull the trigger, and out comes a little bullet. But what then?

My ice cream is beginning to melt down the sides of the cone and onto my hand. I lick it. Delicious. A man eating an ice cream with a gun in front of him. Put it away, a voice inside me says. But I look up at the mirror at that moment, and see a face. It is gentle, careworn. The face of a woman who has known pain, cared for loved ones, protected her family from the dangers and evils of the world. It is vulnerable. It is Anna's face as I've never seen it.

The face disappears, and the next thing I know is the cold breeze on my back as the ice cream parlour door opens, and Anna's voice as she orders an espresso.

I look round. She is looking at me. The shrew-like look has returned, and she has one hand in her pocket. I think it's a gun, and that she's going to shoot me there and then – third time lucky. I have my hand on my Glock, knowing it would be too late to stop her, but she brings out her wallet to pay for her coffee, picks up her cup, and comes to sit on the other side of my table.

Her eyes widen as she sees my gun lying on the table in front of me. I still have my hand on it. Ready.

"So," she says, by way of an opening.

"So?" I reply. I look at her face, trying to see the person I saw in the mirror. It must be there, just beneath the surface.

"What you want?"

"To stop you."

"Stop…me? Ha!"

I try to read her face. There's a flicker of uncertainty there – something of the face in the mirror there.

"Why do you want to do it? To murder all these people?"

"Murder? That's word you always use. Is not murder, is assassinate," she hisses.

"Call it what you like: assassinate, eliminate, take out, remove, it's still killing them. Wrecking their families." I feel a warm muzzle resting on my knee. "You killed my dog."

"Dog?" she spits out. "What's that you have under table?"

"The ghost of my dog, he comes back…"

"You worry about dog? You have no idea…"

"You've tried to kill me…"

"Yes, but you're like cat. You have, how they say, nine lives…"

"Nine lives? But my wife…"

"Your wife?" she hisses. "You no love your wife. She no love you. Don't give me your wife."

The bodies in the cave come back to me – her warmth. The last chance of love. I did love her then, when she was dead. I look down at my gun, and to my dismay it is covered in melted chocolate ice cream. This interchange with Anna, has caused me to lose my concentration on what I came here to do – eat ice cream. Most of it has fallen out of the cone and onto my gun. I look at what's left in the cone and take a bite. Anna has got her iPad out and is looking at it intently.

My phone vibrates. I gobble the last of the ice cream down, and reach in my pocket with sticky fingers. Looking at the little screen, all I can see is rows of numbers that mean nothing.

Anna's pad vibrates on the table. She looks down sharply and quickly covers the screen with its protective flap.

"So," I say. "Why kill all these people? People who want peace."

"Peace?" She pronounces it 'piss'. "Peace? What you know about peace? You live your little safe suburban life in your little middle-class town. Yes I know all about your little town. Very good place for us to operate. Right under your nose."

335

"But… why…kill?"

"I tell you story. You listen good?"

"Hang on." The sea of melted chocolate is gradually spreading across the table. I get up and walk to the counter, careful to keep my body between the waitress and my gun. I ask for a cloth and turn abruptly, hoping that she doesn't glimpse what's on the table. I sit down and start to mop.

"When I am young, Latvia is good place to be if you like music. I study piano and teach for living. But I am always thinking about politics, more important for me, and Latvia bad place to be under the Russians, so when I get older, and it's easier to leave, I go to join Red Cross. Save lives. I work as nurse for long time, very long time…"

"But if you are a nurse, why didn't you help Stash? You just ran away."

"I can't… go… near… I can't do it any more. Listen," she looks me in the eyes. "I tell… in that time, those many years, I see things change. Red Cross is respect once, but then hospitals get attacked. More and more. I am addict, I have to keep going back, to see more death and suffering. If I stay away, I can't sleep. Have nightmares. Go crazy. So I go back. We have campaign to try to get things changed. Peace negotiators say they will make better. Nothing gets better. They are useless. They make noises, but do nothing. I hate."

"But they try, don't they? It's better than doing nothing."

"No, no, no!" Anna hisses. "Is worse. It make the powers look like they try to make better, but they never. It make them look good, but they are bad. Very bad."

My phone buzzes. I decide to ignore it. "So how?"

Her iPad bleeps, but she carries on. "When I work in hospital I meet many people who fight against superpower aggressors. They are tired, wounded, many die when our hospital is bombed, but some survive. We meet. We talk.

336

We want to bring the powerful to their knees. Their peace talk is a sham, and we know it. They want oil, they want control.

"Then one day this man contact us. He is very powerful, and he agree our view. He want to help, to fund us. He has contact in UK. He says we get organize. We make list of the powerful and the peacemakers. Is the only way, he says. There's too much suffering in the world. The poor, the starving, caught in war made by superpowers, as they use these people, these parts of world to fight for domination. They do what they like, the powerful, and they use their so-called negotiators to pretend to try and stop killing. But they don't stop."

"But you kill."

"But only few. You go out there and see what it's like. Thousands die. Women, children. Your country bomb and kill and spread disease. Your press don't report, but if someone die here, is all over papers. Your country is disgusting, it gets machines to do its killings, while you sit here in your comfortable houses, pointing at us, calling us the terrorists."

"But how did you expect to improve things by more killing? Surely..."

"We want to bring world to its knees, like after World War. Then we can start new order. Fairer. New United Nations, not toothless one we have now."

"So you kill. I am surprised you have so many..."

"Why you surprised? You harm so many people with your professional killers. We have recruits from all over: Kosovo, Azerbaijan, Albania, Iraq. We have experienced fighters from old Yugoslavia, and we have people in Britain. We have one of yours, at least."

"Who?"

"Son of door. He protect me. He like ice cream. He would be here now, but..."

337

"But?" I look round at the door, expecting him to come in any moment.

"But... I don't know. I think he's dead."

"Dawson?" I remember the shots fired at my car. The helicopter. The armed convoy. I wonder if *our* killers got him, then.

"So this list. How long have you been..?"

"Couple of years, but only now we have effect. Then we discover..."

"What?"

On a whim, I delve inside my coat pocket and take out a crumpled piece of paper, smooth it out, and place it in front of Anna.

"Very good. You do?"

"Yes. Who is that?"

"You don't know?" She smiles, and I notice for the first time that she has a front tooth missing.

"It's him, isn't it? Your man, your funder."

She nods. "Yes, is him. It doesn't matter now. Your people know. They don't tell you?"

"No. They don't trust me."

"No trust you – why?"

"I make mistakes."

"We all make mistakes. We made mistake with him. Big mistake."

"I thought he helped you."

Anna pushes her iPad towards me. "Look. Those numbers. That is arms sales. His arms sales. He deal in arms. He sell to one side, then he sell to the other. People like him make the best profit out of these wars. We should have known. He give us such good modern weapons."

"Like the one that shot down that helicopter."

"Like that... but he just wants to make sure there are no negotiations, so he can sell more arms. He doesn't care

338

about us. He leads us up garden path. He gets us to do his dirty work so he can make more money."

"Why did you believe he would help you?"

"He is politician, adviser to government. Very big, important man, and we are in, what you say, maelstrom, and along he comes with plan. We need someone like this. This focus us, and we decide to trust him. He give us what we need, and says he agrees with us, it all seems to work until…"

"Until?"

"Until now. Now we discover that it is not working. Nothing works. Nothing." She looks distractedly out of the window, and I wonder if she's seen something, or if it's the drone of a helicopter close overhead that has attracted her attention. The thought comes to me that it might be Grimwode's team and they might catch up with us. They will know where the car is.

My phone vibrates again. I look down and see the text message:

Where are you?

"What about the paintings?" I try to distract her.

"Painting?" she looks disgusted. "You and your painting. Is big mistake. We should have leave them, but instead spend too much time trying to sell. Is very difficult. We have no contacts, but this man, he say he help." Her iPad makes a sound, and she looks down at it and then at me.

"And did he?" I try to keep things going.

"He take one that we get back from O'Connell's friend. But say it is too risky for him to have it on yacht so we hide it in cave. You know…"

"It has a bullet through it now."

"Waste of time, we should have concentrated… is no good now. Nothing works. The killing goes on. No-one is on their knees. We have been led up garden…" She looks

339

out of the window again – is she expecting one of hers or one of mine?

"Listen. I must go. I tell you everything. You have man now."

"Stone? You mean Stone don't you? We need you. I need you to stay here." I look down at my phone, ready to reply to the text.

"Don't tell them."

"Tell them what?"

"Where you are. Your text is on my iPad."

"How…?" I realise that we are getting the same info on our devices. "So you have cracked into our secure communication?"

"We have, how you say, underground animal in your system. She keep us in your loop. She is friend of Stone."

"A mole?"

"Yes, mole, that's it."

"So if I reply to this text, you will go." I am thinking they will find us anyway. They know where the car is, it's only a matter of time.

"I go, I must stop all this."

"But I can stop you going." I put my hand on the sticky cloth that covers my gun.

"What?" she looks at me with a rueful smile. For the first time, our eyes meet, and I see pain rather than anger. "You would use gun, a weapon, to stop me? What are you going to do? Shoot me? Here, in ice cream shop? No, I don't think you will shoot."

"But I have killed before. Just like you. Why shouldn't I just finish it now?" I say this, but I don't make any effort to take my gun from under the cloth.

"You have killed, but you don't mean to kill, do you? You never like arms." As I look at her, she splits into two. There are two images of her and I can't quite seem to focus on either. I close one eye in an attempt to see her properly.

340

"Arms," she goes on. "Isn't this what it's all about? He sell arms. We all kill each other with them. Who sells that gun to police? Who makes them? The man who betrays us."

"So it's Stone, Sir Reginald Stone. But who betrayed us?" I ask, as everything starts to swim in front of my eyes. "Who is the mole?" The room is starting to sway alarmingly. "How did you break into... our... communi...cations?"

"Son of Jack. I go before she gets me. Before any of you..." the room is a river. Ice cream flows across the walls, the table, and I can't keep my head up.

She is close to me now and I hear her whisper in my ear, "I've got to stop this. All of it. Finish."

I hear a clatter as she gets up out of her chair. I manage to look up. There is no Anna any more. She has disappeared. I slump down again, trying to stop the room spinning round.

I feel a hand on my shoulder. "Are you alright, sir?" A girl's Polish accent. Then the hand reaches under my head and pulls out the sticky cloth. There's a shriek and a clunk as my gun falls to the floor, and then I hear the door bang open, and someone shouts, "Down. Get down on the floor."

But I am down.

Them or us? Them or us? It goes round and round in my head for what seems an eternity.

Another hand on my shoulder. "Are you alright, sir?" A man's voice this time. Sounds like one of ours.

"What's happened to Anna? Have you got her?" I manage to say. I am beginning to feel rather sick.

"Yes, sir. We have her."

I look round and see a frightened-looking waitress sitting on the floor.

341

"You think that's her?" I ask. The nausea begins to subside as I feel myself coming together again, but I don't attempt to sit up.

"Yes, sir. She had a gun."

"That's my gun. That's not Anna. That's a waitress."

There's a sudden explosion of voices from behind the counter. The manageress has risen from the floor, and is shouting at the armed police.

The door opens again, and there's sudden silence. A dark figure comes into my view. I can only see him from the waist down, but I know who he is.

"Ah, Rackham. Lost her again, have you?" Grimwode's sarcastic tones are close to my ear.

I grab hold of him, and pull myself up so that I can whisper in his ear. "Son of Jack."

"What? What are you talking about Rackham?"

With extreme effort I try again. "It's son of... it's Jackson... their mole is Jack... son." The room starts to swim again, and I give up.

11.00am 18th December

"A holiday, Rackham. That's what you need."

We're sitting in Grimwode's office. He is twiddling his pen, sitting behind his desk in his chair. The sound of London traffic comes through from the window behind him. Everything is old and tatty – a lifetime of policing leaving its residue around him. Books and files take up much of the wall space, leaving room for the odd framed photo of this prime minister or that. I'd half expect to see some old fishing trophy in a frame – a huge trout maybe – but Grimwode has never had time for leisure activities.

"So how are you?" He asks.

I can't believe he's actually asked that.

"Much better. Nothing that a good bit of food and sleep couldn't sort out. The sugar from the ice cream must have hit my sugar levels and…"

"Yes, listen," he wasn't really interested – just suffering from a rare moment of politeness. "We will have to clear up a few things, and I'll need to hold onto you for a few more days till you can see your… um… loved ones."

For the first time I wonder if there's a Mrs Grimwode. Maybe some young Grimwodes. Then I dismiss the thought. Dick Grimwode is a natural celibate – his work is his life.

"Do I have to stay locked up?"

"In protective custody, you mean? Not for much longer. We just need to pin down the main players. We

343

don't want any of Stone's lot taking you out, although," Grimwode smiles, "I am hoping Anna's done her work, and disbanded the group that were carrying out his wishes. In fact I suspect, from what you've told us, that Stone is the one who's in real need of protective custody. But it's Jackson's lot that we need to be wary of. We still don't know how deep that's gone. So if you don't mind, we'll keep you here out of harm's way. Just my men around you."

"But Dawson…"

"Dawson was seconded to me by Jackson. He only became part of my team after the shooting in your home town."

"How long did you suspect Jackson?"

"Oh, you know me," he taps his bony beak of a nose. "I don't trust anyone. But all the same, it came as a bit of a surprise."

"So are you sure you can trust my… er… keepers?"

"They're my old team. A bit like you, Rackham. Tried and tested, though," and he looks at me with a scowl, "not quite so unreliable or… imaginative."

"How's the man I shot outside our cottage?" The one who killed my dog, I reflect.

"Much recovered, and singing like a bird now he knows we have Stone. I wonder if Anna got a message to him. We're so leaky at the moment."

Grimwode gets out of his chair and looks out of the window. "But that's going to change," he says to the traffic as it passes below him.

"And Stash, Anna's nephew, how's he? I'd like to thank him, he saved my life, you know…"

"He also led you to her…"

"Still, I'd like to thank him…"

"That's the trouble with you, Rackham, you're so trusting of people…"

344

"Oh, I don't know, perhaps…" more trusting than you, I say to myself.

There's a knock on the door – an armed policeman enters, followed by a girl in leather motorbike gear. She hands Grimwode an envelope.

"A moment, Rackham." Grimwode sits down and rips it open with a paper knife. He glances over the contents, while we all wait in tense silence.

"OK, we're on," he says to the girl, who nods and leaves the room without a word. The armed officer goes out and closes the door.

"Christmas."

"What?"

"We should be safe by Christmas," says Grimwode. "We'll need you till then. And your loved ones…"

"Can I..?"

"No you can't. I'll send all your… er… love, shall I?"

He stands up. I stand up. Then he leans over his desk and we shake hands. "Thank you Rackham. You've been… most valuable."

I turn, and leave to go back to my cell – my only company, a ghost-dog. Seven more days, then I will be free. At least the food's good.

11.30am 25th December

I feel awkward, shy, as I walk through the token sprinkling of snow towards the front door of our cottage, my ghostly dog at my side. I haven't been able to speak to Peggy for two weeks. The last time we were together I was carrying the bloody corpse of my dead dog, and had more time for that than I did for her. Where's she been? What has she been thinking? I've been through so much, it has changed me. There's a steeliness in me now – I opened a door, found the killer in me, then closed it again and locked it. But I know it's there. But the loveable fuzzy old Arnold, is he still there?

The past week has been a fury of secret hearings, well away from the prying press. Stone and Jackson both looked as though they were carved from granite, and refused to answer any questions. But the evidence was stacked against them. Not just mine, but other bits and pieces have come together to make the picture. We now have knowledge of a web of deceit that has been sabotaging our force for years. There have been others – quite a number of them. Grimwode spared no effort in tracking down the people who had infiltrated his kingdom. It was truly a purge, and I am glad I was on the right side of that kind of ruthlessness.

I shudder at the memory of all that experience that I cannot share with Peggy or Paul, and I knock on the door of the cottage.

There's a scuffling from inside, and the door opens.

"Arne." Paul's arms are around me. He holds me so tight he almost lifts me off my feet.

Peggy is getting stiffly up off the sofa. She looks at me with shiny eyes.

"I'm sorry," I say. "They wouldn't allow me…"

"They wouldn't allow us either. I…we were so worried about you. I thought I'd never see you again." Her voice rises in pitch as she struggles to keep control. I grip Paul's arms and look into his eyes, and then let go and walk to Peggy. She throws her arms around me and buries her face in my chest. I can still feel the bruising from the shot that should have killed me, but I hold her there as I feel her shake with the emotion she must have bottled up for a fortnight.

"How have you been? Have they looked after you?" I hold her shoulders, and push her back to look into her eyes.

"They kept us…" Paul starts, and then sees Peggy shake her head.

"We can't tell you where we've been staying," Peggy says quietly. "The whole thing's been a bit of a nightmare."

"It's alright. I can't tell you much about what I've been involved in, either. The amount of stuff that's been going on behind our backs. Even the old fox, Grimwode, was surprised. But I've said enough." I notice a slight twitchiness in the way both Peggy and Paul are behaving.

"Would you like a drink?" Paul asks, moving over to the Welsh dresser.

"Isn't it a bit early?"

"It's Christmas Day, and anyway, I don't recall you ever turning down the offer of a drink," says Paul. "Sit down and I'll get you something. G&T? Wine? Beer?"

"Beer."

"I'll leave it for a bit," Peggy says as I sit down on the sofa beside her. I look at her, taking her in.

"But…" Paul looks at her.

"Oh go on then. Open the Prosecco. We need to celebrate…"

She's about to say something else, when the sound of a dog whining, followed by a scuffling and someone going shush, comes from upstairs. Simultaneously I feel the familiar pressure of the dog's muzzle on my knee. So if my ghost dog is here…?

"Where's Hannah?" I ask.

"Oh, she's just upstairs." Peggy is finding it hard not to grin all over her face.

"Is she OK?"

"Yes, she's…"

Peggy is interrupted by a bumping noise, as something small descends the staircase. The door bursts open, and a small dark object hurtles round the room making whining noises. It has a tail, which is wagging. It rushes over to Paul, who points it my direction, but it rushes past me and back to Hannah, who has just emerged from the bottom of the stairs.

"Kip." She picks up the puppy, and brings him over to be introduced. "A local farmer had one too many, and Kip's no good with sheep, but great with people. We thought you might like…"

The puppy struggles out of her arms and jumps up at me. I hold him, and he licks my nose. It's difficult to tell exactly what breed he is, but something linked to a Welsh sheepdog. Probably.

"Hey Kip," I say lifting him up. "Come with me." I hold him under one arm, and open the front door, letting in a gust of cold air and a little flurry of snow. Outside the door is the place where my dog died. I place Kip on the spot, and he just sits there sniffing the air. Then he stands

349

up, wagging his tail, and moves round in a circle, his nose raised. Stops, turns, and walks back, standing as though listening to some doggy conversation. Then he barks, once, twice, three times, and sits down on my foot.

Acknowledgements

With thanks to Helen Spencer for help with editing; Tony Vaux for his valuable advice regarding a major plot issue; Alice Stainer and Susanna Jordan for proof reading; Francis Lovel for showing me how to aim a pistol; Chris Lethbridge for being happy for me to quote his brilliant song, *'Granite is the Hardest Stone'*.

And in Hay-on-Wye: our friend James Kennett of 'The Thoughtful Gardener' for selling *The Occasional Gardener*; Tomatitos for their beautiful Tapas; and Shepherds for the best sheep's ice cream in the world, and for having mirrors by their windows.

About Nick Hooper

Nick Hooper (known as Nicholas Hooper in the film world) is a BAFTA award-winning composer, and has written the music for two of the Harry Potter films. Inspired by working so closely with J K Rowling's stories, he has turned to writing words as well as music.

Nick published his first novel *Above the Void* in 2017. In 2018 he published *The Occasional Gardener* which introduced Detective Inspector Arnold Rackham – *The Mirror in the Ice Cream Parlour* is the second in the series. Nick plans to continue with the Inspector Arnold series, and other writings.